A WINTER'S MADCAP ESCAPADE

*Brides By Chance
Regency Adventures
Book Four*

Elizabeth Bailey

SAPERE BOOKS

Also in the Brides By Chance Series
In Honour Bound
A Chance Gone By
Knight For A Lady
Marriage for Music
Damsel to the Rescue
Widow in Mistletoe
His Auction Prize
Disaster and the Duke
Taming the Vulture

A WINTER'S MADCAP ESCAPADE

Published by Sapere Books.

20 Windermere Drive, Leeds, England, LS17 7UZ, United Kingdom

saperebooks.com

Copyright © Elizabeth Bailey, 2017
Elizabeth Bailey has asserted her right to be identified as the author of this work.
All rights reserved.

No part of this publication may be reproduced, stored in any retrieval system, or transmitted, in any form, or by any means, electronic, mechanical, photocopying, recording, or otherwise, without the prior written permission of the publishers.
This book is a work of fiction. Names, characters, businesses, organisations, places and events, other than those clearly in the public domain, are either the product of the author's imagination, or are used fictitiously.
Any resemblances to actual persons, living or dead, events or locales are purely coincidental.

ISBN: 978-1-913335-09-0

Chapter One

The fine sleet beyond the window did not beckon. Alexander, Lord Dymond, comfortable and warm in the coffee room of the Swan, regarded it with distaste.

Replete with a sustaining meal of a thick wedge of an excellent pigeon pie and several slices of ham, washed down with a flagon of ale, he found the prospect of resuming his journey unwelcome.

On the other hand, if the sleet should turn to snow, he might be forced to remain at Alton for several days. Best to make all speed home. Or risk his mother's wrath. She'd kick up stiff if he was not at hand with Christmas in the offing and all the bother of entertaining the gentry round about Dymond Garth.

Sighing, he picked up the hand bell and sent a peremptory summons pealing through the inn. He'd lingered too long at Purford Park, seduced by the warmth of his cousin's domestic felicity. Truth to tell, he envied Justin. A quirk of circumstance had given him his heart's desire, lucky dog. Marianne too. To see the two of them, one would never suppose there'd been a moment when Fortune had not blessed them.

His reminiscences were interrupted as the door opened to admit the waiter.

"Ah. Tell my fellows to put the horses to. And bring me the reckoning, if you will."

Alex rose from the table and picked up his greatcoat, shrugging himself into it. Absently, he fastened the buttons, his mind dwelling on images from his visit to Purford Park. Small chance of his acquiring such happiness. In all his years on the Town, he'd not found one eligible damsel who caused his heart to flutter. Pity, because he'd got to throw the handkerchief at some point. Even his father was showing signs of impatience. As for his mother —

The landlord appeared, thankfully cutting off the memories of the last lecture Lady Luthrie had read him on the subject of what she called his dilettante attitude towards the future of the earldom.

"It's none too pleasant out there, my lord."

Alex ignored the hopeful note and took the scribbled paper the fellow was holding out. He pulled a roll of bills from one of his capacious pockets and peeled off the necessary amount, waving away the landlord's bleat about getting his change.

"Keep it. An excellent luncheon, my dear Hawkins. Compliments to your cook."

The landlord thanked him and pointed out that his coach had just come through from the yard.

Glancing out of the window, Alex saw two coaches and a gig outside, and a glimpse of the Luthrie crest on the panel reassured him as to the presence of his own. Satisfied, he donned his gloves and hat, which he'd left on a side chair, and wrapped a muffler around his neck, which he was heartily glad of the moment he stepped out of the inn into the biting cold. He was relieved to find the sleet had stopped, though the air was damp and it looked as if the day would remain overcast.

His groom hailed him and moved to open the coach door.

"A bit brisk, my lord, but we've plenty of daylight left. Laycock thinks he can make two stages before dark, if the sleet don't come back. We can change at Winchester and carry on to Romsey. I know you'd prefer to stay at the White Horse if we can't get through to Salisbury."

"Doubt we'll make Salisbury. Tell him to go steady. Don't want to come to grief in this lot."

"No fear of that, my lord. Laycock has 'em well in hand."

A glance at the restive team harnessed to the coach, shifting but quiet enough, reassured Alex that his coachman was more than capable of controlling them.

He put his foot on the step, leapt nimbly into the coach and took his seat, blowing out air and rubbing his gloved hands together. Only then did he see there was another occupant in the coach.

Crouched in the opposite corner of the forward seat sat a slight figure wrapped in a cloak, its face almost entirely concealed by the hood.

"What the deuce?"

The figure shrank back, shifting a fold of the cloak so that it fell away to reveal a dark-coloured gown beneath.

"Good Lord! A female? Who the devil are you? And what in the world are you doing in my coach?"

A hushed voice answered him. "Oh, pray don't betray me! They will come looking for me at any moment."

She sounded young, and scared. His brain seething with question, Alex went straight to the point. "Who will?"

"My guardian and Mr Cumberledge. Pray, pray don't give me up to them!"

Bewilderment wreathed Alex's brain. Was the girl off her head? The coach began to move, and he shifted to the window and let it down, sticking his head out.

"Hi, Carver! Hold a moment!"

As he drew in his head, the girl's hushed tones assailed him again.

"No, no! Tell them to drive on! We have not a moment to lose!"

Cold whooshed in from the open window, and Alex shoved it back up as the coach came to a standstill. At any moment,

Carver would be jumping down to come and find out what the problem was.

"Look here. I don't know who you are, but if you are indeed running away from your guardian, I've no choice but to return you to him at once."

The girl leaned forward and her hood fell back a little, revealing a pale countenance and a pair of large, pleading eyes. "You must not! It would be too cruel. I am escaping from horrible persecution!"

Alex sighed. "Didn't suppose you don't have reason. But you must see how impossible it is for me to aid and abet you."

"But I only want to ride with you for a short time. Just to the next stage. Surely that isn't so much to ask?"

The plea in the tone had lessened, and Alex detected the beginnings of irritation. He struck back. "Don't you get uppity with me, young lady. Must see it's the height of idiocy to expect me to carry off a complete stranger. Especially if you're running away from school or some such thing."

The girl sat up, indignant now. "I'm not a schoolgirl! I am one and twenty all but a matter of weeks."

"Then you should have more sense." He reached for the door handle and turned it. "Now, out you get, and go right back where you came from."

The intruder's manner altered. She did not move from where she sat, but her right hand emerged from beneath the cloak and she raised it. Alex found himself staring into the mouth of a small but serviceable pistol.

"Order your servants to drive on, if you please."

The politesse at the end did nothing to take away from the tone of command. The girl's voice had changed, losing the plea and gaining an edge. There was no trace of her former fear.

Alex did not move, but his fingers tightened on the door handle and he felt a pulse spring to life at his throat. No doubt he could overpower her. Could he take the chance? If she fired at this close range, she could not miss. His tongue followed an instant thought.

"Is that thing loaded?"

Her eyes widened. "Why wouldn't it be?"

"Where did you get it?"

Her brows drew together. "Why ask me? It's not your concern."

"Very much my concern if you mean to shoot me with it."

"Then do as I asked."

Alex released his hold on the door handle and sat back. "What if I don't?"

For a moment, she looked nonplussed. Then she rallied, bringing up her other hand to help support her hold on the gun. She lifted it higher, her chin rising along with the gesture. "Then I will fire."

Footsteps scraped outside and his groom's voice sounded. "What's to do, my lord?"

The girl flicked a glance towards the door. "Tell him to drive on!"

Was there panic now? At any moment, Carver would become concerned and open the door. Alex seized the handle and held it fast. Then he pulled down the blind, raising his voice to be heard on the other side of the door.

"All's right, Carver. Just wait, will you?" There was a mutter from outside, and the stranger visibly blew out a breath. Alex dropped his tone. "Listen, you madcap child, this won't do. Might as well give it up, for you ain't going to fire that thing and you know it."

"Yes, I shall!"

"What, and cause enough stir to bring the whole place out on you? And if I'm dead or wounded, how do you propose to explain yourself?"

For a moment, she did not speak. Her eyes never left his, and Alex thought he saw the matter turning over in her head. The barrel of the pistol wavered and he saw a slight rise and fall in the folds of the cloak.

Unwillingly, he began to feel sorry for the chit. She'd put herself in an impossible situation. If he didn't miss his guess, she'd no idea how to get herself out of it.

To his reluctant admiration, she did not buckle. That determined chin lifted again and she gripped the gun more firmly.

"I will take my chance."

Exasperation seized Alex. "You won't have one, you birdwit!"

"Nor will you."

"Want to spend your life in prison? Or hang, more like?"

"Even hanging would be preferable to marrying Mr Cumberledge!"

"You're off your head, my girl!"

"And you are wasting time!"

Alex threw up his eyes. "I don't believe this."

He heard a click and his veins froze. She'd cocked the gun!

"I will say it only once more, sir. Tell them to drive on."

Why he did it, Alex was never afterwards able to fathom. He released the blind and his hand went to the catch to drop the window down. At the same time, he moved his body to cover the opening and block the girl from the groom's sight.

"All's right, Carver. Up you get, and tell Laycock to proceed."

He raised the window and sat back, regarding the girl in silence. She held her posture until the coach began to move, when she was obliged to adjust it.

Alex watched her push back into the seat, waiting for the moment when she would lose concentration and lower the pistol. Her wrists must be aching by now from holding it aloft. Inevitable she would tire.

His chance came sooner than he hoped. One of the coach wheels struck a rut, and the subsequent lurch set the girl off balance.

Alex swung himself across to the other seat, dropped into it beside her and at the same moment, grabbed the barrel of the gun and wrenched the weapon out of her hands.

She gave a gasp, but to her credit, did not shriek.

Without waiting for her reaction, he got back into his own seat and made himself comfortable, the pistol in his grasp. He released the hammer with care, letting out a breath of relief. He'd half-forgotten she'd cocked it.

"Lucky it didn't go off just then."

She did not reply, huddling back into her corner and wrapping the cloak about her. She pulled the hood forward, and Alex could no longer see much of her face.

What the deuce he was to do with the chit, he had no notion. Probably have to turn around and take her back. He remembered there had been a second coach pulled up before the inn. Had she come out of that? In all the kerfuffle, he hadn't thought to ask.

He inspected the weapon in his hand. No ball. No powder in the pan either. He looked across at the girl. "Wouldn't have done much damage with this."

Her head came up. "Of course not. I am not a murderer."

"You knew it wasn't loaded?"

"My guardian has never loaded it, as far as I know."

"Ah. Stole it from him, did you?"

"I am not a thief!"

She had straightened in the seat, the hood falling back.

"Whatever you're not, one thing you are is a runaway."

The defiant chin lifted and she closed her lips firmly together.

Alex sighed. "Suppose you tell me why you did such a mad-brained thing?"

"I told you already. I am being persecuted."

"By this guardian, I suppose?"

She became animated, waving her gloved hands for emphasis. "Yes, and also by Mr Cumberledge. He is Cousin Walter's partner, and of course he wishes me to marry him so they may both benefit from my trust."

Alex could not forbear a disbelieving laugh. "An heiress, are you?"

She drew in a breath and sighed it out. "I don't know. No one will tell me how much Papa left for me. I must guess it is substantial, or they would not be worrying me to marry that oafish beast."

"Which oafish beast? This Cumberledge?"

Her gloved fingers curled into fists. "I hate him! He tried to paw me and pretend he was in love with me, but it is no such thing."

"This is why you ran away?"

"I'm not running away. I am going to London to see the lawyer."

Alex began to feel a touch light-headed. What had he got himself mixed up in? Why had he let the wench persuade him into this?

"I must have taken leave of my senses," he muttered. A tiny giggle drew his attention. He cocked an eyebrow. "Find that amusing? Suppose I should count myself fortunate if I don't come out of this with a charge of kidnapping."

"Oh, it will not come to that, sir. I shall slip out at the next stage, and no one will know I was ever in your carriage."

For a moment, Alex allowed himself the luxury of relief, but it was short-lived. Under no circumstances could he let the silly chit go off on her own. She'd come to grief in no time. Best to keep this reflection to himself for the moment. Didn't want her doing something idiotic, like trying to jump from the coach. She'd shown herself capable of any sort of crazy conduct.

"What's your name?"

A wary look entered her face. "Why should I tell you?"

"Why shouldn't you? Considering the way you were willing to trust yourself to a strange man, can't see why you'd balk at telling me your name."

"I didn't trust you! Besides, I had the pistol."

"Which wasn't loaded, birdwit."

"How dare you call me birdwit?"

"What else am I to call you if I don't know your name?"

"Well, it's Apple."

Alex let out a snorting laugh. "Wish you won't be so stubborn! Apple? No one's called Apple."

Her eyes flashed. "I *am* called Apple. It's my papa's fault. He began it when I was a child and it stuck."

"Oh, it's a pet name? What's your real name?"

"It's Appoline, if you must know. Appoline Greenaway."

"Ah, I see. Makes a bit more sense now." He doffed his hat and made a little bow. "Miss Greenaway. I'm Dymond. Alexander Dymond. My friends call me Alex."

She inclined her head in a manner that struck him as a touch imperious. He tried not to laugh. A little out of place for a girl of her class. Though was it?

"What's your station, Miss Greenaway? I mean, who was your father?"

"John Greenaway."

"That tells me a lot."

Miss Greenaway huffed a little. "I don't see why I should tell you anything."

"Suit yourself. Only I can't help you if I don't know the half of it."

She eyed him with suspicion. "Why should you wish to help me?"

"Well, if that don't beat all! Didn't you throw yourself on my mercy?"

"No, I did not. I merely asked you to convey me a little way in your coach. That does not give you the right to demand the history of my life."

"First off, you didn't ask me. You ordered me at gunpoint. Second, if you don't stop trying to run rings round me, I'll set you down in the middle of the countryside and leave you there."

Miss Greenaway's obstinate little chin came up. "No, you won't. You are not that sort of man."

"How would you know?"

"If you were, you'd have given me back at once."

"Ha! I may still do so."

"You can't. You don't know where to take me."

Alex cursed and smote himself on the knee. "Devious little monkey! Should have guessed it when you wouldn't open up about your father. Well, don't think you'll get the better of me, young bufflehead, because you won't."

To his chagrin, a mischievous look flitted across her face. It made her eyes sparkle and her lips quirk. Alex's gaze became riveted upon her mouth and a ripple of sensation startled him. The lower lip curved prettily, and a neat little cleft made a bow of the upper.

Dragging his eyes away, Alex chided himself. It was a child. And under his protection, however unwilling he'd been to assume it. With an effort, he recalled what he'd said, and the symptoms vanished. Why, the little minx! So she thought she'd got the better of him already, did she? They'd see about that.

He adopted a casual tone. "What do you mean to do when we part company?"

He was careful not to mention when that might be, but Miss Greenaway did not hesitate.

"I shall take the stagecoach to London."

"You do realise we're going the wrong way?"

"It makes no matter, as long as you set me down at a coaching inn."

"And when you get to London?"

"I told you. I'm going to seek out Mr Vergette."

"Who's he? The lawyer you spoke of?"

"Yes, and I think he is my trustee. I am persuaded he will feel for me."

If Alex knew anything of the matter, the fellow was more likely to return Miss Greenaway at once to her guardians. Which was exactly what he ought to do himself. But it was scarcely politic to say so.

"Not sure what you expect your Mr Vergette to do for you, but a conscientious lawyer won't be persuaded to break the trust, you know."

"He won't need to. It comes to an end the moment I attain my majority."

Alex could have slapped the girl. "Then, for the Lord's sake, what possessed you to play this fool's trick? If you're very nearly one and twenty, as you told me — not that I believe a word you say! — you've only to wait a short time to be free of any persecution."

Miss Greenaway did not appear to be in the least perturbed by his statement that he did not believe her. She waved this away in an airy fashion. "No, because there is a stupid caveat. The trust may be broken if I marry before that date."

Enlightenment dawned. "Hence the attempt to get you to accept Mr Cumberledge."

"Exactly so." Miss Greenaway became cordial. "I'm so glad you understand my predicament at last. You must concede that I had no choice but to escape."

"Dare say I must, but I can't conceive why you must choose to do so in my coach!"

"Well, I am sorry, but yours was the only other coach. And when I saw them make ready to get you away, I slipped from ours while they were in the inn and crept around the back so that your coachman would not see me. Marjorie was in our coach, but she'd dropped asleep. Was ever anything more fortunate?"

Alex could think of a number of things that were a good deal more fortunate, but he did not say so. He regarded her with a resurgence of exasperation, tempered by that sliver of admiration. "You do realise you're completely feather-brained, don't you? I could have been anybody."

The mischievous look reappeared, and Alex had to exercise severe self-control not to laugh.

"Well, you aren't anybody. You're you. I expect it was fate."

Chapter Two

While she could not help a little flush of triumph at the success of her tactic, Apple was conscious of inordinate relief. This Mr Dymond had fathomed it exactly, for her apprehension had indeed centred upon what sort of person she might encounter in the coach. She'd been prepared for an amorous villain, which was why she'd had the forethought to provide herself with the pistol.

She had not known whether it was loaded, but suspected not. It had been sitting in the holster in the coach for all of the three years she'd lived with her cousins, and she'd never seen Walter remove it. She'd remembered it when she was making her plan and resolved to possess herself of it before her escape.

She would have to make Mr Dymond give it back to her before she left his coach. It was her only protection. An idea occurred, and she gave voice to it at once.

"Will you show me how to load the pistol, if you please?"

"No, I will not."

A flurry of annoyance entered her breast. "You are very disobliging."

"More than you think, because I ain't about to give it back to you either."

She was chagrined, but it was plainly useless to argue with him. Apple regarded him from under her lashes. The gloom outside the window made the coach dark, his features unclear. She was able to note the strength in the line of his jaw, however, and the beak of a nose. He was not unattractive, in an odd, saturnine way. His eyes were keen. She rather thought they saw too much, but strangely, they'd made her trust him. He did not hide what he thought.

Apple had been hedged by people keeping things from her all her life. Even her papa had caught himself up time and again, beginning to say something and clamming up.

"Well, that's neither here nor there, Apple, my dear. You'll not regard it."

How could she regard it when she didn't know what he was about to say? But it had rankled every time. Cousin Walter was as bad. Saying how clever she was and how useful and helpful, and then starting to mention Mr Cumberledge and stopping himself when Cousin Marjorie gave him a look.

They thought she did not notice, but it had put Apple on her guard. She had long suspected there was some plot afoot. Especially when Mr Cumberledge began to show her attention. She had managed to evade him for some time. Only Walter grew impatient and showed his hand. Foolish of him. They might have succeeded otherwise. She shuddered at the thought.

"Cold, Miss Greenaway?"

Startled, she looked across at Mr Dymond. Lost in remembrance, she'd not realised he was watching her.

"I am well enough, thank you." A thought surfaced. "How far to the next stage?"

"Winchester? A few miles yet. I'll be pushing on to Romsey if I can."

Apple considered. Romsey would put her further out of reach of Cousin Walter and they had been heading for Winchester. Romsey might be better. They were bound to pursue her, but Walter would surely waste time hunting around Alton before setting out. He was impetuous enough to take off at once, but Cousin Marjorie had a head on her shoulders. She would not jump to conclusions. She'd think Apple had gone into the inn, so they must search for her there first. Or she might have slipped off to one of the shops.

"They will scour the town first," she said aloud, forgetting she was not alone.

"Your people?"

Mr Dymond was acute, she had to give him that. He'd grasped her meaning at once. She could make use of his intelligence at least.

"I was trying to work out how long a start I have over them."

"Well, if they don't set out soon, they'll not do so at all. Weather's worsening."

Apple looked out of the window. A fine trickle of snow was falling. Her heart pumped painfully. "But the stage won't run in snow!"

"Only sleet so far. They've to keep to the waybill if they possibly can."

That gave little comfort. Her whole scheme depended upon catching the stagecoach. Of course it was a boon that the weather would keep pursuit at bay, at least for a time, but if she was marooned, she stood in danger of recapture at any moment. Walter's lumbering old coach might not make very good speed, but it was fast enough to catch her up if she was stuck in some inn somewhere. Besides, she had insufficient means to pay her shot for days. She'd counted on the meagre amount she'd been able to extract from Cousin Walter's desk to see her through to the capital.

"I should have broken into his strongbox."

"Thought you said you aren't a thief."

She had not realised she'd muttered aloud. She must be more careful. "I'm not."

"Whose strongbox? Your guardian's?"

Apple was surprised into answering truthfully, giving way to indignation. "Cousin Walter's. And it wouldn't be stealing because it was Papa's, and he wouldn't have kept me short of pin money. But they give me disgracefully little ready money, and Cousin Marjorie has the tradesmen send the bills to her. It is all of a piece and I should have guessed what they meant to do long ago."

Realising she was revealing far more than she'd intended, Apple clammed up. It was no concern of Mr Dymond's after all.

"Cousin Marjorie married to this Walter, is she?"

"She is his sister. And if I'd known what a hypocrite she is, I'd have asked Papa to be rid of her long since."

Mr Dymond's penetrating gaze intensified. "Seems to me you're a deal too hot at hand, young lady. Take it this Marjorie has been your chaperon?"

Wrath rose in Apple's bosom and she could not refrain from bursting out, "How dare you judge me when you know nothing of the matter? I wish I'd had a chance to be hot at hand. And Papa only dragged in Marjorie when I came home from school, for he insisted I must have a female at sixteen. Besides, he was ailing already and Cousin Walter was his heir and Papa said it would serve me better if I was acquainted with Marjorie before — before…"

She stopped, her voice suspended. Apple swallowed down the rising lump in her throat, sniffing as she struggled to suppress the rush of grief.

Mr Dymond said nothing, but he shifted in his seat and a folded handkerchief appeared in front of Apple's face. She took it, torn between gratitude and defiance. She blew her nose, dabbed the wetness from her eyes and sniffed again, crumpling the handkerchief into a ball. She felt impelled to offer an explanation for her lapse. Not that it was any of his business, but she hated to seem weak. "You need not imagine I'm in the habit of crying about it."

"I don't."

"Well, I haven't done so for ages. I promised Papa and I've kept my word. Only he didn't know what those wretches had planned for me."

Mr Dymond, to her surprise, let out a crack of laughter. He held up a hand. "Beg pardon, Miss Greenaway, but there's no need to sound so begrudging. I'm ready to believe you ain't in the habit of turning into a watering pot."

"Well, I'm not," said Apple, mollified. "Besides, what's the use of crying? It doesn't help."

An odd smile curved his lip. "Very true. Tell me this, child. Have you any money with you at all?"

The lurking apprehension returned. "I have what was in Cousin Walter's desk, but I'm afraid it won't be enough if it comes on to snow and I can't get to London tonight."

"How much have you got?"

"A few guineas only." Apple regretted the words as soon as they were out. "But you need not regard it. I don't know why I told you."

He ignored this. "You propose to travel to London, alone, with no other destination than this lawyer fellow's office, I presume, with just a few guineas in your pocket?"

Apple lifted her chin. "Yes, I do."

Mr Dymond whistled. "You're not just hot at hand, my girl. If you're not off your head, you're the most feather-brained female I've ever met!"

"I am not! It's a perfectly good scheme — if only it doesn't come on to snow."

"How far do you think you'll get, you widgeon? And even if you do reach London, what if this lawyer fellow ain't there? Where will you stay? Have you any acquaintance in London?"

"Of course I have not. But I can stay at an inn, can't I?"

"What sort of inn? No respectable house will take in a lone female. You've not even got any baggage, let alone a maid."

Apple's heart dropped, but she rallied. "Then I shall stay at some inn that will take me."

"Yes, and become a target for thieves and marauding males. Good God, girl, have you no sense at all?"

Since she had never considered this aspect of the matter, Apple had no means of refuting the horrid picture Mr Dymond conjured up. She was not so ignorant she did not understand what he meant. Indeed, Cousin Marjorie had laid a deal of emphasis on her dismal prospects if she didn't choose to marry Mr Cumberledge and carried out her threat to leave the family home. But she had left, and in such circumstances as rendered her acutely vulnerable. She fought against the sinking feeling in her stomach. She would not be defeated.

"Well, it won't come to that. You said the stagecoach must keep to its waybill."

"Listen to me, my dear girl." Mr Dymond's tone had softened and Apple experienced an odd shiver, as if her veins were heated. "You must see your scheme is flawed beyond reason. Perfectly understand you felt compelled to escape, but these guardians of yours can't force you to the altar. Only have to stand firm. You said it won't be long before you attain your majority, and then you can do as you please."

Dismay engulfed Apple. He meant to make her go back! She broke into impetuous speech. "It isn't as easy as that. I've said I won't do it I don't know how many times. I told them they can't make me say the words, even if they drag me to church. I swore I would tell the pastor I was being forced. But they only laughed at me!"

"I dare say, but —"

"It's of no use to try and persuade me, sir, for I'm not going back. In any event, I don't mean to remain away. I am only going to see Mr Vergette. Once I have him on my side, they won't be able to do anything for he will refuse to break the trust."

"How do you know that? Are you acquainted with the fellow?"

"No, but I have corresponded with him."

"Then, in God's name, why didn't you write to tell him what was going forward?"

"I did. He wrote that I should consider the offer, for I might not get another."

Mr Dymond expelled what sounded like a snort. "And you expect to get him on your side?"

"I must! I am persuaded, once he understands the circumstances, he will not fail me."

Mr Dymond was silent for a moment and Apple waited, feeling a lift of hope. If he chose to try to take her back, she might have a difficult time escaping him. He would not be as easy to dupe as her cousins. At last he looked across at her.

"When did your father set up this trust of yours?"

"I don't know."

"Well, was it when he began to ail? Did he know he would not recover?"

The question recalled her papa's words to her mind. *No need to trouble your head, my dear. Your future is assured.* He had never spoken of his future, but Apple had known he was going to die. He would not otherwise have spent so much time arranging for the transfer of the business. In the event, he was gone before the lawyers had completed their work.

"He knew," she told Mr Dymond, "but I think he may have set up the trust earlier, for Marjorie said Papa had been building a nest egg for years. And Walter believes his inheritance has been siphoned off into my trust. I heard them talking once."

"You mean you were eavesdropping."

Apple's better opinion of Mr Dymond dissipated. "I had every reason to do so. I had to find out what they intended."

"Incorrigible is what you are, my girl."

"I am not your girl and I wish you won't keep telling me what I am! You don't know anything about me."

"Matter of fact, I know far more about you than you do about me." He brought a fist down on one knee. "Tottyheaded chit! What possessed you to take such a risk? And don't bleat about your pistol, for what use is it if the thing isn't loaded? What's more, if I'd known I'd be saddled with such a birdwit, I would have stayed the night at the Swan."

Apple fairly gasped. "Saddled with me? You are not in the least saddled with me!"

"Aren't I just! Don't suppose I can let you go careering off around the country by yourself, do you?"

"Yes, you can. It's got nothing to do with you."

"I know, and that makes it worse."

Bereft of words, Apple could only gaze at him.

But Mr Dymond was not done. "What's more, I'm supposed to get home for Christmas and now I'll have to scratch that and post off to London to see this lawyer of yours. And what the deuce I'm to do with you in the meantime, I haven't the foggiest."

Torn between indignation and a sneaking thread of relief, Apple seethed for a while in silence. At least Mr Dymond had abandoned the notion of returning her to Walter's care. Or had he? Was it a trick? She gave immediate voice to her suspicion. "Is this a scheme to lull me?"

He let out another of those snorting laughs of his. "Lull you? What nonsense is this, pray?"

"Are you trying to make me believe you wish to help me, only to trick me after?"

"No wish about it, my dear girl. Let's be clear about that for a start."

"Then you do mean to trick me!"

"Don't be such a widgeon! Not going to give you back to your guardian, if that's what you mean."

Relief swept through Apple. "Thank you. But please just drop me off when the coach stops, and I shall do very well by myself."

"You won't, because I'm not letting you go."

"But you must!"

"Already told you what I mean to do. Only thing is, how to keep you safe while I'm doing it."

"But you can't see Mr Vergette on my behalf. He doesn't know you. He wouldn't tell you anything."

"You'll write a letter of authority to say I'm acting for you."

Apple thought about it, and found her spirits lifting. She was sorely tempted to accept Mr Dymond's help, however grudgingly offered. Yet she was reluctant to put her affairs in anyone's hands than her own. After all, what did she know of this man?

"How do I know I can trust you?"

"A little late to be thinking of that, ain't it?"

She could not deny it. What in the world should she do?

She was still pondering when the coach began to slow and drew up at last before the Dragon at Winchester. Apple sat up, leaning forward to look out of the window. If the stagecoach was already here, it would make things a lot simpler. She could slip off when Mr Dymond was occupied — for he must wish to refresh himself or answer the call of nature at least — and then she had only to find the guard and purchase a seat on the coach.

The matter was taken out of her hands as Mr Dymond reached for the door handle. "No use your scheming, Miss Mischief. I have your measure."

Apple looked at him with reproach. "I don't know what you mean."

By this time, the groom was at the open door, letting down the steps.

"Yes, you do. Come along. We'll take a refresher here while I decide what's best to do."

Seething, Apple gathered her dignity and prepared to exit the coach. She caught sight of the groom's staring face, his mouth at half-cock.

Before he could voice his astonishment, Mr Dymond took a hand. "Mum's the word, Carver. Explain it to you presently."

The groom's eyes turned to his master and his brows climbed under the brim of his hat. "I hope you can, my lord. Nor I never suspicioned you'd had a drop too much back at the Swan."

With a start, Apple took in the groom's form of address. *My lord?* Was he not then Mr Dymond? He was swinging himself out of the coach, but took time to glare at his groom.

"Damn your eyes, of course I'm not foxed! Just keep your trap shut for now, will you?"

He turned to offer his hand to Apple, helping her to alight. She looked eagerly about, but the only other vehicles were a gig and a chaise to which ostlers were harnessing a new pair. No sign of the stagecoach. She would have to find an opportunity to ask the landlord when it was due.

Meanwhile, she had nothing to do but submit to her captor's firm hand on her elbow, ushering her into the inn.

Chapter Three

Having procured a private parlour and requested the necessary refreshments, Alex obliged his unwilling charge to sit down at a neat round table and himself took the chair opposite, closest to the door.

The moment they entered the inn, she'd asked to use the facilities of the house. He'd immediately suspected her of trying to give him the slip and had frustrated any such design by ordering a maid to go with her and remain to escort her back to him. The dagger look Miss Greenaway had cast at him was enough to convince him he'd gauged her state of mind with accuracy.

He had taken the chance to relieve himself and was back in time to receive her from the cheerful maid and escort her into the parlour.

That he had not won her trust was no surprise. From what she had let fall, Alex gathered she'd been deceived enough to be wary. How he was to convince her to put herself under his protection, he had no notion. But his determination was fixed. As a man of honour, he could not permit a genteel girl to blunder about on her own. Especially one as buffleheaded as Appoline Greenaway. She might be only a few weeks short of her majority, but she was naïve to the point of lunacy. Else she would not have undertaken such a ridiculous and dangerous adventure.

She appeared to have gone into a fit of the sulks, for she did not speak until the waiter came in with a laden tray. Her eyes, which — conveniently, from Alex's point of view — gave away what she was thinking, brightened at the sight. He grinned. "Hungry?"

A tiny smile flitted across her mouth. Alex was conscious of a riffle of warmth in his chest.

"Yes, I am. I hardly ate any breakfast, I was too wound up. What did you order?"

"Some patties, rolls and tarts."

The smile reappeared, wider and accompanied by a sparkle in those big eyes. "Excellent."

Such a mercurial little chit! She swept up and down like a vivacious monkey, chattering in heat at one moment, in cold the next. He was amused and exasperated by her at one and the same time.

She watched as the waiter laid dishes on the table, and Alex saw her eyes brighten again at sight of the coffee pot. As the waiter finished and moved to the door, Alex took up the pot and poured out a cupful. "Cream and sugar?"

"Yes, please."

He added a quantity of both and passed the cup and saucer across to her. Miss Greenaway took the cup in both hands and lifted it to her lips, sipped a couple of times and let out a sigh of satisfaction.

He had to laugh. "Good, is it?"

She twinkled. "I need reviving."

"You mean you aren't at your brightest? God help me then!"

A giggle escaped her. "Oh, I have plenty of surprises up my sleeve."

"That's what worries me."

Her eyes acknowledged a hit, but she made no reply, addressing herself to the food. Having made a substantial meal at the inn where she'd hidden in his coach, Alex ate sparingly himself and took time to observe the girl in the better light of the inn parlour, where a couple of candelabra helped against the dimness of a gloomy day.

She'd doffed her cloak, revealing a dull, dark gown made for warmth rather than fashion, with long sleeves and unadorned except for a splatter of embroidery around the neck, which was made high to the throat. She was slight, with few curves and even less bosom. A mop of curls, dusky and dishevelled, fell about her face, the rest caught up at the back. Not a remarkable countenance in Alex's judgement, though her mouth was pretty and she had that determined little chin. But those large eyes, grey he now saw, lifted her out of the ordinary. And her face was mobile, reflecting her thoughts. How had she managed to fool her relatives?

"Didn't these guardians of yours suspect you might try something like this?"

She looked up from her plate, which was nearly empty. "No, for they have not the least understanding of my character."

"Why not, if this Marjorie has been taking care of you?"

Her eyes lit with wrath and she set down the end of the roll she'd been eating. "Taking care of me? When all she can do is try to force me to marry a man I can't abide? For all she is sharp, she doesn't notice what is under her nose."

Alex had no difficulty in interpreting this. "What you mean is, you put on a show of submissiveness for her benefit."

"I did not!" Then the mischief appeared. "Well, I said I would consider the matter. But only after I was set upon what I meant to do. Only it did not serve, because she told Walter and he immediately went to ask the pastor to read the banns."

Startled, Alex set down his tankard. "A trifle premature."

"That is Cousin Walter all over. When I learned what he'd done, I had to bring my scheme forward. I wouldn't have set out in such weather otherwise."

He raised his brows. "You mean you actually took that into account?"

That resolute little chin thrust up again. "Of course I did! I am not a complete idiot!"

"Not *complete*, perhaps."

He'd expected an explosion of wrath, but to his surprise, Miss Greenaway bubbled with mirth.

"I dare say I must seem idiotic to you, but I was desperate. Have you never done anything out of the way?"

Taken aback, Alex thought for a moment. "Afraid I haven't. Been a dull dog all my life. By Gad, I never realised it before!"

Her smile warmed him. "Then you should be grateful to me for bringing adventure into your life."

He laughed. "Perhaps I will be."

She drank her coffee, regarding him over the rim of her cup in a way Alex found singularly unnerving. She surprised him yet again.

"Your people must be quite gothic in their ways. Or else very strict. Are they?"

Alex's mind went to his mother. Lady Luthrie's had been the guiding hand throughout his life. He lived by her maxims rather than his father's. Strict? Forthright rather. Made her wishes known and expected them to be met. Alex had learned it was preferable to fall in with them than engage in the sort of wrangle that ensued when he rebelled.

"Could say my mother's controlling, if you like. My father keeps his attention on running the estates. That and his dratted exotic plants."

Her eyes had widened. "Estates? Who are you?"

"Told you. I'm Dymond."

"Yes, but if there are estates, you must be someone important."

He let out a snorting laugh. "Hardly. My father's a peer."

"That's why your groom called you 'my lord'."

"Ah, you noticed that?"

"Of course I did. What sort of peer?"

"Don't be inquisitive."

Miss Greenaway did not appear to be in the least crushed by this snub. She was eyeing him with new interest, as if she was turning something over in her mind. Alarm gripped him. What the deuce was she scheming now?

"If you've any notion of embroiling me any further in your wretched plots, my girl, let me tell you here and now that I won't be party to any nonsense."

She gave him a look compound of innocence and astonishment. "Why in the world should you imagine I want to embroil you?"

"You look as if you're plotting, that's why."

"I am not." She hesitated, taking another sip of her coffee. Then she set down the cup and gave him a bright smile. "I was only thinking that if you are usefully high in the peerage, Mr Vergette might be more inclined to listen to you."

Ignoring most of this speech, Alex fixed upon the nub. "Usefully high? How high is useful? And I'll thank you not to start imagining I'm a soft touch, because I ain't."

"But you said you would go and see the lawyer on my behalf."

"Yes, but I'd no notion of pulling rank on the fellow."

"Well, you must tell him who you are, must you not?"

"Yes, but I'm not in the habit of puffing off my father's earldom in hopes of securing an advantage. What do you take me for? Ain't the thing at all."

Miss Greenaway's big eyes gazed at him with a hint of the plea she'd adopted at the first. But her voice remained steady.

"Well, but only a moment ago you were deploring your dullness. If you insist upon only doing what is the thing, you will never shake off your shackles."

"Shackles?" Alex did not know whether to give in to exasperation or laughter. "You conniving little devil! I've a good mind to wash my hands of you."

The light in her eyes dimmed a trifle, and Alex felt an impulse to retract.

"Well, I said you should let me go on my way. Will you ask the landlord when the stage is due, if you please?"

Alex threw his hands in the air. "Incorrigible little monkey! If I don't end by slaughtering you, it will be a miracle!"

To his mingled relief and frustration, she erupted into giggles. Spying the tarts, she took one and nibbled at it. "Mmm, these are good, Mr — I mean, Lord Dymond, if that is who you are. You should have one."

On the words, she urged the dish in his direction. Alex reached out for one, cocking an eyebrow. "Trying to turn me up sweet?"

The mischievous look reappeared. "I just wanted you to share in the treat."

"Too kind, Miss Greenaway." He mimicked her, nibbling at the tart. "Mmm, very good indeed."

For an instant, a flash showed in her eyes. But the expected protest did not come. Instead she chewed in silence for a moment. Alex received a limpid look of innocence.

"May I have more coffee, if you please?"

He eyed her with suspicion as he poured her another cup. "What are you up to?"

Her brows rose. "Nothing at all."

She sipped the coffee. Her fingers hovered over the tarts again, and then drew back. She looked at him. "So you are going to be an earl?"

Surprised, he flicked back in memory through what he'd said. Had he given it away? With caution, he acknowledged it. "In due course."

"Are you married?"

"Not that it's any of your concern, but no."

Her tone changed. "Well, it wasn't any of your concern to ask me questions, was it?"

"That's a different matter."

"It would be."

He was nettled. "What the deuce does that mean?"

The air of interest disappeared. "It's all of a piece. You may demand answers from me, but the moment I have a question, it's none of my concern. I had thought you different, but now I see you are just like Walter and Marjorie. Papa too. No one ever tells me anything. I didn't know I was going to have to live with Walter and Marjorie until it happened, and I'm not even allowed to know how much is in the trust — and it's my money. And now, when I try at least to know a little about a horrid man who refuses to let me go on my way, you behave as if I am plotting something and I'm not!"

The tirade ended on a distinct sob, and Alex was thrown into disorder. "Hey! No need to cry about it."

"I'm not crying!" But she was hunting for the handkerchief he'd given her. An image popped into his head. She'd stuffed it into the pocket of her cloak. Probably without thinking. Alex got up and went across to where she'd discarded it and found the crumpled ball. Miss Greenaway snatched it from his hand when he presented it, glaring up at him as she blew her nose with defiance.

Alex re-seated himself and took a draught from his abandoned ale, feeling in need of a restorative. Then he eyed the girl in some frustration. "Beg pardon if I seem horrid to you, but I'm trying to help."

She sniffed, a flush mantling her cheeks. "I didn't really mean that. You're not horrid. At least, not as horrid as Walter."

Alex managed to refrain from laughing. "Obliged to you."

She eyed him, doubt in her face.

He lifted an eyebrow. "Well, what?"

She drew an audible breath. "If you really are heir to an earl, you ought not to be doing this."

"Doing what?"

"Helping me — if you can call it that."

He ignored the rider. "I know I ought not, but I don't have a choice."

"That's ridiculous. Of course you do. All you need do is find out about the stagecoach and set me on my way."

"Yes, and toss and turn all night worrying about what's happened to you."

"Why should you? You don't know me, and you most certainly have no authority over me."

"That's as may be, but I ain't such a care-for-nobody as to leave you in the suds. Besides, I do know you. Couldn't unknow you now if I tried."

A giggle escaped her, and Alex was relieved at her lift of mood.

"That's not even a word."

"Not going to brangle with you over words, so don't start."

"Well, what are you going to do with me then?"

Alex sighed. "That's just the vexed question exercising my mind."

35

Chapter Four

Apple was secretly so relieved to find Lord Dymond adamant, she abandoned any further effort to dissuade him. How it was she felt she could trust him, she did not know. Instinct? It was most odd, but almost from the first she'd felt it, and she'd not been in the least afraid of him.

On the other hand, she could not judge whether his interference was to her advantage or not. If he truly went to Mr Vergette on her behalf, would he put her case in a way that would win his support?

"If you are set on seeing my lawyer, why don't we go to London in your coach?"

This produced one of his snorts. "That would mean the devil to pay."

"I don't see why."

"You wouldn't."

He really was perfectly irritating. "I wish you won't treat me like a child!"

"Like your guardians, you mean?"

Incensed, Apple let fly. "They might not tell me things, but they don't behave as if I were fifteen instead of twenty!"

"They obviously don't know you."

"That's what I said in the first place. But if you mean to imply that I act like a fifteen-year-old, I'll thank you not to be insulting!" He did not look chastened, and Apple caught a giveaway twitch at his lip. Exasperation seized her. "You are the most infuriating person, Lord Dymond! And if you think you're going to dictate what I must do, you may think again."

He held up his hands. "Peace, young Apple! If it makes you happy, I'll engage to treat you with all the courtesy at my command."

Apple eyed him, her bosom still bursting with resentment. She dared say he didn't mean it. Or if he did, he'd forget the moment she said anything he thought foolish. And if he was in the least bit inclined to consider her feelings, he wouldn't smile at her like that.

"Better?"

"No!"

"Oh. Feel free to abuse me a bit more then."

Despite herself, Apple could not withstand the bubble of mirth. "You are quite hateful!"

Lord Dymond put his fingers to his brow and shook his head. "Alas! I've known it any time this past hour."

Try as she might, Apple could not hold on to her justifiable annoyance, though she was sure he was behaving in this fashion only to win her out of it. "I know what you are at. And I know you won't treat me with courtesy, so you need not pretend."

A rueful look came into his face. "Dare say that's true. Wandered far from the point, however, and it's high time we were setting forward."

"Where? To London?"

"Taking you to my sister's. Tell you all about it when we're away."

He got up as he spoke, going across to pick up her cloak. Too startled to think what to say for the moment, Apple allowed him to place it about her, wondering when and how he'd made this decision.

By the time Lord Dymond had arranged for his coach to be readied, paid their shot and was ushering her out into the darkening afternoon, she had so many questions she didn't know where to start.

Her escort handed her into the coach and stayed to give instructions to his servants. Then he jumped in and took his seat beside her. "Fortunately, my sister's home is much quicker to reach than my own. It's a short way beyond Romsey. Should be there in a little over an hour."

Apple could no longer contain herself. "Who is your sister? Won't she object? She might not wish to have me foisted upon her."

"Oh, Georgy won't object. Thing is, she's increasing so she and my brother-in-law ain't coming home for Christmas. Fortunate I remembered that, for I couldn't possibly take you home. My mother would cut up stiff. And I can't say I'd blame her."

Apple was conscious of a drop in spirits. Not that she'd expected Lord Dymond to present her to his mother. But it was not pleasant to hear that the countess would not welcome her presence. "I suppose I am too lowly for her."

"Suppose it no longer. It ain't that."

"What, then?"

"For the same reason I can't take you with me to London, greenhead."

Beginning to feel resentful all over again, Apple balked. "What is the reason? And pray don't say I wouldn't know in that odious way. It's not my fault I don't know."

"Suppose that's true. Though it beats me why you weren't taught. Where did you go to school?"

"In Bath, of course. Like everyone else. There must be five hundred academies like Miss Godfrey's."

"Don't exaggerate."

"Well, fifty at least. We were always meeting girls from other schools."

"What sort of girls went to yours?"

"Girls like me." Apple sighed. "There weren't any titled girls, if that's what you mean. Though Sally claimed her uncle was a viscount."

Lord Dymond said nothing for a moment, and Apple regretted saying as much. She had not envied the pupils in the more select academies. Most of them held themselves on too high a form to notice Miss Godfrey's girls. But her fellow pupils at the Academy were genteel, even if their parents were of less account than the lords and ladies of the ton. Only Jenny had a father in trade like Papa. But Jenny's father was so wealthy, it had puzzled Apple how Papa managed to afford the fees. She'd asked him once and he'd brushed it off, saying he would not have her attend the nearby school where she'd meet only with cits' daughters. She deserved better.

How or why she deserved better, Apple was never able to work out. It had not saved her from the hideous prospect of marriage with Mr Cumberledge. But she couldn't blame Papa for that. He hadn't known what was in the wind. If he had, would he have tried to arrange something better for her?

"You're very quiet, young Apple."

She jumped. "I was thinking." She recalled how she'd been pitched into reverie. "And you haven't answered my question."

"Which one?"

"You said your mother wouldn't welcome me for the same reason you won't take me to London."

"Ah. Simple enough, my dear. You can't jaunter about the country alone with a gentleman. Ain't the thing."

"Oh, we are back to the *thing* again. I told you I don't care about your *thing*."

observed to her friend Jenny. But Jenny, who cherished ambitions of rising out of her sphere, was determined to cultivate all the genteel qualities she could and did not hesitate to ape the manners and bearing of any high-born females who came within their orbit whenever they were permitted to venture out into Bath's more fashionable quarter. Jenny made it her business to study the Peerage to find out who was who and try to identify any females they encountered. Apple's interest in the ramifications of the families of peers had been tepid, until this moment.

"Have you only the one sister?"

"No, there's two of 'em. Charlotte's the elder. Got two young 'uns already and a new babe."

"What about brothers?"

"None that lived."

"I suppose your other sister is married to a peer as well."

Lord Dymond turned his head. "What's to do? Why should it throw you into gloom?"

"Because I don't belong!"

For once he did not laugh. To Apple's shock, he found her hand and squeezed it. A flutter disturbed her heartbeat.

"Don't let it worry you. Georgy's a touch flighty, but she ain't in the least starched up. Wouldn't take you to Charlotte, even if she didn't live too far away. Too much like my mother. She'd be bound to take it in snuff and kick up a dust."

His fingers had left hers, but Apple felt their comforting pressure still. His words, however, did nothing to settle her growing agitation. Almost she wished for the familiarity of home, even though it contained Marjorie and Walter. At least she was not made to feel an intruder.

Chapter Five

Alex greeted the Edgintons' butler in his usual insouciant fashion, ignoring the man's curious glance at the cloaked and shrinking figure beside him.

"Evening, Berryman. Trust her ladyship ain't dined yet?"

The butler took his hat and coat, setting them aside. "No, sir. Captain Edginton has not yet come in. I will apprise Cook that there are two more for dinner and ensure covers are laid."

"You're a good fellow. Where's my sister to be found?"

"Her ladyship is resting, sir. If you will be so good as to wait in the saloon, I will inform her of your arrival."

He made for the large room off the hall, but a mental image of the place caused Alex to stop him. Apple would be overawed in there, what with the Adam curlicues and garlands all over the walls and all that elegant painted and moulded furniture of Georgy's with its striped brocade upholstery. The chit was already scared to death.

"We'll wait in the little parlour, Berryman."

The butler bowed and led the way upstairs to the cosy room Georgy had set aside for daily use. It was much less intimidating, with informally scattered tables and easy chairs, and his sister's ancient harpsichord. Apple might readily regain her confidence. He'd been exasperated by her impertinence and argumentative attitude, but he found it decidedly disturbing to see her subdued like this.

He ushered his charge into the room and held out an imperative hand. "Let's have your cloak."

"Must I?"

"Ain't going to dine in it, are you?"

With obvious reluctance, she slipped back the hood and emerged from its enveloping folds. Alex took it and handed it over to the butler. "Dare say you'll arrange for a chamber for Miss Greenaway, Berryman."

"And yourself, my lord?"

"Well, of course. Do you think I'm going to sleep in the coach? Tell my fellows to bring in my gear, will you?"

The butler bowed and withdrew.

Alex urged the girl into a chair by the fire. She sat on its edge, looking about her with a gaze compound of interest and apprehension.

"Nervous as a cat, ain't you? There's no need. Told you my sister's a right one."

Apple's grey gaze came to rest on his face. "She may not wish to have me here."

"Balderdash, why shouldn't she? Dare say she'll be delighted. Must be dull work for her alone here if Rob's off on duty at the moment."

The stiff pose relaxed a little and Alex gave her a reassuring smile, devoutly hoping Georgy would not make him look nohow by setting up some objection. Not that he supposed she would. Much more likely to take the chit to her bosom once she heard of her mad exploits.

"Is your sister very young?"

"Much of your age, why?"

Apple's hand made a sweep to encompass the parlour. "This place. It's — it's frivolous."

He cast a glance about, taking in the billowy pink curtains looped at the windows, the motley chairs of different design, some thinly striped with little flowers threaded through, others chintz, and Georgy's pink and gold chaise longue which in no way matched the rest.

"Suppose it is. I'd not noticed before. You don't like it?"

A smile crept into her face, which brightened under the light from the candelabrum on the mantel. "Oh, I like it. It's just I've never seen such a room before. At home, everything is neat and terribly ordinary. Marjorie is such a nipcheese, she won't waste a penny on what she calls unnecessary frills and furbelows. Though Papa kept one parlour looking the way Mama had made it, for visitors, you know. But it's dark and horridly old-fashioned."

Letting the rest pass, Alex fastened on the one thing she'd not mentioned before. "Take it your mother died some years ago?"

Apple showed no grief as she had done over her father. "When I was little. I don't remember much about her."

"Who looked after you then?"

"The maids mostly, though Papa always made time for me." Her eyes sparkled. "Reading fairy stories and later there was *Robinson Crusoe*. Papa used to draw pictures of the island for me so I could better imagine his adventures. I have some of them still."

Alex let out a crack of laughter. "No longer wonder at your plunging into adventure yourself. *Robinson Crusoe!*"

She looked indignant, but before she could give voice to whatever protest had leapt into her head, his sister Georgy tripped into the room.

"Alex! Good gracious, what in the world are you doing here?"

He received her in a brotherly embrace, the golden curls, worn loose about her face, tickling his chin. As usual, she was off again before he could open his mouth.

"I could scarcely believe it when Berryman said you'd arrived. Not that I'm not delighted to see you, but I cannot

"The devil!" Deep disappointment swept through Alex. "If that isn't the most curst mischance!"

"I'm so sorry, Alex." She turned to Apple. "But of course you may remain here until I must leave."

"When are you going?" Alex asked.

"In two days."

"*Two days?* Hang it, not sure I can do the business in that time! Now what are we to do?" He saw Apple's dismay and pulled himself together. Time enough to find another solution. "I'll think of something, Apple, never fear. Meanwhile, dare say you'd like to freshen up before you dine. Georgy?"

His sister rose at once to the occasion. "Of course. Come with me, Apple — if you don't object to my calling you so? — and we'll arrange for your accommodation and —" with another deprecating look at the other girl's costume — "I'm sure I can find something of mine that will fit you. Perhaps not tonight, but I'll look in my wardrobe tomorrow. But at the least I can lend you a nightgown and anything else you need."

Her voice, still chattering, receded down the corridor as she hustled Apple away.

Alex sank into a chair and set his mind to profound cogitation.

Chapter Six

A very few minutes in Lady Georgiana's company sufficed to erode the shyness that had overtaken Apple on arrival at Merrivale House. She chattered nonstop, so that one did not actually have to answer many questions since she was in the habit of asking one and then saying something else. Except when it came to Apple's lack of luggage, which she harped on several times.

"How in the world did you come to set forward without even a bandbox? I dare not take a foot from my door unless I have everything I may need, even if I am only going out for the day."

Apple was looking about the bedchamber to which her hostess had led her, after a brief colloquy with a maid detailed by the butler to prepare the Blue Room for the guest. This large term turned out to designate a cosy chamber containing a tent bed with pretty lacy hangings, beribboned in blue and a blue velvet-covered base. It was not grand at all. Indeed, Apple again stigmatised it as frivolous, which she suspected was typical of her hostess.

"I hope you will be comfortable in here, Apple. I have not yet had all the rooms changed, but at least I was able to get rid of the ancient bed that used to be in here. It was quite gothic and horridly huge."

Apple assured her she would be perfectly comfortable. "I have never been in a bedchamber half as pretty."

"Have you not? Poor thing! Now see, if only you had some clothes, there is this charming press. I love the Chinese look, don't you?" Hustled onto a dressing stool, Apple could hardly believe it when her hostess began deftly removing the pins in her hair. "We will comb it out and redo it. Oh, I had best ring for Nelly to bring you hot water for washing."

Leaving Apple with her hair half falling down, she flitted to the bell-pull and tugged on it. Relieved at the notion of being able to wash the travel stains away, Apple started to remove the rest of her hairpins.

"But you haven't yet told me about the luggage," complained Georgy, coming back to her and examining Apple's features in the mirror. "Gracious, you are not in the least the sort of girl I would expect Alex to befriend."

A bubble of resentment loosened Apple's tongue. "Why not? What sort of girl should I be?"

"Oh, dear, have I offended you?" Georgy looked contrite. "To be truthful, I'm not sure I even know what Alex likes. Mama is in despair about him, I must tell you, for he ought to have married ages ago."

Apple was conscious of a rise of interest. "He is not all that old, surely?"

"He will be thirty in a year or two, and it's perfectly ridiculous of him not to have secured the succession by this time. Instead, he's evidently going about rescuing stray damsels and risking a horrid scandal."

Apple's cheeks warmed and she drew herself up. "There will be no scandal on my account, I assure you. And it's not my fault he chose to insist on bringing me here."

Georgy immediately became penitent, plonking down on the bed. "Oh, dear, I did not mean to be such a cat. I am very glad to have you, and of course it's much less scandalous if you are with me."

Apple swivelled to face her. "Besides, he has not rescued me. I rescued myself. Not that I have run away, if that is what you think, because it isn't so."

Georgy's blue eyes widened. "But if you haven't run away, why are you utterly without luggage?"

"If I was running away, I would have taken as much as I could carry, wouldn't I?"

"Would you? Oh, dear, I am perfectly bewildered!"

Fortunately, at this point the maid Nelly appeared and Georgy broke off the conversation to instruct her to fill the jug with hot water and also to find a brush and comb.

"Oh, and fetch my shawl, Nelly, the one all over flowers. That will brighten up your gown, Apple. And I won't change for dinner either," she added as the maid dashed off upon her errands, "so you need not be put to the blush. We will wait upon the water before doing your hair up again, and in the meanwhile do for heaven's sake tell me everything, for I am dying of curiosity."

"There's not much to tell," said Apple with reluctance. "I have to go and see a — a certain lawyer in London, and — and your brother decided he ought to go in my stead."

Georgy threw up her hands. "But that can't be all! How did Alex find out what you meant to do? Have you known him long?"

"Known him? No! We only met this afternoon. At least, we didn't meet exactly. He happened to be in the coach I chose and I — I waylaid him."

"Waylaid him? Gracious, what in the world do you mean? Why — oh, tell me everything at once or I shall burst!"

Apple could not help laughing, but she obediently gave her hostess a somewhat expurgated version of events, omitting all mention of pistols and certain exchanges made between herself and Lord Dymond.

"So when your brother discovered what I meant to do, he decided it would be more seemly if he visited Mr Vergette on my behalf."

"That's the mission he spoke of?"

"Yes. I wanted to go with him, but he insists upon my remaining here."

"Oh, dear, I wish it were possible for you to do so, only Rob insists upon securing me at Dymond Garth before he goes. I am increasing, you see, and he is worried about me being left alone, poor lamb."

Apple said all that was proper, but she could not conjure up more than a tepid interest in Georgy's pregnancy, her mind taken up with what was to happen now. At last Georgy left her to her ablutions, saying she must tidy her own costume, and she was glad of the privacy to make use of the chamber pot.

Without the distraction of Georgy's incessant chatter, however, she became prey to foreboding and regret while she washed her face and hands and re-pinned her hair, her hostess fortuitously having forgotten her intention to do it for her.

The thought could not but obtrude that if Lord Dymond had not insisted upon interfering, she might have been well on her way to London by now. Of course it would have been too late to seek out Mr Vergette tonight, and Apple had to acknowledge the force of Lord Dymond's arguments if she'd had to stay at some inferior inn. She was obliged to admit there was some justification for his uncomplimentary remarks upon her escapade. She had not sufficiently thought it through. At least, she hadn't known how odd a lone female without luggage must appear. Lady Georgiana's scandalised reaction had brought it home to her, and Apple felt a sneaking gratitude towards Alex.

He'd been kind, even though he was disgracefully autocratic. And he had not been at all high in the instep. Nor had Georgy. Apple was surprised, never having encountered anyone in the aristocracy in any close capacity. From Miss Godfrey's discourse, she'd expected a different reception. It was both refreshing and alarming in an odd way.

Knowing herself to be born of inferior stock — even her fellow students had thrown up hands of horror upon learning her papa was merely a wine merchant — she'd had little expectation of removing from that circle. Unlike Jenny, whose ambition centred upon rising in the world. Apple had no such ambition. She'd hoped only for a trifle of independence, at the least in her choice of husband. The trust, Papa said, would provide her with a dowry.

Her secret hope she'd confided in no one. Until she knew the extent of the trust, it remained a pipe dream. Unless she succeeded in outwitting Walter and Marjorie in this horrible scheme to marry her to Mr Cumberledge, there was no earthly possibility of securing any such future.

Well, if Alex — or rather, Lord Dymond, for she must not allow herself to become too familiar — had no solution to the present difficulty, she must once more fend for herself.

Chapter Seven

Alex was no nearer solving the problem, since the arrival of his brother-in-law within a few moments of Georgy taking Apple off had at once involved him in protracted explanations.

An easy-going fellow, Rob only laughed at his escapade, observing that he'd never taken Alex for a knight errant. He was apologetic that the scheme must come to naught.

"For I don't mind owning to you, Alex, I couldn't rest easy leaving Georgy with none but a chit of a girl to keep her from doing anything imprudent. You know what she is."

Alex knew only too well. "And no hope of Apple curbing her, old fellow. She's about ten times worse than Georgy."

Rob burst out laughing. "Heaven help you then! I'd not be in your shoes for a fortune."

Oddly, this remark caused Alex a twinge of conscience. It was not Apple's fault he'd taken her in charge. Dealing with her affairs was becoming a curst nuisance, but to do her justice, she'd never meant to embroil him this far.

Dinner in Georgy's company could never be dull, and her husband was inclined to be indulgent. She'd married Captain Robert Edginton for love, in the teeth of her mother's opposition, having refused every eligible offer over two seasons. Lady Luthrie, fearing her wayward daughter might persuade her lover to elope, had given in at last. Alex was glad for his sister's sake, for he was fond of the girl, and it was plain the couple were inordinately happy. Like his cousin Justin and his wife Marianne. Once again, that flicker of envy arose in him, but he banished it. He was not now concerned with his own prospects, but with Apple's even less promising future.

Which brought him full circle to the problem of what he was going to do if he couldn't leave her with Georgiana. He'd discarded at once the notion of taking her to Charlotte after all. His elder sister would be shocked by the chit's exploits and even more by his having become involved. And his mother was out, full stop. Besides, he'd not subject poor little Apple to what Lady Luthrie could dish out.

He watched her surreptitiously while she ate. She did not talk a great deal, but who could when Georgy was about? She and her cousin Jocasta, now also settled and likewise expecting her first child, were used to be a perfect pair when they got together. Wasn't like Apple to be so silent. She could chatter with the best of them. Was she worried? Of course she must be. Hang it, he had to leave her here! Something must be done.

Inspiration came with the second course, which consisted of a ragout of veal, artichoke pie, stewed damsons and orange tarts of which Apple was at that moment partaking. He butted into his sister's discourse without ceremony.

"Quiet for a minute, Georgy! Need to ask you something."

Her mouth remained open, and she blinked at him from the foot of the table. Apple, sitting opposite, paused with a half-bitten tart in her fingers and shot him a hopeful look.

"Is it about me?"

"Of course it is. Georgy, doesn't that old nurse of yours live nearby? Can't remember the woman's name."

His sister's blue orbs widened. "Reddy, do you mean?"

"Mrs Reddicliffe, that's it. Retired, didn't she? My father pensioned her off as I remember, settled her somewhere round here."

"Yes, at Romsey, but what in the world has she to say to anything?"

Alex turned to his brother-in-law. "I'll fetch her over, Rob. She can take care of the girls while I'm in London, and I'll escort Georgy home when I get back. Will that fit?"

Predictably, Georgy chimed in. "Bring Reddy here? Good heavens, Alex, she'll hedge me so about I won't be able to do a thing!"

"Precisely my point. Woman was a tartar, so Charlotte always said."

"Yes, but a very kind one. I mean, I loved Reddy, but she was ever so strict."

"Ha! Just what you need, my lovely," said her husband, with a grin.

"I'll not have her here, Rob, carrying on as if I was five!"

"Dash it, Georgy, it's only for a day or two! But if it makes Rob easier…"

"Well, I would be easier in my mind if there was a sensible woman on the premises, I must say."

"Oh, and I suppose I'm stupid, am I?"

"My darling, you may not be stupid, but you're reckless and you're carrying my heir."

"What do you mean, *may* not be stupid, you horrid creature? And I hope it's a daughter, just to teach you a lesson!"

Rob grinned down the table at her. "No, you don't. You've been nagging on about it being a boy since you found out."

Georgy stuck her nose in the air. "I can change my mind, can't I?"

"Every day. Now stop making difficulties, there's a good girl. You're not being very kind to our guest."

Contrite, Georgy at once put out a hand towards Apple. "Oh, I don't mean to be difficult, dear Apple. Only you don't know Reddy. You just wait and see." She flung a rebellious look at her husband. "And it's no good expecting me to be kind to Alex, for I won't. It's his fault I've to put up with Reddy hedging me about, and I shan't forgive him."

Alex laughed. "Yes, you will, silly chit. Only think how you're getting a few more days free of Mama's restrictions."

Georgy's face of dismay was so comical, even Apple joined in the general laughter.

"I hadn't thought of that. How right you are, Alex. Mama will drive me into a frenzy. Apple, wouldn't you like to stay with me for a few weeks while Rob is off on his duties?"

But at this, her husband balked, throwing up his hands. "No, no, no, my sweet, you don't get off as lightly as that. I'll concede enough for the time it takes Alex to do his business in Town, but that's all. I want you under your mother's eye."

"But I'll be under Reddy's eye, Rob, isn't that enough?"

His smile was wry. "I don't doubt you're able to twist the woman round your little finger, just as you twist me. But you won't do it with my formidable mother-in-law, and much as I hate to subject you to it, I'll sleep better for knowing you are safe."

Which settled the matter. Recognising defeat, Georgy subsided, turning her attention instead to Apple's wardrobe. A matter which had been exercising Alex somewhat when he wasn't occupied with working out what to do.

"Georgy, do you have a seamstress or some such in the area?"

"Not that I know of. Nelly does my mending, but she couldn't fashion a gown, if that's what you're thinking."

"Well, what about the nearest town? Must be one of these dressmaking places somewhere near."

His sister wrinkled her nose. "The nearest modiste is Emmeline's in Romsey, but if I'm to judge by her made-up dresses, I shouldn't care to have her make me a gown."

"*You* might not. I dare say Apple ain't so nice." He caught an odd look from across the table. "No need to take a pet. Only trying to get you geared up with a couple of extra gowns."

"But I haven't enough money for gowns!"

"Don't let that worry you. I'll frank you."

Apple began to look agitated. "No, Lord Dymond! I can't be so beholden to you. It's bad enough as it is."

"Won't be beholden. I'll keep a tally, and you can pay me back when your trust comes free."

"Trust? What trust?"

Apple's eyes lit, and she ignored Georgy's interjection. "Indeed I can. That's a splendid notion. But you must be sure to keep a strict accounting. Or rather, Georgy must do so if she is going to help me buy some things."

A shout of laughter came from Rob at the end of the table. "Georgy? Good God, no. My wife has no head for business at all, Miss Greenaway. You'd best keep the tally yourself."

Georgy picked up a fragment of left-over tart and threw it down the table at her teasing husband, who batted it away with ease.

"Wretch! But what is all this about a trust, Apple?"

Alex cast a significant glance at the butler, who had re-entered the room with a laden tray. "She'll tell you presently."

He watched Berryman take away all but the sweets. In place of the remove, he set out dishes of fruit and cheese, along with a plate of sweetmeats.

Recalling her duties as hostess, Georgy glanced at Apple's empty plate. "Rob, give Apple another of those tarts, will you? And would you care for cheese, Apple? I will take a spoonful of the damson stew, Alex. Oh, and pray pass me one of the sweetmeats." While he served her, Georgy reverted to the matter of Apple's wardrobe. "I can lend her what she needs for the time being. We are much of a height."

"Yes, but you're much more buxom and your gowns will hang off Apple," said Alex with brotherly candour.

"Beast! I suppose you mean to say I am plump."

"A cosy armful, my darling," cut in Rob in a placating tone. "I wouldn't have you any other way."

"Well, you will if she is increasing," Apple cut in. "She'll be about as cosy as a pig at a fair!"

Georgy blinked and Rob stared, but Alex laughed.

"Knew that unaccustomed curb on your tongue would break at last, Apple. She's nothing if not forthright, when she ain't feeling shy."

"I'm not shy!"

"Not with me, no."

A faint flush mounted to her cheeks, and she glanced from Rob to Georgy. "Was I rude? I beg your pardon."

Rob smiled at her. "Not at all. Merely frank. Feel free to say whatever you wish. We don't stand on ceremony here."

"Gracious, no, for I can't bear it! I was surprised, that's all, Apple. But if you should ever meet Mama, I'd advise you to be more circumspect."

"Good heavens, I hope I don't! Alex — I mean, Lord Dymond — has said enough of your mother to make me glad I never shall meet her."

Georgy immediately launched into a recital of Lady Luthrie's less endearing traits, and Alex listened with only half an ear. His mind was dwelling instead on the sound of his name on Apple's lips, and the swift apologetic look she'd cast at him when she corrected herself. It had slipped out and it gave him an odd feeling of warmth to think she felt sufficiently at ease with him to use it unthinkingly. Hard to remember he'd only known her a matter of hours. He'd been irritated by the necessity to play the knight errant, as Rob called it. He was astonished to realise that if he could extricate himself now, he wouldn't wish to.

Chapter Eight

The departure of the gentlemen two days later released Apple from one fear at least. It had occurred to her that if Marjorie put two and two together, Walter might chase down to London and try to suborn Mr Vergette to his scheme. Since the lawyer had already suggested she consider Mr Cumberledge's offer, Walter might well succeed. But Alex was bound to get there ahead of the Greenaways' ancient coach.

He'd wasted no time, setting off after breakfast, hard on the heels of Captain Edginton, who would be away to the coast by nightfall, satisfied with the presence of the old nurse, Mrs Reddicliffe, installed in the house by Lord Dymond.

Alex had surprised Apple by returning her pistol, but his farewell had included an admonishment to stay put. "Don't go getting some odd fancy into your head and taking off."

"What fancy?"

"I don't know, but don't think I trust you, for I don't."

"Then why did you give me back my pistol?"

"Because it's useless without ball and powder. But like me at the outset, your victim won't know that."

"I can't imagine what you mean. Why should I have any victim?"

"Well, you had me, didn't you?"

"Yes, but you are on my side now."

"Ah, but I told you I don't trust you. And remember this, for I mean it."

Apple eyed his wagging forefinger with a rise of apprehension. "Remember what?"

"If you try to escape me, Apple, I'll come after you. And I'll find you, if I have to search the length and breadth of the country."

A weird mix of apprehension and delight ran through Apple. "You wouldn't!"

His frown was direful. "Don't try me, I'm warning you."

Shock entered in. "But why, Alex? I should have thought you'd be pleased to be well rid of me."

"Think it no longer. Taken responsibility for you and that's that."

"Well, I can't see why you should. I mean, it's one thing to go and see Mr Vergette on my behalf, and I'm grateful for it. But afterwards, we are bound to part company."

"When I see you safe back to your guardians, yes."

"*Safe!* If that's your notion of safety, you've failed to understand a word I've said."

"Understood only too well. And if this lawyer of yours ain't willing to stand buff, we'll have to keep you out of their clutches until your birthday. All there is to it."

Apple's heart swelled. "You'd do that for me?"

"Why wouldn't I? How many times do I have to say it?"

"You've taken responsibility for me, you mean?"

He grinned. "Good girl. Knew you'd got enough gumption to get it into your head eventually."

Apple erupted into giggles. "You are perfectly high-handed, Lord Dymond, and rude into the bargain."

He cocked an eyebrow and a gleam appeared. To her astonishment, he took her hand and lifted it to his lips. "Only too happy to be of service, Miss Greenaway."

He left her mystified and not a little disturbed. But she was obliged to set this aside and attend to her hostess, whose lamentations at the loss of her husband were sincere, if voluble.

"Oh, Apple, I have the greatest fear he will be wounded! If not killed. What in the world should I do without my dearest Rob?"

Mrs Reddicliffe, a rotund and comfortable woman, though elderly, patted her charge's shoulder. "Now then, Lady Georgiana, that's quite enough nonsense. The captain isn't going to war now, is he?"

"How do you know, Reddy? He may be sent to Pomerania and the French are there! Who is to say shots won't be fired?"

"Well, your husband said so, didn't he?" Apple put in on a bracing note. "He says it's a precaution and he's only going to the coast. They won't send him across the sea unless it's absolutely necessary, he said. And he must know, Georgy."

"Now, no more megrims, my lady, it's not fitting in your situation. You don't want to go upsetting the babe inside you."

This had the effect of turning Georgy's tears to laughter. "Why, Reddy, how can you? It's scarcely a babe yet. I'm only three months gone."

"'Tis a babe the moment it begins, Lady Georgiana, and don't you forget it."

Apple listened, fascinated, to a lecture on the trials and duties to be undergone by an expectant mother on behalf of her unborn infant. She was glad to think she was not likely to experience them herself. She would hate to have been obliged to suffer all that for Mr Cumberledge's offspring. Thank heavens Lord Dymond had taken her affairs in hand!

With the hope of diverting Georgy, she suggested a trip to Emmeline's. "For your brother was quite right, Georgy. I can't thank you enough for lending me this gown, but it is a little loose."

This was an understatement, for the maid Nelly had been obliged to pin her into the garment to make it fit and then tack the pleats in place, but the lumps so made were uncomfortable.

Already less tearful, Georgy jumped at the scheme. "Oh yes, Apple, do let us go! I am game for any diversion."

In the event, they did not make the trip until the following day, Georgy proving incapable of setting forward, just as Apple had been warned, without a great deal of fidgeting preparation, most of which was undoubtedly unnecessary for such a minor excursion. By the time she had recalled half a dozen things that must be done before she could leave the house — including consultations with her personal maid, the cook and the groom who would drive the carriage — and then insisted upon a light luncheon to stave off hunger until dinner, it was time for her obligatory afternoon nap.

"Not that I shall sleep a wink, but I promised Rob I would rest, and I have the second volume of my novel. I am halfway through, and I must say I should enjoy a chance to continue. Do you care for Fanny Burney's tales, Apple?"

By this time thoroughly exasperated, Apple found it hard to summon enough patience to explain that she preferred robust tales of adventure. "When I was a child, *Robinson Crusoe* was my very favourite story. And I love *Gulliver's Travels*."

Georgy blinked at her as if she were confronted by a freak. "Prefer such stories to Fanny Burney? Don't tell me you have not fallen utterly in love with Lord Orville?"

"Who's he?"

"*Apple!* He is the hero of Evelina, and so very noble!"

"I thought that was Sir Charles Grandison."

"No, he is Richardson's hero. Good heavens, Apple, how could you possibly mistake them?"

"Well, as I haven't read either, I only know of the latter from the raptures of my school friends."

Her stock with Georgy had evidently taken a dive, but her hostess bore up well under the blow and suggested Apple might like to look among Rob's books for something to interest her.

"The library is his especial domain, for the wretch insists upon having somewhere quiet where he may escape from my chatter."

Apple could not entirely blame Captain Edginton, although she felt a trifle shy of poking about in his library. The room, situated across the hall from Georgy's cosy parlour, was its counterpart in size and furnished in a masculine fashion, with a desk, a couple of deep leather-covered chairs before the fireplace and several closed bookcases around the walls. Very like Papa's study, Apple thought, with a hint of nostalgia and more resentment at the changes Walter had effected when he took it over. For one thing, he'd jettisoned some of Papa's books in favour of his own, and Apple had only just been in time to prevent her favourites from being sold, along with various pieces of furniture Walter considered redundant.

In the event — although she found a copy of one of Smollett's stories she had not read, though she would have preferred Swift or Fielding — she could not settle to reading. Instead, she sat with *Humphrey Clinker* open before her and her mind on Alex's mission, wondering whether he had yet reached London and if, when he did, he would find Mr Vergette.

Only now did it occur to her that the lawyer might not be there. She remembered Papa saying he was obliged to travel to serve certain clients whose high status merited more trouble than he was prepared to take for lesser men. He never came to

Portsea to see Papa, for example, although her father had known him personally. They must have met at some point, and Apple concluded he had been the one to travel to London to see Mr Vergette. Perhaps when the trust was begun? It was strange Papa had not used the man of business who carried out his workaday contracts. She'd met Mr Twitchin often enough and since he lived in Portsea, he made no bones about coming to his client's premises.

Why in the world had she not thought to ask Papa about all this? Of course it had not occurred to her that it might be necessary for her to make contact with Mr Vergette. Moreover, it was probable Papa would have brushed it off had she asked. There were some questions he never would answer, deftly redirecting the conversation into other channels. Papa supposed she was distracted, but instead they niggled, storing up in a pocket of her mind where a number of anomalies centred, making no sense.

Why did she not resemble the portrait of Mama that hung upon the wall in the good parlour? She certainly looked nothing like Papa, who'd had reddish hair while his wife was fair. She'd questioned him once, fearing she'd been adopted.

"Adopted? Nonsense, Apple! Just because your hair is dark? A throwback, that's what you are. Plenty of dark heads in my ancestry."

Only there were no old portraits to substantiate this claim. Having no desire to find out the worst, Apple did not pursue it. But it raised its head again now, when the matter of her trust had assumed such importance.

There was also the matter of Papa's will. It contained no word of the trust or her inheritance, only stipulating that the Greenaways must protect Apple until she came of age when she would be free to decide her own future.

Apple had been subjected to a catechism about the trust, for of course Marjorie knew of it.

"All I know is what Papa told me, and the name and direction of the lawyer in London," she'd told them.

Already suspicious, Apple had not disclosed the existence of the box containing Papa's exchange of letters with Mr Vergette. Not that there was anything in these to tell her more than that the matter of the trust was completely separate to John Greenaway's business affairs. But his heir refused to believe it. He had insisted on Apple giving him the necessary information so that he could write to Mr Vergette and find out the truth for himself.

To Apple's satisfaction, he got nothing by that beyond a brief letter stating that unless he had John Greenaway's authority to act in the matter, no information about the trust could be disclosed to him. Balked, he'd fallen back on what Marjorie already knew, which was when the trust was due to end and that it might only be broken if Apple chose to marry before that date.

Apple had not known anything about that until Walter had let it slip, after Mr Cumberledge's attentions became marked and she'd refused to entertain his offer. Had she known, she would have contacted Mr Vergette much sooner. He'd shaken her faith in his willingness to help her, and her flight had been an act of desperation.

At which point in her cogitations, Apple was conscious of a huge wash of relief that she had providentially fallen in with Alex. His promise to keep her hidden from the Greenaways until her birthday could not but change the whole nature of her escapade. She no longer needed Mr Vergette's doubtful assistance. She need only wait out the time.

Except that she could not think where in the world Alex could hide her. Georgy must go to her mother's as soon as he returned. And he'd made it clear she must have a chaperon.

Oh, dear, she was causing him no end of difficulties! And wasn't he also supposed to be going home for Christmas? Apple sighed. It would not do. She could not impose upon him to that extent. Only if Mr Vergette proved obdurate, what was she to do?

She was no nearer thinking up a solution when she and Georgy set out upon the following day. Apple had to chivvy her hostess to ensure they left in reasonable time, and succeeded so well that she found herself in Romsey and browsing in Emmeline's little premises above the papermakers in Bell Street by eleven o'clock.

Georgy might disparage the quality of the sample garments on display, but Apple was in a fever of delight. Papa had never been ungenerous, but while he was alive she'd only worn gowns suited to a schoolgirl. When she came home, she'd had no choice but to bow to Marjorie's judgement and her notion of what was appropriate to her station.

But that was at an end. Knowing she would be able to repay Lord Dymond within weeks, she was free to select just what she liked.

She would have preferred to browse quietly with the attendance of the proprietress — who turned out to be a Miss Emma Sharpe and looked nothing like an Emmeline — to show her the samples in made-up gowns. But the moment Miss Sharpe realised Lady Georgiana Edginton had deigned to patronise her tiny salon, she addressed herself almost exclusively to Georgy, whose intervention did little to assist Apple.

Although she listened and dutifully examined whatever the two women put in front of her, Apple was not to be persuaded into buying anything she disliked. Georgy thankfully refrained from openly criticising Miss Sharpe's creations, though she whispered in Apple's ear from time to time.

"Don't buy that, Apple. The cut is perfectly dreadful and it will not hang well."

Despite refusing to try on anything she didn't like, Apple was bundled in and out of half a dozen sample gowns with little opportunity to make up her mind about which she preferred. She refused to consider the light muslins Georgy favoured with tiny puff sleeves.

"I'll freeze to death! I must have long sleeves and a warmer material than muslin."

"Well, you may wear a shawl, Apple, don't be silly!"

But Apple remained adamant. In the end, she opted for a round gown with a modest neckline in russet-coloured poplin for day wear and, for evening, a white full-sleeved gown embellished with tiers of ruffles and knots of green ribbon. It was indeed of muslin, but double-layered and at least the sleeves were long. Neither of the samples fitted her slim form, but "Emmeline" pinned them where needed, took her measurements and promised the new gowns would be made up and delivered to Merrivale House by the following day.

Apple was astonished. "How will you manage that?"

Miss Sharpe gave her a pitying smile. "My sewing women will keep at it until they are done, ma'am. I will do the cutting, of course."

She could not but pity these unfortunates, obliged to sew half the night and likely for a pittance. But she was not granted the opportunity to dwell on the thought as Georgy exclaimed all at once, "You ought to have a new hat, Apple!"

But Apple had no notion of indulging in unnecessary extravagance. "This one will suffice for the time being. But I must get a nightgown and a couple of shifts perhaps. I can't keep wearing yours."

"Oh, you may have them, for I am well supplied. But I can do with more stockings myself, so let us repair to Dawes's in Market Place. They are mercers, but they sell all manner of things and you may purchase a toothbrush and anything else you need there."

It did not take Apple long to make her purchases. She added a couple of handkerchiefs and a small valise to the necessities and was then ready to depart from Dawes's. But Georgy, a dawdling shopper, had discovered a tray of colourful ribbons and another containing a selection of cheap fans, brooches and such and was engaged in rummaging and exclaiming, encouraged by the proprietor who lost no time in finding more trays to lay before her.

Losing interest, Apple wandered to the front of the shop and looked idly into Market Place through the windows in the door, watching the passing traffic and pedestrians strolling through. Her gazed passed over a weighty woman in a purple pelisse and a large bonnet, who was crossing the open space from across the street. Apple caught sight of her face and the whole figure became abruptly familiar.

"Marjorie!"

Apple's shriek attracted Georgy's attention.

"Why, Apple, what is the matter?"

Marjorie — for it was indeed she, Apple now realising she knew those particular clothes only too well — was moving out of her line of sight and she had to lean into the glass to see her.

By this time, Georgy was at her elbow, trying to peer through the door. "What is it? What did you see?"

Apple fell back from the door, her heart pounding. "It's my cousin, Marjorie Greenaway! She must have come after me. That means Walter is here too. Oh, Georgy, what shall we do? If they see me, I am sunk!"

Georgy gripped her wrist. "They shan't see you! Come away!"

Hustled to the back of the shop, Apple saw the proprietor's shocked features, his eyebrows climbing up his forehead.

"My lady?"

Georgy flapped a hand at him. "Shush! There is someone outside we don't wish to meet."

Apple began to feel faint. "I need to sit down."

Georgy snapped her fingers at the man. "A chair, quickly!"

In a moment, Apple was able to sink into a cane chair, Georgy bending solicitously over her, and the proprietor offering to fetch a glass of water.

"Yes, please do so," said Georgy. "But lock the door first!"

The man stared. "Lock the door? But, my lady…"

"Only for a moment while we decide what is best to do. Hurry, man!"

Apple had cause to be grateful for Georgy's status, for the proprietor, looking bemused, went to do her bidding and then disappeared into his back premises, presumably to fetch the water. She held a hand to her palpitating bosom. "What shall we do? I must escape, Georgy!"

"We'll sneak into the carriage before she can see you."

"But the carriage is at the other end of the town!"

"I'll send Herbert to bring it here."

Apple breathed a little more easily. The footman who accompanied them was waiting outside the shop. Captain Edginton's instructions were clear and, rather to Apple's surprise, Georgy obeyed them.

"Rob won't let me venture out all alone, especially now. I tell him I am not made of china, but he is adamant. He says Mama would expect it, and that is perfectly true."

Yet even the thought of negotiating the few feet from the shop to the carriage caused Apple a shiver of fear. "Suppose Marjorie is passing just at that moment? She will see me and all will be in vain."

"She won't see you. Why should she? Which way did she go?"

"Oh, down towards Emmeline's. How does she come to be here? She ought to have turned for Portsea from Winchester. Or tried along the road towards London."

The proprietor returned at this moment and Georgy took the glass he held, handing it to Apple. "Drink this. I will go and tell Herbert to bring the carriage."

Apple seized her arm. "Wait! Couldn't we sneak out the back way? Is there a street behind where the carriage could wait for us?" She turned to the proprietor as she spoke. Seeming to catch something of the prevailing excitement, he gestured vaguely in the direction behind the shop.

"Indeed there is, ma'am. If your coachman can find his way there. It's a narrow street, but I think it may be wide enough."

But Georgy took a hand. "Oh, this is silly! We are not going to go creeping about like a set of criminals. I will tell Herbert to choose a moment when there is no one in sight and we will be out of here in a trice." So saying, she bade the proprietor open the door again and sallied forth to arrange everything. Apple could not withstand a rise of dread that Marjorie would walk into the shop. Why in the world had she to arrive in this place just at this moment? The workings of Providence were not going in Apple's favour. Which did not augur well for Alex's mission.

Chapter Nine

Reaching the capital far too late to go seeking out Apple's lawyer, Alex betook himself to an ordinary inn for a meal and sent Carver to book a room at Stephen's in Bond Street. He'd already decided not to venture anywhere near the London house. For one thing, it was shut up and he was not expected. The few servants remaining would be put into too much of a flurry by having to serve his needs. Besides, he didn't want any word of his activities getting back to Dymond Garth. His mother would infallibly hit the roof if she knew what he was up to.

His stomach satisfied, the thought of a dull evening on his own drove him to seek amusement at Brooks's, reflecting that few people he knew would be in Town at this season. Almost at once, he ran into a friend, who offered him a bed for the night.

"Good God, no, Vincent! Couldn't impose."

Lord Wintringham waved his protestations aside. "There's plenty of room in my lodging, and I can do with the company."

Alex eyed him, realising the fellow looked decidedly hangdog. "Blue-devilled, Vince? What's to do?"

Vincent took a gulp of wine and sighed. "Parson's mousetrap, my friend. It looms."

Alex stared. "Don't say you've got yourself betrothed? Never saw any announcement."

"Not yet, but if I don't manage to cajole one of the eligibles this coming season into taking me, I'll be well and truly in the suds."

"Why?" He noted his friend was wearing colours, so he must be out of mourning. "Thought you came into the title and property more than a year back."

"I did, but my father tied the funds up so I've got to marry to untie them. And he put a time limit in the damned codicil. If I don't do it, I'll lose the lot."

"Ah, yes, I recall you saying something of the sort."

"I should just think you do recall it! I was wild when I found out, I don't mind telling you."

Which just about described his old schoolfellow, Alex reflected. As wild as bedamned was Vince. He could not say he was surprised at the late Lord Wintringham taking measures to curb him. He'd often enough deplored his friend's dissipated habits. He downed his wine and poured another glass.

"Well, you get no sympathy from me, old fellow. Time you settled down."

Lord Wintringham gave him a glare. "I've a good mind to retract my offer of a bed if that's your attitude. What are you doing here out of season anyhow? Up to some trick yourself, I'll be bound."

Alex laughed. "Nothing out of the way. Merely carrying out a commission."

Vincent eyed him with suspicion. "No, you're not. You'd not be putting up at a hotel if you weren't up to something. Why shouldn't you stay in Berkeley Square?"

"Because the place is shut up. I'm not like you, Vince, kicking up larks. Just the same at Oxford, you madcap loon!"

Vincent laughed. "Well, what are you doing then?"

"Got to see this Vergette fellow, that's all."

To his surprise, Vincent snorted, throwing up his eyes. "Vergette the lawyer? You'll be lucky! Unless he's your father's man of business, which I strongly doubt."

Intrigued, and a good deal dismayed, Alex demanded enlightenment.

"What, you've not heard of Vergette?"

"I did think the name was familiar."

"Familiar? Good God, man, he's the most exclusive lawyer in London!"

A vague memory surfaced in Alex's mind, even as his disquiet increased. "Well, if I have heard of him, I can't think in what connection. But never mind that. What's all this about him being exclusive?"

"You've to be at least a duke before you get Vergette to handle your affairs."

Alex's heart dropped. What the deuce had he got himself into? Or was this one of Vincent's starts? "That can't be right. Know for a fact he's served a fellow who's no better than a wine merchant."

Vincent's disbelieving stare was disconcerting. "Wine merchant? Impossible! I tell you, Alex, my father tried for years to get Vergette, but the fellow wouldn't look at him."

"But your father was of a rank with mine, though I believe our title is older."

"Considerably. But that's not it. I told you. Vergette is practically royalty in the legal world. Dukes, yes. Possibly a marquis or two. Nothing less, I assure you."

Bemused, Alex could only gaze at the man. To say this put a whole new complexion on Apple's trust was an understatement. What the deuce kind of a bumblebroth he'd stumbled on, he dreaded to think.

"No wine merchants then?"

"Not unless Vergette was in his cups when he agreed to serve the fellow, and that's not likely. By all accounts, he's as sober as a Methodist."

The development gave Alex furiously to think, but he was obliged to change the subject when Vincent showed an alarming curiosity in his mission. Fortunately, he was readily diverted into a discussion of his own troubles. While Alex responded suitably, however, he was distrait, his mind revolving the mystery of Greenaway having placed his daughter's trust in the hands of the exclusive Vergette.

After a rough night, disturbed by unquiet dreams of chasing a fugitive Apple through uncharted and unfamiliar territory, Alex set forth in no optimistic frame of mind, after a breakfast in the company of a morose and sleepy host, who was suffering in his usual fashion of a morning from having thoroughly drowned his troubles the night before.

He had Vergette's direction from Apple, and he was armed with her letter of authority. But Vincent's revelations had left him doubtful of his reception, even if the wretched fellow was available. If he'd gone off somewhere, what the devil was Alex to do? Chase him down? Resolving to cross that bridge if and when he came to it, he called up a hackney carriage and gave the address to the jarvey.

Alex had dismissed his servants, telling Carver to come to Lord Wintringham's lodging in Ryder Street for instructions in the afternoon. There was no avoiding sending the coach and horses to the Luthrie stables in the mews behind Berkeley Square. Carver and Laycock could put up in the rooms above, and Alex only hoped the groom left to keep the place in order could be induced to keep his mouth shut. He'd supplied Carver with the means to bribe the man, and must hope it would serve.

On the other hand, he was less than sanguine about how matters would fare with Vergette, and it might become impossible to keep the whole affair from the ears of his parents. If he was obliged to look after Apple until her birthday in January, there would be no keeping his activities secret.

The address, in a quiet leafy lane not far from the Inns of Court, proved to be a well-kept house of imposing grandeur. Alex paused before it, looking up at the tall façade with its arched and pillared windows, no longer in doubt of Vincent's assertion of the lawyer's high status.

He walked up the steps and rang the bell in a mood of growing discomfort. A porter opened the door and politely enquired his business.

"Is Mr Vergette in?"

The fellow eyed him in a fashion which instantly put up Alex's back.

"Well, don't stare at me as if I was a snake, man! Is he here or not?"

This form of address appeared to reassure the fellow, who assumed a more respectful mien at once and gave a small bow. "If you'd care to come in, sir."

Alex followed him through a vestibule. Through an open door at the back, he glimpsed an office with desk clerks busily at work, backed by bookshelves thick with huge tomes and piled boxes. The porter ushered him into a pleasant front room furnished for comfort but in a business-like fashion, with crimson-upholstered chairs ranged around a baize-topped table, and two easy chairs in similar style set either side of a marbled fireplace. Clearly this was a venue for meetings, as well as a waiting area for clients.

Alex took up a stance before the fire, warming his hands and feeling a touch relieved. It looked as if Mr Vergette was here at least. He began to have doubts of actually getting in to see the fellow, if the porter's attitude was anything to go by. Well, if necessary, he'd have to take a high hand. He could have laughed, recalling how he'd told Apple he wasn't in the habit of puffing off his consequence. Hoist with his own petard. How she'd crow if she knew!

At this point, the door opened to admit a fellow of middle years, well-dressed and with a benevolent manner.

"How do you do, sir? I understand you are wishful of seeing Mr Vergette?"

Ah, so this wasn't the man himself. Should have known it wouldn't be as easy as all that. "I have urgent business with him."

The man smiled his understanding. "You have no appointment, of course.."

Alex lifted his chin. "Didn't suppose I'd need one."

The clerk, or assistant, or whatever he was, did not bat an eye. "May I ask your name, sir?"

"I'm Dymond. Alexander Dymond."

He was about to add his father's credentials when the fellow's brows rose. "Ah yes, sir, you'll be the heir to the Earl of Luthrie."

Surprised, Alex cocked an eyebrow. "You know him?"

"Not personally, my lord. It is our business to know the workings of the world, however."

Alex stared. "Don't tell me you carry the whole peerage in your head?"

The fellow smiled. "Perhaps not all. But I've been doing this for a very long time, Lord Dymond."

Alex frowned. "Who are you?"

The smile grew. "I'm Vergette, my lord Dymond. Shall we sit?"

Astounded, Alex could only stare at the man. "Why the deuce didn't you say so in the first place?"

"But then you would have had the advantage of me, my lord."

Feeling flustered, Alex took the indicated chair to one side of the fire and watched Vergette take his seat opposite. The lawyer crossed one leg over the other and smiled across the small divide, for all the world as if he meant to entertain a guest.

Thrown, Alex knew not how to begin. In all his experience of the legal profession, he'd never met a lawyer who behaved in such a fashion. He'd fully expected to be shown into one of those intimidating offices, all red tape and fusty documents inhabited by a prim and proper, and probably severe, individual who would peer at him over the top of a pair of spectacles.

The image made him laugh, and Vergette gave him an enquiring look.

"Something amuses you, Lord Dymond?"

Alex cleared his throat, feeling his cheeks warm a little. Not so benevolent after all. He would swear those eyes could pierce one at ten paces! He opted for frankness. "Never met a lawyer like you. Not what I expected at all."

The smile reappeared. "In my line of work, my lord, a relaxed atmosphere is essential. Now, what can I do for you?"

Brought to a sense of his duty, Alex pulled himself together. It was evident plain speaking was in order with this man. "It's about Miss Appoline Greenaway."

An intent look came into Vergette's eyes, which did not veer from Alex's face. It was singularly unnerving.

"Indeed, my lord Dymond. And what have you to do with Miss Greenaway?"

Alex's neck-cloth felt a trifle tight. Ridiculous. He had nothing of which to be ashamed. "I'm acting for her. That's why I wanted to see you. She's given me an authority for you to disclose her affairs to me."

He fished in his pocket for the letter he'd directed Apple to write and drew it out. Vergette made no move to take it.

"I repeat, my lord, what is your interest in Miss Greenaway?"

Incensed now, Alex hit back. "None, sir! Happened upon her by accident, if you must know, when she was trying to make her way to London to see you."

The unnerving stillness of the man caused Alex to clam up, unwilling to expose Apple's folly to a fellow he was fast coming to believe would prove wholly unsympathetic. His silent glare at last brought the smile back into Vergette's face, though it was only faintly reflected in his eyes, which remained wary.

"I do beg your pardon, Lord Dymond. I'm afraid I harboured unworthy thoughts of your motives for a moment."

"My motives? What the deuce are you talking about?"

Vergette inclined his head. "How did it come about that you happened upon Miss Greenaway, my lord?"

Thoroughly ruffled, Alex brought it out flat. "She held me up!"

The brows rose. "Held you up?"

"She sneaked into my coach and asked me to take her to the next stage. When I refused, she produced a pistol."

Vergette's lips twitched and his shoulders shook. The fellow was amused. Relief swept through Alex.

"An enterprising young lady, Miss Greenaway."

"You don't know the half of it," said Alex with feeling.

"No doubt you will enlighten me further as to Miss Greenaway's present whereabouts?"

"Took her to my sister's. She'll be safe enough there and chaperoned, which is more to the point."

Vergette nodded. "Do I assume rightly that your business with me is to press her request for me to intervene on her behalf with these marriage plans?"

The fellow was astute, one had to give him that. Alex resolved to put his cards on the table. "Point is, she don't like this Cumberledge fellow. No reason why she should. And these guardians of hers appear to be intent upon getting hold of her trust by means of marrying her off to him. As I understand it, he's Greenaway's partner in the wine business Apple's father left."

"Yes, she told me as much in her letter."

Something in Vergette's voice made Alex suspicious. "You knew already? Before she wrote, I mean."

He chose not to answer this, giving that enigmatic smile again. "My lord Dymond, may I ask what you intend by Miss Greenaway?"

"I mean to keep her safe from her people until she's of age. That is, if you won't stand her friend and refuse to break the trust."

"You do realise the trust comes into its own in a matter of weeks, do you not?"

"Apple thinks so, yes."

The lawyer's brows drew together. "A singular pet name, my lord?"

He laughed. "Nothing to do with me. By Miss Greenaway's account, it was her father's invention."

Vergette fell silent again, the fingers of one hand drumming on the arm of his chair. His gaze never left his guest's face, and Alex felt compelled to break that intent stare.

"What I don't understand is why you consented to act for Greenaway in the first place, sir. By all accounts, he ain't the sort of client you'd choose."

The lawyer's features took on an odd expression, as if he was considering whether to answer this. At length, his fingers became still and an edge entered his voice.

"Mr John Greenaway was never my client, my lord. He was merely the instrument through which I served Miss Greenaway."

Mystified, Alex could only stare at the man. Vergette's brows rose. "You are wondering how I should come to be serving Miss Greenaway. That, my lord Dymond, is a matter I could reveal only under particular circumstances."

A sliver of apprehension ran through Alex. "What circumstances?"

Vergette put his hands together and steepled his fingers, the sphinx-like smile coming into play. "Until they arise, my lord, my lips are, so to speak, sealed."

Baffled, his earlier disquiet rising to the surface, Alex knew not what to think, much less what to say. But one thing he could pursue. "Will you act for Miss Greenaway and set her mind at rest?"

"Act how, my lord Dymond?"

"What I mean is, will you refuse to break the trust if these wretched fellows come to you on the matter?"

"They may come, my lord, but they will not find me."

"But you won't break the trust," Alex insisted.

"It is out of my power to do so. Where this notion came from that I could, I cannot imagine."

Bewilderment wreathed Alex's brain. "Getting confused here, Vergette. Apple's Cousin Marjorie seemed to think the trust would be broken if she married before her twenty-first birthday."

"There is no mystery. The trust is purely for the benefit of Miss Greenaway. It may not be touched by another, regardless of her circumstances. My task is merely to hold it until she wishes to make use of the articles therein. That is all."

"Articles?"

"There are provisions made."

More and more baffling. "Provisions? I thought it was money. That's what Miss Greenaway supposes. At least, it's what her father told her."

Vergette merely tapped his fingers together, his features resuming that carefully blank expression. But he was not apparently as divorced from Apple's future prospects as he appeared.

"What will your lordship do with Miss Greenaway in these next weeks?"

"To tell you the truth, I've no notion. My sister has to go to my mother's for Christmas. And so have I, come to that." He gave the man a look. "But one thing I won't do is give her back to those schemers."

Vergette fell into one of his habitual silences for a space. Alex half ignored him, his mind busy with the problem that now confronted him. He almost started when the lawyer spoke.

"If I might make a suggestion?"

Alex eyed him, mistrusting the resumption of the friendly manner. "Go on."

"If I cannot prevail upon you to return Miss Greenaway to her home —"

"You can't, for I've given my word."

"Yes, I rather thought you might have done. In that case, may I request you to return to me in the New Year."

"What, bring Apple to you, do you mean? When the time is right?"

Vergette pursed his lips. "I think not. Initially, I must ask you to come alone. By that time, I trust Miss Greenaway may have thought better of her rash action."

"Doubt it, to be frank. But I did say I'd take her back once she was her own mistress. Got to see her safe."

A purely genuine smile creased the lawyer's mouth. Alex found it singularly charming and no longer wondered how it came about that this urbane and astute man had risen so high in his profession.

"An excellent idea, my lord. But before you do so, I suggest you bring Miss Greenaway to Town. I would prefer to see you first, and then you may bring her to me."

A resurgence of Alex's initial apprehension surfaced. "Dashed if I see why you'd need to see me first. Nothing to do with me. It's Apple's inheritance, not mine."

Again the smile, this time with a distinct air of reassurance. "I acquit you of any unnatural design upon her fortune, my lord Dymond."

"Fortune?"

His brows rose and he remained wholly unmoved. "Did I say fortune? I meant in the sense of future prospects."

Alex was having none of it. "No, you didn't. Worth a good deal, is she? It's what the Greenaways think."

"Then they are misinformed."

Alex regarded him stonily. The fellow was lying. He'd slipped up. Refreshing to find he could slip up! "Well, I'll accept that for the time being, Vergette, since you insist."

A slight twitch of the lips acknowledged a hit, and Alex nearly laughed out.

Vergette rose, holding out his hand. "My compliments to Miss Greenaway."

Alex shook the hand. "Not that she'll be any too pleased with what you've told me."

"Then you will word it with care, my lord. I must rely upon you for that."

"I ain't lying to the chit, if that's what you mean."

"Nothing so uncouth, my lord Dymond. Bear in mind that in a matter of weeks, Miss Greenaway will be fully informed."

"Not sure she's got the patience to wait."

"I feel certain you will persuade her." The fellow gave a slight bow. "Until we meet again, my lord."

Escorted to the door by his host — for such Alex felt his attitude to be — he departed, as much infuriated as puzzled by the outcome of his visit.

Chapter Ten

On tenterhooks, Apple found it impossible to settle. In vain did Georgy remind her that their escape had been carried out without the smallest difficulty. Yes, it was true there'd been no sign of Marjorie when she slipped out of the shop, huddled in her cloak with the hood well forward, and leapt into the carriage with more haste than grace. They had been away in minutes, trotting out of the town at a sedate speed that accorded ill with Apple's panicked desire to race back to the safety of Merrivale House as fast as the horses could go.

She knew it was ridiculous to suppose her cousins could be hard on her heels, but the apprehension persisted. If Marjorie could track her to the town, what should stop her discovering her present whereabouts?

"Good heavens, Apple, how should she? I wish you won't be so fidgety."

"I can't help it. You don't know Marjorie."

"No, and I am not likely to either," said Georgy with asperity. "How in the world should she know you are here? She doesn't even know you were with Alex, does she?"

Which was true, but it was of no comfort to Apple. "It wouldn't be difficult to find out, would it? After all, she has only to make enquiries at the inn where we stopped. Alex may have given his name."

"But not yours."

"If she asked whether he had a female with him and someone described me…"

"I think you are being very silly. Even if she is clever enough to think of that —"

"Which she is."

"— she can't possibly know Alex has a sister living here."

"Then what was she doing in Romsey? It's entirely in the wrong direction for London."

Georgy remained unconvinced, arguing hotly against any possibility of Marjorie turning up on her doorstep. After a light repast, of which Apple was only able to swallow a mouthful or two, Georgy went off for her nap, recommending her guest to delve into *Humphrey Clinker* — a volume of which Apple knew she would have thoroughly disapproved did she know its contents — as an antidote to anxiety. Instead, Apple paced the parlour floor, the book lying unopened on a chair.

As the day wore on, doubt crept in and her anxiety began to subside. Had it been Marjorie? She'd had time only for a brief peek. Had she been mistaken? She must suppose there were other women in possession of a purple pelisse and a large brown hat. Though to be sure Marjorie had been wearing the self-same outfit when Apple sneaked out of their coach. Suppose it was Marjorie, where then was Walter? Or Mr Cumberledge, come to that? Both had been with her. Would they have come on together, having discovered no trace of her in Alton? Or had they returned home, leaving Mr Cumberledge in charge at the shop?

She'd not before considered the matter, beyond supposing they would scour the town before coming after her. Even then, she'd thought they must make for London rather than trying to locate her on the road. Only they had no notion where she meant to go. Had Marjorie not guessed her destination? Had she noticed her correspondence with Mr Vergette? The seal of his letter had not been broken admittedly, but Apple would not put it past Marjorie to read the letter after it was opened, could she but find it in the secret cache in her chamber.

A horrible fear clutched in her chest. Had Marjorie ransacked her room? Had the precious box Papa gave her been found? Walter and Marjorie would know everything Papa had known about the trust if that were so. They would realise it had no bearing on the takings of the winery. In which case, they would be even more determined upon her marriage to Mr Cumberledge, for he'd become master of whatever inheritance was to come her way.

This reflection served to increase her agitation, and she could not help wishing Alex had not left her here while he went to see Mr Vergette. She'd battled with him over being high-handed, but in his absence, it came home to her how safe she'd felt with Alex at her back.

When Georgy entered the parlour, refreshed and ready for her dinner, Apple did her best to appear calm. She was hungry enough by this time to make a reasonable meal, but if she'd been asked, she could not have said what she ate, and she could not help starting at every untoward sound until Georgy became exasperated.

"Stop it, Apple! You will have me on the fidgets too, if you don't take care. Then Reddy will scold and send me to bed and make me drink warm milk or a horrid tisane."

This made Apple laugh despite her fears. "She won't send you to bed, don't be ridiculous. You aren't a child."

"She thinks I am. She cossets me as if I were two, not twenty. And I hate warm milk!"

Apple was conscious of a twinge of envy. No one had ever cosseted her, or not that she could remember. Perhaps her mother had done, but she had not the benefit of knowing about it. Papa had been good to her, but he was never a demonstrative parent and he'd left it to the maids to supply her needs. After that, there had been only Mrs Hatherley and

Marjorie, neither of whom had shown the least disposition to treat her with the sort of smothering care that Georgy's old nurse displayed. What was more, it was plain Captain Edginton was an indulgent husband who was inordinately fond of his wife. Georgy didn't know how lucky she was.

A wave of ancient loneliness almost overcame Apple, and she was hard put to it to keep her countenance. She'd ever been resilient and resourceful, but the deep-seated feeling of isolation that had plagued her from her earliest years could never be wholly shaken off.

Fortunately, she was not called upon to contribute very much to the conversation, and Georgy's prattle served to lull her unease. It was not long after the tea tray had been brought in that Mrs Reddicliffe appeared to drag Georgy off to bed.

"And you ought not to be drinking tea, Lady Georgiana, for it's no good for the infant. I'll fetch you up a glass of warm milk directly, once I have you nicely tucked in."

Georgy submitted, but threw a comical grimace over her shoulder at Apple as she left the parlour, which made her laugh out the moment the door was closed. She was not long behind, preferring bed to intrusive thoughts of pursuit and capture while she was deprived of Alex's protection. In the event, the day's anxiety had taken its toll and she slept the night through, waking refreshed and much inclined to think she'd been indulging fears as foolish as Georgy had thought them.

Apple continued in this better frame of mind until the middle of the afternoon, when the sound of a carriage and horses sent her flying to the parlour window.

"Oh, I do hope it is your brother returned from London!"

But one look at the ancient coach rumbling slowly down the drive and her heart leapt into her throat. "Oh, dear lord, it is them! Georgy, it's my cousins!"

She turned briefly to where her hostess was lounging on the chaise longue, with her feet up. Georgy sat up in a bang.

"You don't mean it! How do you know?"

"It's their coach. I could not mistake. What in the world shall I do? Where can I hide?"

Distracted, Apple continued watching as the lumbering vehicle slowed down on its approach to the entrance of the house, her heart thumping in her chest.

"Come away from the window, Apple!"

Georgy was up, moving across the room. She pulled Apple back and took her place, peering down. "They are stopping. Yes, the groom is jumping down. He has let down the steps. Oh, gracious! There is a female getting out."

"Marjorie! Quick, Georgy, what shall we do? If she finds me, all will be lost!"

"I have it!" Coming away from the window, Georgy dashed to a panel in the back wall. "This will serve excellently." She pressed the panel and it slid open like a door, revealing an aperture. "See, it is the servant entrance. You hardly notice it when it's closed."

Apple had not noticed it at all. She went to the concealed door and looked through to where Georgy was standing in a narrow hallway. "Where does it lead?"

"To the back stairs and then down to the scullery. You can escape and hide in the kitchen."

Apple followed her into the passage, squeezing past Georgy and running to the end. Another door revealed a short landing leading down a dark and narrow stairway. Satisfied, Apple closed the door and returned to Georgy.

The peal of the doorbell sounded from the hall downstairs. The flurry of Apple's pulse increased. "Could I be seen if I stood behind this door?"

"Good heavens, Apple, what are you thinking? You must run and conceal yourself at once!"

"No! I want to hear what is said. They won't see me, I'm persuaded. I never even knew there was a door here."

"Oh, very well, if you must." Georgy went back into the parlour and made ready to close the door. "But I doubt they will even come up here. Berryman will deny me. He knows better than to allow undesirable persons to come in."

"He won't put Marjorie off. What will you say, Georgy? You must decide at once."

"Say? Goodness, I don't know."

"Well, think!"

Georgy's blue orbs sparkled. "Oh, I do know. I shall deny knowing anything about you, of course. If I refuse to acknowledge knowing you, what can this Marjorie of yours do?"

"I don't know, but I feel sure she will think of something," said Apple on a pessimistic note. Footsteps sounded on the stairs, and her fright revived. "Close the door, Georgy!"

Georgy hesitated. "If I can't put them off, you'd best run down to the kitchen and hide in any event, Apple."

"Yes, yes, but someone is coming! Close the door quickly!" As the light began to fade as the door came to, she added, "And sit down! Pretend you are resting. You are not expecting visitors."

"Yes, all right. Now be quiet, Apple!"

The light vanished and Apple was plunged into stifling gloom.

For several moments, Apple was completely disoriented, closed in as she was without light or sound. A penetrating chill crept into her feet, and her fright augmented the feeling of being stifled.

Muffled sounds came from the other side of the panel door. She put her ear to the wood and recognised Berryman in the slight distortion of his voice.

"So I said, my lady, but the lady claimed cousinship to Miss Greenaway, and as she has the same name —"

"Good heavens, Berryman, don't say you told her Miss Greenaway is here?"

"Certainly not, my lady. I merely desired them to wait in the hall while I ascertained —"

"You should have said I was indisposed. Or dead!"

Apple threw up her eyes in the darkness. *Georgy, for heaven's sake!* But Berryman was patience itself.

"If you will give me leave, my lady, I was about to explain that I gave no hint of your ladyship's presence or otherwise. I told them I would ascertain whether anyone was able to receive them."

Apple let out a silent breath of relief, but Georgy's was clearly audible.

"Thank goodness! Well, go and tell them no one can see them at all."

Berryman's footsteps retreated. There was a swish and patter and the panel door was jerked open.

"There, Apple, you can come out. Isn't Berryman wonderful? They will be gone in a flash."

Blinking in the sudden light, Apple remained just where she was. "Not until we hear the carriage and I know they've truly gone."

"Berryman will get rid of them, never fear. After all, they can't force their way into my parlour, can they?"

Apple agreed to this, though her doubts were not entirely suppressed.

"I'll watch for them coming out," Georgy said, running to the window.

But any notion Apple had indulged of emerging from her hiding place was quashed by the unmistakeable sounds of an altercation coming from downstairs.

"I knew it! Marjorie is too stubborn to take no for an answer."

The voices were getting louder and Georgy, with a small shriek, scuttled back to the chaise longue, flapping her hand and hissing at Apple, "Close the door, quick!"

Apple found the knob on her side and pulled the door to, hearing it close again with a soft click that echoed in her head even as the voice she'd dreaded hearing came through loud and clear.

"It's no use barring the door, my man, for I'll see this Lady Georgiana of yours or die in the attempt!"

Apple heard Georgy's frightened squeak, several male grunts and then the thunk of the parlour door banging open. Instinct sent her backing down the passage, her mind freezing on the possibility of Marjorie's stalking instantly to the panel and wrenching open the door to find her.

"I beg pardon, my lady, but I did my best to stop them." Berryman was abnormally loud and slightly out of breath.

"Ho, yes, you did that all right! To no avail. You don't know who you're dealing with."

Walter! Oh, heavens, she was undone!

Marjorie took over, speaking with belligerence. "I'm Miss Greenaway, ma'am, and if that isn't enough to give me entrance here, then I'm sorry for it, but I'll not be put off finding out for myself."

"Will you have the goodness, madam, to allow me to edge in a word?"

An arctic voice, in which Apple barely recognised the flighty Georgy she knew.

"Well, I will, but don't think to pull the wool over my eyes, for you won't."

"I have no desire to pull the wool over your eyes. Perhaps you will be good enough, madam, to explain why you have forced your way into my house."

"She'll tell you all right," came in a growl from Walter, "if you'll have this fellow desist so I can let him go."

There was a short silence. Only half realising she did so, Apple crept back towards the door.

"You may leave us, Berryman. Remain within call, if you please."

Apple could hear the faint fear under Georgy's brave words and a wash of remorse swept through her. This was her fault. Georgy should not have to endure Marjorie and Walter all by herself. Especially when she'd been so good and kind. Apple hovered on the brink of revealing herself, only to spare her hostess. But Marjorie's voice, calmer now, gave her pause.

"That's better. Now we may thrash this out between us, my lady."

"Certainly, if I understood what it is you wish to thrash out. So far I am at a loss."

Apple could have laughed out at the tone. Georgy was playing the *grande dame* to perfection. Unfortunately it had the effect of ruffling Marjorie's feathers.

"I wish you won't come all highty-tighty with me, ma'am. I may not be your equal, but I'm sorely beset and I'd take it kind in you to listen without prejudice."

"How dare you?" Georgy sounded much more her usual self, clearly genuinely annoyed. "Your insolence passes all bounds, madam, barging into my private apartments and having your escort stand there like a gaoler!"

Another short silence ensued. Apple could almost hear her cousin struggling with herself.

"Walter, leave the room. I'll handle this."

"But I want to hear this as much as you do."

"Then get away from the door." Apple could hear Walter grumbling and his clumping steps. "Now, my lady. I've reason to believe your brother abducted my cousin."

"Abducted? My brother? I don't know what you're talking about."

"He's Lord Dymond, isn't he? Your brother, I mean."

"What of it?"

Marjorie's patience snapped. "Oh, don't play the innocent, my lady! I know Apple was with him. The innkeeper at the Dragon in Winchester was explicit, and I know the villain must have taken her up at Alton when she left our coach. It's taken hours of hunting and question, but that much I've ascertained, so it's no use your denying it."

A trill of laughter came from Georgy. "What a perfectly bewildering story! My brother to behave in such a way? You must have taken leave of your senses."

Careful, Georgy, thought Apple. This style of speech would only infuriate Marjorie. So it proved.

"So that's your attitude, is it? I'm more than seven, Lady Georgiana Edginton, and your name has come up in my investigations more than once, I'll have you know."

"*My name?*" Georgy's tone was a model of disbelief. "I cannot imagine what you mean."

"She's lying!" Walter was in again. "She can't keep her eyes still, watch."

Oh, this was intolerable! Poor Georgy! What should Apple do? If she burst out to succour her friend, all would be lost.

"Lady Georgiana, I'll ask you straight," said Marjorie with deliberation, "where is your brother?"

"I have not the least idea," Georgy snapped, abandoning her pose of outraged aristocracy. "Nor do I know why you should suppose I keep track of his movements."

"He's been here, though, and within the last few days."

Georgy remained silent. Again, Apple was hard put to it not to enter the scene. Her fright had given way to fury. It was monstrous of Marjorie to subject Georgy to this rude catechism.

"And he had my cousin with him when he came, that much I do know."

Georgy rallied. "Do you indeed? Then you know a deal more than I."

"What's more," pursued Marjorie in that inexorable way that had so often driven Apple into frenzy, "I've since discovered you've a young girl staying with you."

"Indeed?"

"You were at Emmeline's with her. The woman couldn't wait to boast of having your custom. That's how we found you, Lady Georgiana. Not that we wouldn't have done in any event, but it was a deal easier to follow the delivery boy than to cast about asking all and sundry how to find Merrivale House."

From Georgy's silence, it was evident this impertinence had flummoxed her. In all the panic and flurry, Apple had not noticed the cart that must have come through either ahead or before the Greenaway's coach. It would have gone around the back of the house in any event, though Apple was surprised none of them had heard a clopping horse.

"Well?" Walter spoke again, in a horrid crowing growl, as if he knew Georgy was beaten. "Nothing to say, eh? I wasn't convinced, Marje, but I am now."

It was too much. Apple set her hand on the door knob. She was stayed by the sound of the parlour door opening, and a new voice spoke.

"What the deuce is to do here? Who are you people? And what the devil do you mean by badgering my sister?"

Chapter Eleven

Satisfied to see the stunned expressions of the unwelcome visitors, Alex stalked into the parlour, sizing them up. The woman, whom he took to be Apple's cousin Marjorie, was of middling stature but rather too much girth and a large bosom, with hard grey eyes in a round countenance, high-coloured just now and hostile.

The man was stocky, but a protruding belly indicated an addiction to the fleshpots and veining to his nose and cheeks suggested an avid partiality to the wine he sold. Since he resembled the female in face if not form, Alex took him for Walter Greenaway rather than the despised Cumberledge.

Before he could say anything further, Georgy chimed in.

"Thank goodness you are here, Alex! How you came so opportunely I have no notion, but I am so glad and I wish you will rid me of these people at once!"

His arrival on the scene was not as fortuitous as it appeared, but he could explain all that later. No time now, when Marjorie Greenaway, having evidently recovered from surprise, was turning on him with an ominous look.

"So am I glad to see you, Lord Dymond, if that is who you are. Answer me this. Where is my cousin?"

Alex regarded her with hauteur. "Ain't about to answer your question, ma'am, until you've answered mine. Who are you?"

"We're Appoline's cousins, sir, as you must very well guess. It's no use denying you abducted Apple because we've followed your movements from Winchester, and we know you brought her here."

"My movements ain't your concern, ma'am, and as for abduction, boot's on the other leg."

The woman's jaw dropped open. "Well, if I ever heard the like!"

Here the fellow Walter took a hand, jerking forward. "What's this? What are you saying? What does he mean, Marje?"

Alex began to enjoy himself. "I mean, Mr Greenaway, that Apple abducted me. At pistol point, if you must know."

"Ha! The minx! I told you she'd taken the pistol out of my coach, Marje, and you wouldn't believe me."

"Be silent, Walter!" Glaring at Alex, Marjorie went into the attack. "So you admit she was with you, Lord Dymond?"

"Never denied it. But if you think I had anything to do with her escape from you, you're fair and far off."

"That won't fadge," snapped Walter. "If you didn't help her escape, why didn't you bring her back?"

Marjorie's eyes lit with triumph. "Just so. Answer that, if you can, my lord girl-stealing Dymond!"

Alex almost laughed out at this masterly description. "With ease, Miss Greenaway. Apple don't wish to marry Mr Cumberledge and if I'd brought her back to you, she'd have been constrained to do so. Besides, she wasn't running away, merely going to London to see Vergette."

He could see his candour was having the effect of baffling the enemy and congratulated himself on his tactics.

"Vergette?" Walter looked from him to his sister. "I said that too. I knew she'd head for that lawyer fellow. Told you we should have gone there at once."

Miss Greenaway did not trouble to reply, instead fixing Alex with a hard glare. "You're aiding and abetting a minor, Lord Dymond."

"Not for much longer."

Marjorie looked taken aback. "You're going to give her back?"

"When she's past her birthday and only if she wishes it. But that ain't what I meant."

Walter Greenaway exploded. "You've no right to keep her from us! I'm her guardian and I demand you produce her instantly. Where is she?"

"A very good question, brother. Where is she, Lord Dymond? In London?"

"No, she's here all right and tight. Keeping out of sight, I don't doubt. What, did you think I'd less than common sense, Miss Greenaway? Couldn't jaunter about the country with the chit unchaperoned. Left her with my sister while I did the business with Vergette."

As he'd confidently expected, this information took the wind out of their sails. Walter spluttered like a landed fish, and Marjorie blinked at him for several moments in a dazed fashion.

Georgy took the opportunity to jump in. "Oh, have you seen him, Alex? Was your mission successful?"

Alex frowned her down. "Tell you later."

But the intervention had the effect of reviving Marjorie.

"Do you mean to say, sir, you've had the effrontery to see Vergette yourself?"

"You've no right," complained Walter again, his voice a whine. "What did you say to him?"

Alex turned to the man. "Told him what was afoot and asked if he'd support Apple, just as she asked me to do."

Under no circumstances was he going to reveal the substance of Vergette's discourse to these vultures. They'd find out for themselves soon enough, no doubt.

Marjorie's colour rose. "You've a deal of brass, Lord Dymond, taking it upon yourself to talk to Vergette. Still, I'll be bound he told you nothing. The wretch is as close as an oyster."

"Oh, he was forthcoming enough."

To his intense pleasure, this caused the woman's cheeks to flame more. He dared swear he'd see sparks coming from her eyes in a moment.

"I don't believe you! You're lying just as surely as this Lady Georgiana wretch here lied in the first place."

Alex's amusement was quenched. "Hey! Leave my sister out of this!"

"Yes, you horrid creature! How dare you speak of me in that fashion?"

"Quiet, Georgy! As for you, Miss Greenaway, you'll keep a civil tongue in your head or you don't get a syllable more out of me."

Marjorie Greenaway visibly struggled with herself. If this was the woman's temperament, Alex was blowed if he gave Apple back to her at all.

"Very well, Lord Dymond," she said at last, her tone as of one gritting her teeth. "Now would you kindly allow me to have a word with my cousin?"

Alex hesitated. He didn't know just where Apple was at this moment, but he doubted she'd wish to see the woman. "You ain't taking her away from here, I'll tell you that now."

"And I'd like to hear that from Apple's lips, sir. How do I know you haven't constrained her?"

"Like your brother, you mean?"

Walter reddened. "I've had enough of this, Marje! We'll go to London and see the lawyer fellow ourselves."

Marjorie flapped a hand at him and continued to stare at Alex. "Yes, we'll see a lawyer all right, but it won't be Vergette. Lord Dymond, if you don't produce my cousin in person, we'll have you up on a charge of kidnapping."

Alex was just about to scarify the woman with a counter threat when the panel at the back of the room sprang open and Apple tumbled into the room.

"No! I won't have it! I won't let you!"

Chapter Twelve

The impulse that had sent her through the door gave way to dismay as Apple saw the effect of her entrance on the assembled company.

Georgy gave a shriek. "Apple, you idiot!"

"Ha!" exploded from Walter. "There you are, you disobedient wench!"

Marjorie glared. "Stupid, stupid girl!"

All of which Apple largely ignored, her gaze riveted on Alex, who cast up his eyes and shook his head at her. She took this up first. "It's no use looking like that, Alex. I couldn't possibly stand by and let them threaten you."

"But, my dear girl —"

Riding over him, Apple turned on Marjorie. "How dare you try and have him charged with such a thing? Of course he didn't kidnap me. I kidnapped him, if you must know, just as he said. And he's looked after me much better than either of you ever did."

She turned on the last, her fury embracing Walter as well, who growled in a fashion with which she was all too familiar.

"There's gratitude for you!"

"I've no reason to be grateful to you, Walter. You've done nothing but try to get at my inheritance from the start."

She came under instant fire from Marjorie.

"Will you be quiet, Apple? Your conduct is disgraceful. Anyone would suppose you'd been taught nothing of decency and maidenly modesty. Running off by yourself? Taking up with a strange man? What were you thinking?"

"Just what Lord Dymond told you. I wanted to see Mr Vergette. You wouldn't support me when I told you I couldn't stand the notion of marrying Mr Cumberledge. What else could I do?"

"You deserve a good slapping, girl! And when I get you home —"

"That will do, Miss Greenaway!"

The command came from Alex in a tone Apple had never heard from him. Marjorie stopped mid-sentence, her mouth still open as her head whipped round. Alex took a step towards her, and Apple almost quailed at the look in his face.

"You'll raise a hand to the chit over my dead body, understand?"

A thrill shot through Apple's veins and her heart began to pump hard. It was like having her very own champion, as if she was a medieval lady.

Marjorie was not visibly cowed and Walter squared up to him.

"You've no say in the matter, Lord Dymond. I keep telling you, I'm Apple's guardian."

"A pretty sort of guardian to be selling the girl off to your partner only to get your hands on her trust!"

Sarcasm was rife in Alex's tone, and Apple saw how both her cousins reddened. Her satisfaction was short-lived, for his words unleashed Marjorie's fury.

"And what if he did? It's his due as John's heir. Salting away his substance into a trust for his daughter when the business is suffering? How selfish can a man be?"

"That's right," came in a whine from Walter that set Apple's teeth on edge. "He's done me out of what's mine, and I'll be satisfied if I die in the attempt."

"Suggest you order a coffin then, for you won't be satisfied by way of Apple's trust."

Contempt rode Alex's tone, but it had little effect on her cousins beyond angering Walter even more.

"Because you've chosen to take her part? It won't fadge, sir. You've no rights in the matter."

"Neither have you."

Walter's cheeks suffused. "What the devil do you mean?"

"Go and see Vergette. He'll set you right about your rights."

Apple watched her cousin's jaw working. He looked uncertain and no wonder. What had Mr Vergette told Alex? In all the hubbub, she'd forgotten where he'd been all this time.

Marjorie had been silent, but she rallied. Arms akimbo, she confronted Alex. "Do you think you've got the edge of us, Lord Dymond? You'll learn to know me better."

"My God, I hope not! Know as much of you as I care to already."

Apple stifled a giggle and could not withstand a glance at Georgy, who had plonked down onto her chaise longue, watching the batting back and forth between the combatants as if she were watching them play at shuttlecock and battledore.

"Your insolence passes all bounds, sir!"

"Indeed, Mr Greenaway? More bounds than you barging into my sister's house and badgering her? Could have you arrested for disturbing the peace or something."

Marjorie snorted. "Rubbish! The only person here who is liable to arrest is you, Lord Dymond. It's all very well to scoff, but I reckon it would be a task beyond even your powers to persuade a magistrate that an innocent girl forced you to do her bidding at gunpoint."

"He has no need to persuade anyone," seethed Apple, "for it is the exact truth and so I would tell him, if you do try to haul Alex up before a magistrate."

"You won't get the chance, child. Locked up for your own good and protection is what you'll be."

"Yes, that is just what I'd expect from you, Marjorie. Do you think I'll tamely submit to such treatment?"

A laugh at her back made her whirl to face Alex.

He grinned at her. "You said she don't know you."

Her lips quivered, but she eyed him in some doubt. "Yet I'd best go with them, I think."

"Apple, you can't," shrieked Georgy.

A crease appeared between his brows. "These are empty threats, Apple. No need to trouble your head about me."

"If she comes home, Lord Dymond, there won't be any threat to you," said Marjorie in a voice dripping with false sweetness.

"That's right," said Walter, adding his mite. "We only came to fetch Apple back where she belongs."

Apple's heart sank. The last thing she wished to do was return her person into the hands of her cousins. But she'd rather do that than put Alex at risk. The realisation caused an odd flutter in her bosom, but she had no time to explore what it might mean.

Wholly ignoring the Greenaways, Alex's gaze remained on hers, the frown now reflected in his eyes. "Don't let them manipulate you, Apple. Nothing they can do to me. Or, if it comes to that, to you."

"Oh, I know that. They can't make me marry Mr Cumberledge, and I always meant to go back once I'd seen Mr Vergette."

"Yes, but you don't have to. Told him I'd see you safe and I ain't handing you over to these vultures without a fight."

Her heart felt as if it was being squeezed and Apple struggled to hold onto her resolve. She lowered her voice. "Could we go into Captain Edginton's library for a moment?"

Still frowning, he nodded and turned to her cousins. "Must beg you to excuse us. Apple wants a word alone."

Walter bridled. "So you and she may plot against us?"

"Or she'll disappear again." Marjorie seized Apple's wrist. She flinched. "I wasn't born yesterday, Lord Dymond."

"Let her go, Miss Greenaway!"

There was so much menace in his voice that Marjorie did let her go. He jerked his head at Apple and moved to the window. She followed him swiftly and he spoke in a murmur. "Something you ought to know. Vergette assured me the trust has nothing to do with the winery. You've only to hold out until your birthday and he'll tell you everything, he said."

Apple heard this with considerable disquiet. "What do you mean, everything?"

Alex hesitated. Was he weighing up what he should tell her? "Seems the trust wasn't even set up by your father."

"Not by Papa? But…"

"He wouldn't explain, but the whole thing is devilish mysterious, Apple."

Abruptly apprehensive, those long-held doubts rising to the surface, she cast a quick glance over her shoulder.

"Don't worry, I won't tell them," said Alex. "Nor should you."

"Good heavens, are you mad? I'd never hear the end of it."

He grasped her hand and his touch sent a quiver running through her. "Apple, you don't have to hear a word more from either of them. Swore I'd protect you until you're your own mistress."

"Yes, but Alex, you can't," she uttered, anguished. "You know you can't. You've got to take Georgy to your mother. And you're supposed to be there already to prepare for Christmas. I've delayed you too long as it is."

"Don't matter. Do you think I could rest easy knowing you were in the clutches of this pair? I'll think of something." In an agony of indecision, Apple unknowingly gripped his hand and he winced. "No need to twist my fingers off, young Apple."

"Oh!" She snatched her hand out of his, goaded into a frantic whisper. "Alex, I don't know what to do!"

"Then be guided by me, because I know exactly what you should do." With that, he moved back into the room and faced her guardians, making his stand without preamble. "She's staying."

"What?"

"Apple, you're coming with us!"

"No, she ain't, Miss Greenaway." Striding to the door, he opened it. "Berryman! Ah, there you are. Escort Mr and Miss Greenaway out, if you would."

"Oh, thank goodness," sighed Georgy.

From her stand by the window, Apple saw Marjorie looking nonplussed while Walter turned almost purple. Marjorie recovered first. "You've not heard the last of this, Lord Dymond, I promise you."

"Don't doubt that." Alex gave a mocking laugh. "Come, Miss Greenaway, time to admit yourself beaten. Nothing more you can do here."

Walter bridled. "Ha! You think so, do you?"

Alex hardly spared him a glance. "I know so, Mr Greenaway. You're trespassers in a private residence and we've plenty of servants on call to throw you out if you don't take yourselves off."

"What? What? You — you —"

"Oh, be quiet, Walter! Very well, Lord Dymond, you've won this round." Her eyes veered to Apple and she shrank inwardly at the malevolence in them. "As for you, Appoline Greenaway, there'll be a reckoning between us before too long. You owe me and you'll pay." With which valedictory utterance, she gathered her dignity and, snapping her fingers at her brother, stalked past Berryman waiting patiently by the door.

Walter hesitated, casting a glance of dislike at Alex and a glare at Apple. "Ho! Ingratitude, that's what it is!"

Berryman closed the door behind the couple, but they could be heard arguing all the way down the stairs. "I'm perfectly exhausted," said Georgy, sinking back into the chaise longue.

Alex blew out a breath. "Good riddance! What a devilish pair!"

Glad as she was to be free of them, Apple could not withstand a ripple of anxiety. She looked at Alex. "But she's right, you know. I do owe her a great deal."

"Gracious, Apple, how should you?" protested Georgy. "She's perfectly horrid."

"But she's looked after me for several years. And when Papa died, she was very kind while I was grieving."

"Pooh! I dare say she was merely trying to curry favour with you."

"No, I believe she felt for me. She's not always as belligerent as this."

Alex came to her and, leading her to a chair, obliged her to sit down. "That's as may be, but she ain't well disposed towards you now."

"She never was really, though I didn't realise it until this business with Mr Cumberledge. I confess I never liked her overmuch."

Georgy cast up her eyes. "Liked her? I should think not indeed."

The sound of wheels on the gravel drive took Alex to the window. "They're away all right. Doubt that's the last we'll see of 'em though."

Georgy lifted her head. "That reminds me, Alex. How did you come to arrive just at the right moment? I was so relieved to see you, but I'm sure I never heard your horses or the coach wheels."

Alex turned, a look of unholy glee in his face. "You wouldn't. Left 'em at the gates and came to the house on foot."

Georgy stared. "What a singular thing to do, Alex, are you mad?"

But Apple was ahead of her. "Do you mean you were behind them?"

"That's it. Caught up with their coach a mile or so down the lane. Laycock had to slow down for it."

"He would. It's the most rumbling old thing and only goes at a snail's pace."

"True, and we had to rumble behind for ages. When it slowed almost to a walk, I poked my head out to find out what was toward, which is when Carver said the thing was turning into your drive, Georgy. I guessed it then, of course, and had Laycock stop the coach at once."

Georgy clapped her hands. "How clever of you, Alex. But should we not tell Berryman to send someone up to bring it in now?"

"Lord, they'll be in the stables by this time. Don't suppose I'd leave the horses standing in this weather, do you?"

"And we didn't hear them because of all the row going on in here," said Apple, reflecting that his ingenuity had impressed her at the outset.

"Told them to walk the horses gently once they saw me let into the house." He looked at his sister. "Can you have dinner brought forward, Georgy? I'm devilish sharp-set."

To Apple's disappointment, he then went off to freshen up before the meal. She'd hoped to tackle him not only about his mission with Vergette, but on the vexed question of what was to happen to her now. This loomed so large that it overshadowed the puzzle of what the lawyer might tell her after her twenty-first birthday. She had first to arrive at that date, and what she was to do in the weeks between she could not begin to fathom. Alex had said he would think of something, but for the life of her she could not imagine what.

Since Georgy, having rung for Berryman and given the order about dinner, decided she too would go up to make ready, Apple had nothing to do but to follow her example. When she got to her chamber, she discovered the gowns from Emmeline's had been left in her room. Nelly must have unpacked the bandboxes because they were disposed neatly across the bed with tissue paper lying between them. A sliver of anticipation ran through Apple. It was so long since she'd had new gowns, and never entirely of her own choosing. She lifted up the russet morning gown and ran a hand over the silken feel of the material. Then she turned her attention to the muslin evening gown. Should she change into it? She was still attired in the made-over gown of Georgy's. The notion became irresistible when a sneaking thought came into her head. How would Alex think she looked in such a gown?

Chapter Thirteen

Alex was not nearly as divorced in his mind from Apple's troubles as she supposed. He'd made good his escape on purpose to avoid becoming involved in explanations before he had a chance to think. With the arrival of the Greenaways, matters had taken a turn he'd not anticipated, and he needed time to work out what to do before Apple started bombarding him with questions.

He'd no intention of withholding anything Vergette had said, but the man had been right. He must tell it with care. He wasn't such a nodcock as not to see Apple's rising disquiet the moment he'd spoken of the mystery. She knew more than she'd told him, that was certain. How much more remained to be seen. He might have to find out before he said anything himself.

Would she tell him? He was confident he'd gained her trust, but she was clearly in the habit of keeping her own counsel. No wonder with that pair of schemers in the frame. Whether she'd tell him all remained a question. Mind, it was clear her knowledge was limited. To tell true, he was as much intrigued on his own account as on hers by what Vergette had hinted. Intrigued and a good deal troubled.

He'd not forgotten the astonishment exhibited by his friend Wintringham when he mentioned Vergette. Nor could he shake off the suspicion engendered by the lawyer's saying he served only Apple and not her father. And by Vincent's account, Vergette only served the highest in the land. What had little Miss Appoline Greenaway to do with dukes and marquises?

The last thing he wanted was to burden Apple with the only thing he could think of to explain it. Yet if he was right, his position vis-à-vis the chit was invidious, to say the least.

Alive to all the potential consequences of taking her under his protection, Alex knew he was playing with fire. Yet he also knew he could not abandon the chit. As well kick a puppy. No, not quite that. A resilient little thing, young Apple. She'd not hesitate to take her life back into her own control, especially if she knew she'd put him in a difficult position.

He recalled his exasperation when she'd burst from her hiding place, followed almost instantly by a cascade of warmth in his chest when he realised why she'd done it. Whether it was a sense of obligation or something more was a question he preferred not to attempt to answer. Bad enough as it was. No need to complicate matters even further.

Shoving this aside, he bent his mind to solving the immediate problem. And discovered the idea had crept into his head while he wasn't thinking about it.

He gave it some attention as he completed his toilette, twisting it this way and that, and could find no flaw. Besides, it was only for a matter of two or three weeks. Risky, but better than the notion he'd had while driving back from London. To leave the chit with Mrs Reddicliffe might be safer, but Alex knew it would only result in him chafing because he wouldn't know what Apple might take it into her head to do.

No, this was better. She'd find it more entertaining, for one thing. And for another, it would keep her under his eye. She wouldn't do anything rash while he was by to stop her, and he could take her down to London immediately after her birthday to see Vergette and get the whole business settled all right and tight.

Relieved to have the thing all tied up before he saw Apple again, he went into the parlour to await the announcement of dinner in a much more optimistic frame of mind.

Seated in the chair by the fire was a prettily clad female in whom he barely recognised Apple. Her hair was swept up into some kind of knot, exposing a slim neck and a small expanse of flesh above the slight mound of those pert little breasts.

Cursing a most inappropriate response, Alex hastily lifted his gaze to her face and was surprised to find a look of uncertainty in her eyes. They were emphasised by the hairstyle, seeming enormous in a countenance now piquant with its stubborn little chin and the kissable mouth. Suppressing this thought, Alex found his voice.

"That's a fetching outfit, Apple. Suits you."

She smiled and Alex's mind went blank.

"Thank you. I hoped you might approve. I've never worn such a gown, though Georgy says the cut is far from fashionable and anyone would guess it was made by a country modiste."

The resumption of her usual manner enabled Alex to pull himself together. This was the incorrigible little chit of a girl who'd boldly demanded a ride in his carriage, not some available debutante he might with propriety make the object of his attentions.

Her words floated into his head and he came to the fire. "Just as well for the scheme I have in my head."

Apple's chin jerked up. "What scheme? Have you thought of somewhere to hide me?"

He leaned his elbow on the mantelpiece, relaxing. "Ain't going to hide you. Got a much better notion. I'll tell you at dinner."

A crease appeared between her brows. "And Mr Vergette? Tell me quickly before Georgy comes."

"No time. We'd best talk about that tomorrow."

"I don't think I can stand to wait until tomorrow."

"Then we'll talk after dinner. Georgy won't mind being excluded."

Amusement leapt into Apple's eyes. "She'll be as mad as fire. Don't you know your own sister?"

He had to laugh. "True. Well, she'll have to lump it. Can't trust that wench not to blab it out at the wrong moment. She don't think, that's Georgy's trouble."

"What's my trouble?" demanded his sister from the doorway. "Are you talking secrets? I've a very good mind not to aid and abet you any more, if you are going to do things behind my back."

Apple erupted into giggles and Alex warmed to the chit. She was nothing if not astute. He eyed his sister. "I'm saying I won't talk of my visit to Vergette in front of you, that's all."

Georgy was predictably indignant. "How mean of you, Alex. When I've done everything possible to help."

"You have, Georgy," Apple broke in, controlling her amusement, "and I'm truly grateful to you. But the thing is, I'm afraid Alex has not met with success and anything Mr Vergette told him is probably confidential. Otherwise, I dare say he would have told me himself in his letter."

"Well, I wouldn't tell anyone."

Alex could not let this pass. "Wouldn't mean to, but I know you, Georgy, and the last thing we need is for you to come out with anything about Vergette before my mother. Or my father, come to that. If they're going to accept Apple for a friend of yours, we can't risk them hearing anything untoward."

Both girls blinked at him. Georgy recovered first.

"A friend of mine? What in the world are you at, Alex?"

Rather to Alex's relief, for the coming discussion might well be prolonged, Berryman entered the room.

"Dinner is served, my lady."

Although the females were agog, Alex waited until the first course had been laid out and their plates filled before resuming the subject, first checking that only the butler remained in the dining parlour.

"Had it in mind to ask that nurse of yours to stay here and look after Apple, but that won't fadge now the Greenaways know she's here."

"Good heavens, no. Besides, I have promised the servants a holiday since both Rob and I will be away."

Ignoring this interjection, Alex swept on. "Could send her to stay with the Reddicliffe at her cottage."

"But it's poky, Alex. There's no room."

"Room enough to put young Apple up for a week or two. Saw that when I went to fetch the woman. But that ain't it."

He took a mouthful of roasted fowl and washed it down with a swig of wine. He found Apple regarding him with a frown.

"Why don't you like that scheme? I think it's a very good notion, if Reddy will have me."

"Of course she would. Pay her to have you if need be. But I've had a better notion. Came to me when I was changing. Going to take you to Dymond Garth with us."

Apple's fork stopped halfway to her mouth and she stared at him, speechless. Georgy gave a shriek.

"Have you run mad, Alex? What in the world would Mama say? She'd be horrified by Apple's conduct, you know she would."

"Won't know anything about it. Unless you tell her, and you'd better not."

Georgy remained unmoved by this stern instruction. "How horrid you are! Of course I should say nothing about all that. But even so..." She faded out, evidently turning the thing over in her mind.

Alex didn't wait for her to arrive at her own conclusions. "Thought it all out. We'll say you met in Bath. Where did you say you went to school, Apple?"

"Miss Godfrey's, but this is impossible, Alex. We never met the girls from the exclusive academies, and they wouldn't have noticed us if we had."

Georgy flushed and took refuge in her wine for a moment. Faintly amused, Alex pressed his advantage.

"Don't matter a whit. My mother won't know that. You've only to claim acquaintance somehow. Georgy was at some fancy school there for a couple of years, and you could readily have crossed paths. Leave you to work out a story to suit between you."

"We might very well do that, I suppose," said his sister on a doubtful note. "Though Madame Fribourg would have frowned on us consorting with girls from the merchant class." She then threw a hand to her mouth, gazing at Apple in consternation. "Oh, I beg your pardon, Apple. That was tactless of me."

Alex cast up his eyes. "See what I mean, little sister? Mouth like a runaway horse!"

Before Georgy could protest, Apple cut in. "But what you said is the truth, Lady Georgiana."

"Don't call me that! I don't deserve such a hateful reproach!"

Apple relented, putting out a hand to her. "No, you don't. Forgive me."

"Well, I will if you'll forgive me."

Alex interrupted this nonsense without compunction. "When the two of have quite finished getting maudlin, I wish you'd bend your minds to this scheme of mine."

At this, Apple turned on him. "It's a stupid scheme. I can't possibly come to your home for Christmas. Oh, I don't mean the story about Bath, I can easily concoct something there."

Alex grinned. "I'll go bail you can."

"Yes, but it won't do, Alex, you must see that. I shouldn't know how to behave, and there's no denying I don't belong in your circle. I'd be terrified of doing or saying the wrong thing and I'd be uncomfortable all the time."

"No, you wouldn't, Apple," struck in Georgy, with a lightning volte face. "I can guide you, never fear."

Apple rode over her. "Besides, you've said I don't know how many times how shocked your mother would be at these exploits, and it's ridiculous to be putting your head in the lion's mouth. I won't come!"

"You'll come if I have to drag you there," said Alex. "I'm not leaving you alone to make a dog's biscuit of things, because as sure as check you'll do something silly and I'll have the devil's own work to sort it out afterwards."

Apple's grey eyes flashed. "So that's it. You don't trust me!"

"Why would I? A more hen-witted chit I've never encountered, and that includes my sister here."

"How dare you, Alex?"

"I am not hen-witted! And I don't want to go to Dymond Garth!"

"Well, you're coming and that's that. My mind's made up."

Apple subsided, glowering at him as Alex resumed eating, aware of his sister's astonished gaze going from one to the other. For several moments, they ate in silence, Apple picking at her food in such a desultory fashion that eventually ran Alex out of patience.

"No use you sulking, Apple."

"I'm not."

"Yes, you are. Stop it at once!"

She flashed him a glare. "I wish you won't talk to me as if I was five!"

"Then don't behave as if you were."

To his annoyance, Georgy entered the lists. "How can you be so horrid, Alex? Poor Apple will be wishing she'd gone home with her cousins if you carry on in that style."

He had the grace to feel a touch of remorse. He hadn't meant to command the chit like that. If she hadn't ripped up at him, he'd have used persuasion instead. But the truth was she was a deal too hot at hand and needed taming.

A small voice in the back of his head reminded him that it was scarcely his business to tame the girl, nor indeed to decide what she should do. In fact, he was being as autocratic as her cousins. On impulse, he turned to her. "Beg pardon, Apple. Shouldn't have roared at you like that."

She did not look at him, and her voice was tight and small. "It is of no consequence."

The footman entering at this moment with a laden tray, silence fell again. Alex waited while the second course was laid out, casting a glance at Apple from time to time. Damnation, he'd hurt the chit! Why she'd taken it in snuff when she'd been ready enough to take up the cudgels in the past, he couldn't fathom. She'd paid no heed to his strictures at the outset. But now it was as if he'd crushed her.

He was relieved when Georgy took up the mantle of the discussion the moment the room was clear of all but Berryman. "If Apple is indeed coming with us, Alex, she's going to need more gowns. Two won't suffice at Dymond Garth. We'll have to go back to Emmeline's."

Alex waved this aside. "Do as you must, Georgy, though I'd no expectation of her posing as anything but a female in genteel poverty."

Apple looked up at that, a little of her usual manner returning. "Genteel? But I'm not genteel."

"Yes, but my mother won't know that. Must have some reason you ain't been on the Town. We'll say Georgy befriended you, but lost touch when you left school. Then you sent to congratulate her on her marriage, say, and —"

"And we resumed our friendship," finished Georgy. "Yes, that is excellent, Alex. Oh, and I think you are staying with me because I asked you, as Rob is going away and I didn't want to be alone."

"And when Captain Edginton asked Lord Dymond to take you to your mother's, you felt it rude not to ask me to come for Christmas to your home because you'd already invited me to remain with you for the festive season."

Alex gave a shout of laughter. "See what I mean, Georgy? No shortage of inventive tales when Apple's about."

She'd become animated as she was caught up in the story, but at this Apple's enthusiasm dropped out. "I still think it's a bad idea. I know something dreadful will come of it."

Alex softened his tone. "You're too pessimistic. What could go wrong?"

Even as he spoke, the memory of the mystery entrusted to Vergette cast a cloud over his optimism.

Chapter Fourteen

Apple took no part in the argument going forward between brother and sister on the day the party set off for Dymond Garth. As might have been predicted, Georgy's inability to organise herself in good time drove her brother into frenzy, and his temper worsened by the minute. Tight with anxiety on her own account, Apple perched on a chair in the hall, picking at her mittened fingers.

Her small valise was beside her, packed in a matter of moments, along with the bandbox containing two new gowns from Emmeline's. The valise bulged slightly, her meagre belongings augmented by various undergarments and a couple of shawls Georgy insisted were indispensable. There was also a hat her hostess had bestowed upon her that morning, which she'd stuffed into the bandbox.

"If you need anything else, we'll ransack the trunks in the attics at the Garth. Mama insists everything must be kept, and I'll wager there is oodles of stuff Charlotte and I grew out of that will fit you to admiration."

In vain had Apple protested. "But where shall I put it all?"

"Do you suppose there are not fifty trunks at least in the box room at home? And if you don't wish to be burdened with a trunk, I dare say we can find a portmanteau that will suit. Now don't start making difficulties, Apple, or I shall tell Alex."

This threat shot Apple up into the boughs. "I don't care if you do. He has no authority over me, and so I shall tell him if he starts on at me again."

To her own shock and consternation, Apple's voice broke and unaccountable tears trickled down her cheeks.

Georgy was instantly contrite, enveloping Apple in a stifling hug. "Oh, Apple, don't cry! Of course I wouldn't dream of telling on you to my horrid brother."

"He's not horrid," Apple protested, making a valiant effort to suppress the sobs. Why in the world she was crying about it, she had no notion. "He's b-been very k-kind to me, and he might have b-been so different. He didn't have to choose to look after me, you know. He could easily have given me back to Marjorie and Walter at the outset. He meant to. I don't know why he changed his mind."

"Well, I know why," said Georgy, looking smug.

Apple dragged a pocket handkerchief from her sleeve and wiped her eyes. "I don't see how you should."

"That's because you don't know Alex as well as I do. I know he's a terrible bossy boots, but he's the kindest thing in nature. Whenever I was in disgrace — which I must admit was all too often — Alex never failed to comfort me and tease me out of my misery. I've never forgotten how he mended my doll when Charlotte lost her temper and broke it. And he used to take me up before him on his horse when I hadn't learned to ride. Though he makes me as cross as crabs often and often, he's the best brother in the world and I love him next to Rob."

Much as these revelations intrigued and warmed Apple, she could not forbear to probe further. "That's as may be, but I am not his sister. He'd no reason to take me up."

Georgy fluttered dismissive hands. "Oh, Alex could never turn his back on anyone in trouble; it isn't in his nature. He wouldn't have been easy in his mind if he'd left you to fend for yourself."

As if she was a stray puppy needing succour. The explanation left Apple curiously dissatisfied. Indeed, she could have thought of it for herself, for Alex had said as much several times. She still felt at outs with him for insisting on taking her to his home. However kind he was, he utterly failed to realise how terrified she was at the prospect of entering the milieu he inhabited.

It was one thing to hold her own in company with Alex and Georgy, who were easy and uncritical. Quite another to face their mother, who must be formidable when both of them kept saying how she mustn't know this or that. Even Georgy had not wanted to go back under Lady Luthrie's jurisdiction while her husband was away. And if she felt apprehensive, how did she imagine Apple felt?

Her apprehension had in no way lessened when Alex seized the moment to tell her about his visit to Vergette, after she and Georgy returned from Emmeline's and her hostess went off for her obligatory rest.

Alex took up a stance before the fireplace, looking down at her where she sat in the chair she'd adopted since coming to Merrivale House.

"Emmeline promised to have the gowns delivered tonight," she told him.

"Ah. Then we can leave tomorrow as planned. Excellent."

It was far from excellent to Apple's mind, but she was reluctant to re-open the argument. She'd taken her own measures and had a quiet word with Mrs Reddicliffe before she was returned to her little cottage in Romsey. The visit to Emmeline's was fortuitous, because they were able to drop the old nurse off and save Alex a second journey. Apple had no intention of saying anything about that little discussion to Alex, who would infallibly put a spoke in her wheel if he could. Not that she meant to make use of the scheme unless it became necessary.

"Haven't had a chance to talk to you properly about Vergette," Alex began.

All thought of the forthcoming ordeal at Dymond Garth dropped out of Apple's head. "He refused to support me, didn't he?" She saw the frown gather in Alex's eyes, and her heart pattered uncomfortably. "Oh, pray don't look like that, Alex. You are alarming me horribly. Tell me!"

The frown disappeared and he dropped into Georgy's chair opposite, leaning forward and resting his arms across his knees. "Ain't that much to tell, if you want the truth. Fellow was as close as bedamned. Kept asking what the deuce I had to do with you until I had to tell him the truth."

Apple's alarm increased. "Did he think you were a fortune hunter or something?"

"Don't know what he thought. Fellow was pleasant enough. Too dashed pleasant, if you ask me. Seems to be his stock in trade."

"I don't understand. Wouldn't he accept the letter I gave you?"

"He accepted it, but his manner was a dashed sight too havey-cavey for my money."

"Havey-cavey?" To her surprise and consternation, Alex began to look a little uncomfortable. A horrid presentiment shot into Apple's head and she spoke without thinking. "He told you I am not really John Greenaway's daughter!"

Alex's head shot up and he regarded her with wary eyes. "What makes you say that?"

She drew a shaky breath, unable to meet his gaze. "I suspected it a long time ago. I asked Papa if I was adopted, but he denied it. Only — only it always seemed to me there was something ... secrets ... things I wasn't allowed to know. And I don't look anything like Papa or even Mama's picture, for I hardly remember what she looked like. She was fair and he had reddish hair and — and although he claimed there are dark ancestors, I've never seen a single portrait to support that."

She stopped, wishing she'd held her tongue. She'd never spoken of these fears to anyone before. She dared to raise her eyes to Alex's and found him looking both thoughtful and all too severe.

"Is it — is it true, Alex?"

The alarming look vanished and he smiled. With an effort, Apple thought.

"I've no notion, Apple. Vergette didn't say so at all events."

"What did he say? I wish you won't try to hide anything."

"I'm not, I promise you. Just that there's so little to tell. It was his attitude that gave me to think. But he says he'll tell you everything after your birthday."

"Yes, but what did he say?"

Alex sighed. "Said he didn't serve your father, only you. He also said the business about the trust coming to an end if you were wed while a minor is nonsense."

"Is it? Then they had it wrong!"

"Looks like it. Vergette maintains the trust is purely for your benefit and it don't matter what your status is. Said there are articles in it — don't ask what, for he wouldn't say — and you've only to decide what you want. Nothing to do with anyone else."

The rhythm of Apple's pulses became uneven, her heart jumping. "Then I will have an independence!"

"Seems so."

Her burgeoning excitement dipped. "*Seems?*"

Alex threw up his hands. "Can't be sure, Apple. Vergette let slip the word fortune, but retracted it at once."

Her mind blanked. "Fortune?"

He laughed. "I took him just that way. Vergette insisted he meant it in terms of your future rather than funds, but I'm inclined to believe it is money."

"Then I need only wait for my birthday to be free of the Greenaways forever!"

Alex frowned again. "Ain't that simple, Apple. You have to live somewhere."

"No, I don't. At least," she amended, "only until I can arrange what I mean to do. And if I have the funds, I can stay at an hotel."

"Not without a chaperon you can't."

"Oh, I have that covered, don't worry."

Elation was rising within her. She'd never truly thought she might be able to carry out her scheme. The dreaming images she'd long carried flitted through her head, but for some reason they did not hold quite the same allure.

She came to herself to find Alex regarding her with suspicion. "What?"

"You have it covered, you said."

She blinked. "Have what covered?"

"A chaperon. Are you concealing one somewhere?"

The derisive note was not lost on Apple. She bridled. "Of course not. I shall hire one."

A look of foreboding entered his face. "Just what are you planning, young Apple?"

Almost she told him. Just in time, she remembered how difficult Alex could be. It was none of his concern, of course, but that would not stop him from interfering. She bypassed the question.

"If Mr Vergette means to tell me everything after my birthday, there's no need for me to come with you to Dymond Garth. Can we not revert to your notion of leaving me with

Mrs Reddicliffe? I know we left her at home today, but it would not take you far out of your way."

He snorted. "And have you running off the Lord knows where the moment I'm out of sight?"

"I won't run off! I've no reason to."

"No, not until you get some hare-brained idea into your head which must be carried through on the instant."

"Why should I do so? I've no reason to do anything until my birthday."

"No use asking me why you should, because I don't know what goes on in that excuse you have for a mind, but I know you will if you get half a chance."

Fuming, Apple glared at him. "I don't understand you at all, Alex. What has it to do with you anyhow? And don't say it's because you've taken responsibility for me, because it's ridiculous."

"No, it ain't. Vergette asked me to bring you to him, and that's what I'm going to do."

"Well, you can do so just as well if I'm with Mrs Reddicliffe."

"No, I can't. Can't do anything if you ain't there, which is what will happen sure as check."

"Alex, I keep telling you —"

"Enough!" He rose from the chair, looking down at her over the intimidating nose. "Not going through this argument all over again. It's pointless. Besides, you've put the fear of God into me with this nonsense about a chaperon. Lord knows what the deuce sort of scheme you've cooked up, but one thing I do know. I won't like it."

Apple leapt to her feet, squaring up to him. "I don't care if you like it or not, it's got nothing to do with you. And you needn't think you can plague my life out to tell you, because I won't!"

"Don't worry, I've no wish to hear it. Only drive me up the wall and I've got enough on my hands as it is."

Incensed beyond measure, Apple flounced across the room to the door. She turned there, her fingers already around the handle. "It'll serve you right if I do run away!"

Alex was still standing by the fireplace, but at this he strode forward, holding up a finger. "Warned you about that before. I'll find you, and when I do…"

Apple wrenched open the door and fled, torn between fury at his intransigence and a lively curiosity as to whether he would indeed follow her. Why he should be so adamant, Apple could not understand. But she did not dwell on it for long, the thought of her potential future reviving the bubble of excitement.

A fortune! Though what precisely did that mean? Not that it mattered. Anything that gave her an independence was a fortune in her eyes. It must surely be enough to allow her to embark upon the longed for adventure? Really, Alex supposed her to be the veriest ninnyhammer. Of course she knew she could not set off without a suitable companion. But that was easily resolved. She would advertise.

It was a pity Alex would not countenance her scheme — no use thinking he would because it was obvious he was far too conventional to approve — because she could have used his help in choosing a suitable female. No, the less he knew about it the better. Besides, once she was in possession of her trust — oh, Lord, let it be money! — she would become her own mistress and there was nothing in the world he could do to stop her.

A sneaking doubt crept in at this point. If he chose to, of course Alex would be able to stop her. She would be obliged to prevaricate and pretend to some sensible plan. She'd think of something that would satisfy him sufficiently for him to decide to leave her to her own devices.

Curiously, Apple found this prospect rather bleak. She could not wait to be free of his restraints, of course, but the notion of never seeing him again once her situation was settled was a little disheartening. Even though he was distinctly infuriating half the time.

At dinner, she eyed him warily, but Alex appeared to have recovered his temper and never once referred to their latest argument. He was a trifle stiff, but then Apple could not defend herself against a like accusation. It was left to Georgy to fill the breach. She prattled about the traditions of Christmas upheld at Dymond Garth and seemed oblivious to the prevailing atmosphere.

Prudence kept Apple from intervening when Georgy's dilatory progress sent Alex up into the boughs again. She did not wish to draw his fire and waited as patiently as she could in the hall. Unfortunately, the delay served to revive her apprehensions and she mentally went over all the rules of etiquette she could remember from Miss Godfrey's discourse.

But at last they were settled in the Luthrie coach, the Edginton chariot following behind with Nelly the maid minding Georgy's mountain of baggage. There was no escape now. Apple's nervousness increased with each passing mile.

Chapter Fifteen

To Alex's profound relief, his arrival at Dymond Garth, unheralded and with his sister and her 'friend' in tow, turned out to be an anti-climax. Lady Luthrie was out, and there was no unusual bustle of the household as might have been expected this close to Christmas.

Leaving his charges in the care of the housekeeper, with a brief murmured instruction to his sister to ensure Apple was comfortably housed and under her eye, he went in search of his sire. He ran Lord Luthrie to earth at length in one of his greenhouses, where he was engaged in coaxing a potful of germinating plants to see the light of day.

"Might have guessed I'd find you here, sir. Been searching all over for you."

Lord Luthrie turned his head, his fingers still pressing into the earth around the tiny green shoot just poking through. "Ah, Alex, my boy, good to see you. Your mother's been fretting."

Alex groaned aloud, moving to join his father and casting an eye down at the reluctant plant. "What's to do? This one of your rarities again?"

"*Fuchsia coccinea*, my dear boy, one of Banks's most successful importations from South America. Do you know that when the first one arrived at Kew, he did not choose to entrust it to any other person and carried it to the greenhouse on his head?"

"I didn't know, sir, no, but it don't surprise me," said Alex, inured to this sort of thing and well acquainted with his father's reverence for the eccentric horticulturist Joseph Banks, who, as he'd heard ad nauseam, accompanied Captain Cook upon his epic voyage of discovery in the *Endeavour*. Typically, he turned from plants in an instant to his son's sudden appearance.

"What kept you, my boy? Your mother would have it you'd ignored her claims in favour of your cousin's."

"Nothing of the sort," said Alex, embarking on his prepared explanation. "Thought I'd look in on Georgy and it's a good thing I did. Rob was off to the coast and might have to sail for Pomerania, and meant to bring Georgy home so my mother could keep an eye on her."

"Ah, yes. Your mother always says the first is the hardest."

Thrown for a moment, Alex frowned. "First what?"

"Baby, my dear boy, baby." His father looked up from the plant and gave his sweet, vague smile. "Rather like my little one here. Needs careful nurturing."

"Yes, but she ain't had it yet."

His father wagged a dirt-covered finger. "It's all in the preparation, my boy."

"Well, I don't see it."

"Of course you don't. When you marry, it will all become clear to you." His sire's brows drew together. "Your mother is a trifle anxious on that score, my boy. She says it's high time you settled down and set up your nursery."

"Know that, sir. She's told me often enough." Alex spoke with irritation, but oddly, the usual sense of entrapment he felt at such reminders did not materialise. He wasted no time in wondering why, but reverted to his mission. "Thing is, sir, I told Rob I'd bring Georgy myself so she didn't delay him. You know what she is. Can't set off without finding a dozen things she must do before she leaves."

Lord Luthrie's gentle laugh sounded. "Has she driven you to thoughts of murder, my boy? I can't think where she gets it from. Your mother is efficient to excess in these matters. And Charlotte seems to take after her."

"Good God, yes," Alex agreed with feeling, recalling some of his elder sister's more annoying qualities. "In more ways than one."

The gentle laugh came again. "If you value my advice, Alex, and wish for a comfortable life, when you do come to marry, choose one of these biddable creatures who'll behave just as she ought and be content to do as you wish."

Well aware how much his father had to bear from his headstrong and managing lady, Alex threw him an understanding look. For some reason, though, the notion of this fictitious biddable woman was curiously unsatisfying. Comfortable? Perhaps. But far less invigorating than a woman, for example, who could be counted upon to jump left when he told her right.

Realising where his thoughts were tending, he suppressed a wholly unwanted rise of warmth and ruthlessly dragged them back. "There's a slight complication, sir."

His father's mild look altered, and Alex was subjected to a keen glance.

"Oh?"

Alex was conscious of heat riding his cheeks and fumbled. He had a great deal of affection for his father, who was generally mild and good-tempered. But Alex had learned long ago that his insouciant manner concealed an astute mind and a will of steel at need. He would be less easy to fool than Lady Luthrie, if truth be told.

"Georgy had a friend staying with her. Chit of a girl." He cleared his throat. "Genteel, but the family is all to pieces."

Lord Luthrie's piercing regard did not leave his son's face, and his hands had stilled from kneading earth in the pot. "I see. Am I to understand that we have a guest?"

Alex blew out a breath. "That's it. She ain't up to snuff, which is why…"

"You're concerned your mother will not welcome her." A faint smile lightened the knife-edged look. "Pippa would never repudiate a guest under her own roof, Alex, you should know that."

"Yes, I know, but…" He faded out, stopping himself within an ace of confiding in his sire. He could not wholly trust in Lord Luthrie's engaging to keep the tale from his wife. He would not kick up a dust the way his mother would, but he'd a way of making a fellow devilish uncomfortable when he didn't approve. Not that he'd ring a peal over Alex, but his withdrawal would be enough to kill any hope of reaching an understanding.

His father's gentle voice recalled him to the task at hand. "There is something else?"

"No, of course not," Alex said rather too quickly. He'd never been good at concealing anything under that penetrating gaze. He improvised. "Just that Georgy's hoping you won't make little Apple uncomfortable."

His sire's brows shot up. "Little apple?"

"Appoline, sir. Appoline Greenaway."

"She's a dwarf?"

Alex gave a crack of laughter. "Nothing of the sort. Don't mean little in a literal sense. Just that the chit is such an innocent."

"You seem to have come to know her very well in a matter of a day or so."

Cursing himself and his father's perspicacity, Alex floundered a little as he sought for a plausible explanation. "Well, been a little more than that. Only the two girls and me at Merrivale House, so it was inevitable I'd get the chance to talk to the chit."

For a moment, his father continued to regard him without comment. Alex met that look as best he could, deciding on silence as the simplest defence.

Lord Luthrie smiled at last and gave his plant one last pat. "Let me but get rid of this dirt, my boy, and I'll take up the mantle of host. Though your mother will no doubt return in short order."

Having arranged to bring the girls to the morning room, Alex left his father to follow in his own time and in a few moments was tapping on the door of his sister's old bedchamber.

"Come in," Georgy called, adding as he put his head round the door, "Oh, Alex, is that you? Did you see Papa?"

"He was tending some plant or other, but he's coming in to meet Apple. Where is she?"

"Oh, Mrs Herbert would have had Charlotte's old room made up for her, but I said it wouldn't do."

"Should think not." His elder sister's chamber was fully half a corridor away. "Don't want her feeling isolated."

"Exactly so, which is why I insisted she should be next door."

Leaving Nelly to deal with the collection of clothes strewn across the bed, Georgy came to the door and pushed him into the corridor ahead of her.

"I left her to freshen up, but I dare say she's unpacking by now."

She went to the next chamber door and tapped, calling out as she opened it and entering upon the echo of her knock. "Are you ready, Apple? Here's Alex wanting you to come and meet Papa."

She left the door open, and Alex could see Apple sitting on the end of the big bed, looking a trifle forlorn and lost. Something gave in his chest, and he did not hesitate to walk into the room.

"No need to look like that, Apple. He won't bite. Very gentle fellow, my father."

"Oh, yes, you need have no apprehension, Apple, for Papa is not in the least little bit like Mama."

Apple's gaze went from Alex to Georgy and back again. "What did you tell him?"

"Exactly what we agreed." He refrained from adding anything about his father's evident, if unspoken, suspicion. No need to terrify the girl. "If you're ready, best get it over with."

Apple seemed incapable of moving. She looked peculiarly rigid, and Alex noticed her fingers were digging into the coverlet on the bed. He went up to her and held out a hand. "Come, Apple. Not like you to be a scaredy cat."

Georgy added her mite. "Gracious, are you frightened, Apple? Don't be! I'll support you, never fear."

Apple drew an audible breath and bit her lip. "I shouldn't have come."

"Yes, you should. Alex, for goodness' sake, talk to her!"

Instead, he bent and seized both her hands, forcibly removing her clutching fingers from the coverlet, and pulled her to her feet. "That's it. Now stop being a hen-wit and come on down to the morning room." Putting an arm about her, he gave her a swift reassuring hug. "If anything goes wrong, you can blame me."

"Don't worry, I will," she flashed, in an echo of her usual manner.

But Apple's lively self vanished again as she was herded out of the chamber and along the corridor towards the stairs. Alex did his best to distract her by pointing out the various apartments in the immediate vicinity.

"Main family rooms are on this floor. None of the ground floor rooms are used informally, except my father's library."

Leading the way down the gallery, he stopped at a door halfway along. "My mother calls this the morning room, but to say truth it's where the family sits when there ain't any likelihood of visitors. Most comfortable room in the house, if you ask me."

"Except the old nursery, Alex," said Georgy, a little behind them. "That's where I go when I want to be private."

Alex opened the morning room door and walked in, sighing with relief when he found his father had not yet arrived. He grinned down at Apple. "It's all right. Coast's clear."

Georgy giggled and pushed Apple through the door. "Go in, quick. Then you can sit down and Papa won't be able to see your knees shaking."

"They're not shaking," Apple protested, and Alex was a little amused to see how she glanced about in an awestruck way.

"Don't be put off by the grand style, Apple. You'll soon become accustomed."

She shivered and drew closer to the fireplace. "I never should, I don't think. It's — it's so big."

"Suppose it must seem so to you."

Georgy laughed. "It seems so to me too, let me tell you, Apple. I've grown used to my little house instead."

"Yes, but it's your home, or it was, so it must be natural to you to live in a mansion. I'm sure I shan't be able to find my way about."

There was time for no more as the door opened again to admit Lord Luthrie. He cast a swift glance about the room, his gaze resting for a moment on Apple and then passing on to Georgy. His eyes lit up. "Hello, my darling girl!"

"Papa!" squeaked Georgy and ran across the room to fling herself into her father's arms.

Lord Luthrie received her in a comprehensive embrace, though he entered a protest. "Have a care, my dear, or you'll have me over. Not as young as I was."

Alex could not help smiling at Apple's wide-eyed astonishment. A sliver of compassion slid through him. Had she not known a like affection from John Greenaway? Perhaps not, if the fellow wasn't her real father.

Lord Luthrie was gently extricating himself from his daughter's clinging form.

"Papa, I've missed you!"

"Dear me, that bad, is it? Now I had supposed young Robert would keep you sufficiently entertained to forget your old father."

Georgy bubbled over. "How could I? And of course I adore Rob and he's delightfully entertaining, but I still miss you, Papa."

Her father's indulgent smile embraced her. "Highly gratifying, my sweet. I must say the house is a great deal quieter without you." He laughed at her indignant look and patted her cheek. "Too quiet, I promise you." He put her from him and moved towards Apple, glancing across at Alex. "And this must be your friend, Miss…"

"Greenaway," Alex supplied. "Miss Appoline Greenaway."

"Ah, yes." He smiled down at Apple as he reached her and put out a hand. "A very pretty name, Appoline. Why not use it?"

Apple put her hand into his, looking bemused. "Well, sir, it — it was my father who called me Apple, and it — it stuck, you see."

Alex noted the twinkle enter his father's eye and saw with relief that Apple was visibly relaxing.

"Should you object to it if I were to call you Appoline?"

"No, of course not. I mean — I mean, it is very kind in you to call me anything at all."

One of Lord Luthrie's soft laughs sounded. "Would you expect me to whistle perhaps? I would never be so rude."

A giggle escaped Apple. "What I mean is, sir, it's — it's very good of you to have me to stay."

He gave a small bow. "Not at all. Any friend of my daughter's must always be welcome in my home."

"Th-thank you, my lord."

"Pray don't stand on ceremony, my dear Appoline. Not with me at least." He smiled again and gestured widely. "But should we not sit down? Alex, my boy, set a chair for Appoline, if you will. Near the fire here. The poor child looks half frozen."

Alex shifted a chair closer to the fire, lifting his brows at Apple and grinning as he invited her to take it. She cast him an anxious glance as she sat down. He could not resist a low murmur. "You're doing very well. He likes you."

She flushed and shook her head, but he saw with satisfaction how her gaze drifted to his father, who was seeing to Georgy's comfort and finding himself a chair.

"He's very kind," she whispered, "but if he knew the truth…"

"Shush! He doesn't and won't."

He could not withstand a faint rise of apprehension himself, however, when his father began upon an apparently casual questioning about Georgy and Apple's friendship. Knowing his canny sire, Alex did not doubt he had an end in view.

Georgy, who had ever been their father's pet, saw nothing amiss and embarked upon their agreed story with a glibness Alex hoped would pass muster. Apple, when appealed to, was quick to support Georgy, but Alex realised she was being as reticent as she could and dared not suppose his father would not notice it. The best he could hope for was that Lord Luthrie might take it for shyness, since it was obvious to the meanest intelligence that Apple was ill-at-ease.

She became less so under Lord Luthrie's skilful handling, and Alex was just beginning to entertain the notion that she might cope when his mother's voice sounded in the gallery.

"In the morning room, are they, Meech? Very well, I'll go in. Pray instruct the chef to augment the meal, if Mrs Herbert has not already done so."

Lord Luthrie, alerted to his wife's imminent arrival, broke off what he was saying and turned to the door, rising as it opened and speaking at once as he moved towards his lady. "Ah, my dear, you've returned in good time to welcome our unexpected guest."

Chapter Sixteen

Apple's heart jumped with some violence as she surveyed the lady who had just walked in. This must be the formidable matron of whom it seemed both Alex and Georgy stood in awe. At first glance, this did not surprise her. Lady Luthrie was tall, rather gaunt, with a beak of a nose in an otherwise attractive countenance that strongly resembled Alex. She looked to be quite as autocratic as her son and a good deal less benevolent.

Quaking all over again, Apple could not believe she might find as kind a reception as she'd received from Lord Luthrie. She was proved right almost immediately.

"Good heavens, Luthrie, what in the world do you mean? Meech said Georgiana had arrived with Alexander, of all things."

"Quite so, my dear. It appears young Robert has gone off to Pomerania to fight the French, and Alex engaged to bring his sister home."

"He's not fighting the French, Papa. He's only gone to the coast."

"However that may be, I dare say Robert wishes you to remain under my aegis." Ignoring the rest of the party, Lady Luthrie then crossed to her daughter. "Georgiana, my dear child, what in the world are you doing sitting here? Surely you should be resting after the journey?"

"Oh, Mama, pray don't start fussing. I'm perfectly all right, I promise you."

Georgy got up and gave her mother a chaste salute on the cheek. Quite unlike the way she'd greeted her father. Apple's apprehension increased.

"Nonsense, girl. If there's one thing more certain than another, it's that travelling is bound to tire you. Especially in the early months. It's important to get your rest."

"You sound just like Reddy."

"Mrs Reddicliffe? Pray how should she come into the picture?"

"Oh, Alex brought her to look after me while…"

Apple's heart was in her mouth, but Alex came to the rescue.

"Had to take a bolt to the capital before bringing her here, ma'am. Rob didn't want the girls left on their own, so I fetched her old nurse."

"Girls?" Lady Luthrie had turned to Alex, but at this her glance swept the room and found Apple. "Ah yes, your friend, is it, Georgiana?"

To Apple's relief, Lord Luthrie took a hand, moving to her chair even as she rose from it, twisting her fingers in a nervous fashion.

"My dear, allow me to present Miss Appoline Greenaway. Her friends call her Apple, but you will not regard that."

"Apple? I should think not indeed."

Lady Luthrie's beaky nose pointed itself at Apple in a fashion so like Alex sometimes that she was seized with a most unseemly amusement, and had all to do to prevent herself succumbing to a fit of the giggles.

"My wife, Lady Luthrie," said her lord, ignoring her remark. "Georgy solicits our kindness for her school friend, my dear, who happened to be visiting her when young Robert was called away. We are happy to welcome her, are we not?"

Quick to note the minatory tone, Apple held her breath, all desire to laugh quenched as Lady Luthrie looked her over. She inwardly cringed as that assessing glance took in her attire and rose again to her face.

Apple longed to run to the safety of Alex's side and could barely resist the urge to look at him. But that would ruin their story in an instant.

At last Lady Luthrie smiled. It looked perfunctory to Apple, but the measured words were polite enough. "Of course. You are most welcome, my dear. I could wish Georgiana had sent to warn me, but I dare say it won't incommode us." She turned to her daughter. "Georgiana, has Mrs Herbert seen to Miss Greenaway's comfort?"

"Yes, Mama, all is arranged. She's in the room next to mine."

"Very well. I will see Mrs Herbert and make sure all is in order." Without warning, she turned on her son. "Alexander, I expected you long since."

"Got delayed by a trifle of business, ma'am. Came as soon as I could get Georgy packed up."

That Lady Luthrie was no fool became apparent. "Business that took you to London?"

To Apple's consternation, Alex reddened slightly. But he did not flinch. "Private matter, ma'am. Nothing of importance."

A gimlet gaze bored into him, and Apple could only be thankful it was not directed at her.

"Important enough to keep you from your home when your presence was particularly needed."

"Can't help that, ma'am. In any event, I'm here now, and at your service."

Lady Luthrie sniffed. "Well, I dare say you may still prove useful." She turned on her daughter. "Georgiana, I insist upon you taking a rest. Miss Greenaway will keep you company, I dare say. Alexander, I'll see you in my study in ten minutes and we may go over what needs to be done." Her tone softened as she turned to her husband. "I don't presume to dictate to you, Charles, but if you have finished pottering about in your garden for the day, I would be glad to consult with you upon some of the arrangements for the festivities." With which, she sailed out, leaving Apple feeling as if a strong wind had blown through the room.

Lord Luthrie's glance took in all of them. "There now, we have all our instructions. Let us get to our duties, shall we? Appoline, my dear, I look forward to resuming our interesting conversation at a later date."

Smiling upon them all, he left the room and Alex gave an audible sigh of relief.

"Phew! Brushed through that pretty well, I think." He frowned across at his sister. "Gave me a bad moment there, Georgy. Must be more careful, my dear girl, or you'll undo us all."

"Oh, I am sorry, Alex. It's Mama. She always unsettles me so that I can't think and go saying the wrong thing."

"Well, for the Lord's sake, try and keep calm when she starts up. Can't afford to let her guess there's anything amiss with our story."

At this Apple entered the lists. "I thought your father was going to find something amiss, Alex. He asks such penetrating questions. I hardly knew where to look."

Georgy grabbed her hand. "Come on, Apple. I've got to go and lie down. Mama is quite capable of coming to my room to check that I'm resting."

Alex barred their way. "Yes, but Apple's in the right of it. My father's as shrewd as they come. You'd best talk through the story and work out more details, the two of you. Then you won't be caught out if he does resume his questions as he said."

"Yes, indeed. Papa is so clever."

Apple fell once again under the conviction that she should never have allowed Alex to insist upon her coming with them, but she forbore to speak of it. Alex would only become annoyed, and there was nothing to be done about it now, in any event. It was no use repining, for the thing was done and she must make the best of it.

Once ensconced in a chair by the bed in Georgy's chamber, Apple did her best to keep that erratic damsel focused on the task in hand. Georgy had ordered coffee to be brought to the room, and the interruption when a maid arrived with a laden tray did nothing to help matters.

"Oh, will you pour, if you please, Apple? I must say I am surprised at Mama's accepting you so readily, but I dare say it was because Papa introduced you himself. She always does what Papa wants, you must know."

"You astonish me," said Apple frankly, adding cream and sugar at Georgy's request.

"Yes, but it is so. Of course I have no notion what she says to him in private, but Mama would never behave with impropriety, and I know she considers it's a wife's duty to support her husband because she gave me this huge lecture on the subject when I was going to be married to Rob." She took the cup Apple handed her and sipped. "Oh, that's so good. I do find coffee bucks me up." She continued without a pause. "Charlotte says she was told the same thing as I was, but I doubt she had to endure as much of a scold, for Charlotte is a pattern card of proper conduct and she drives me mad."

Apple could not help laughing. "I can't say I am surprised to hear that."

"Well, it's true. I'm sick to death of having it dinned into my ears. Charlotte this and Charlotte that, until I could scream."

Apple sipped at her own cup. "Was she held up as an example then? Mrs Hatherley was forever doing that with one of our girls, and I must say it made me cordially dislike her."

"Oh, Madame Fribourg was just the same. Of course I was held up as the example of improper behaviour."

Apple's overwrought nerves found release in a burst of giggling, in which Georgy readily joined her. That and the revivifying effects of coffee made Apple feel a good deal better, and she entered with much more enthusiasm into embroidering the details of their supposed long friendship. Georgy became more cheerful.

"One thing is certain, Apple. We are already so much at ease with one another, no one could doubt we are friends."

Warmth crept into Apple's countenance, and she set down her cup and reached out to grasp Georgy's hand. "You've been very much my friend, Georgy, and I'm so grateful. I don't know what I should have done without you."

"Stuff! You were doing well enough with Alex, and I dare say you would have managed."

Apple shook her head. "No, because he could not have remained with me without a chaperon, and he might well have taken me back if he hadn't hit upon leaving me with you."

Georgy beamed. "I am very glad he did, for I've not been so entertained for a twelvemonth. I do hope you won't disappear after all this is over, Apple."

A streak of guilt shot through Apple. "As to that, there's no saying until I've seen Mr Vergette."

Georgy handed her the empty cup. "Would you set that down for me?" As Apple did so, she added, "I wish you will tell me what Alex found out."

Apple shifted her shoulders. "Very little, if you want the truth. Mr Vergette would only say that Alex must take me to him after my birthday."

"But he must have said more. What had he to say about the trust?"

"Only that it doesn't matter whether I am married or not. And that the trust was not set up by Papa. Also, it has nothing to do with the winery, though that I already knew, but my cousins refused to believe it."

"Do you think they will come at you again?"

Apple sighed. "I suppose they might. But I can't think even Cousin Marjorie would dare to beard us in your parents' home. I must think myself safe enough while I am here. Though I still feel this horrid sense of foreboding."

Chapter Seventeen

The succession house was warm. Apple laid down the piece of charcoal and seized the rag she'd begged from the chambermaid, scrubbing at the black on her fingers. With care, she set aside the parchment on which a representation of Lord Luthrie's favourite haunt was emerging and shrugged off her thick cloak. She'd worn it when she did the drawing of the house intended for Lady Luthrie, her fingers slowly freezing as she rapidly sketched the outline of her chosen perspective, depicting the mass of the mansion as it appeared from the other side of the lake. But today it was proving uncomfortable in this hothouse atmosphere.

The portrait of Georgy was done and, like the drawing of the house, had been saturated with milk and then allowed to dry to stop the charcoal from smudging, before being carefully wrapped in tissue acquired from the packing around the gowns from Emmeline's. Once the drawing on which she was engaged was completed, she had only Alex's gift to do. She'd left it until last, hoping the surreptitious pencil sketches she'd caught these last days would be enough for an accurate likeness.

Apple had seen far less of him in the week since he brought her to Dymond Garth, and she'd had to seize moments when his attention was engaged. She could not decide whether it was fortunate or otherwise that his mother kept him so much occupied. Or if not her, Mr Outram had a myriad of tasks for him. She'd met the family steward on a couple of occasions, but as he'd paid little heed to a female in Lady Georgiana's train beyond the commonplace of politeness, Apple had no understanding of his function. Which seemed to her mostly to be removing Alex from the vicinity, much to her chagrin. Infuriating though he could be, she was never as relaxed or comfortable when he was out of her sight and hearing.

"Best if I appear uninterested, Apple," he'd said to her once. "You're Georgy's friend, remember. But I've got my eye on you, never fear."

He'd winked on the last, giving the half-smile that sent a flitter through her veins. Whether it was a warning or a tease Apple remained uncertain, but it was nevertheless reassuring.

The ordeal of being at Dymond Garth had proved to be less testing than she'd expected. Lady Luthrie was too busy to pay her much attention, although she paid a great deal to Georgy, instigating a regime of diet, exercise and rest that sent her daughter into the fidgets.

"Why Rob must needs subject me to this, I truly don't know. I could readily box his ears, if only he were here."

"If he were here, you wouldn't be subjected to it," Apple pointed out.

"Exactly so. I wish to heaven he'd not been obliged to rush off to the coast."

"Well, he has his duty, Georgy. You would not wish him to neglect it."

Georgy gave a fretful sigh, slowing her pace which had speeded up in her agitation.

"In any event," Apple added, "I'm quite glad Lady Luthrie insists upon your walking every day, for it gets me into the fresh air too."

Georgy reached out to clasp her hand for a moment. "Yes, and thank goodness we brought you, Apple. Indeed, if I didn't have you to walk and talk with, Mama would have driven me to screaming point by this time."

It was on one of their meandering walks around the lake that the vexed question of Christmas gifts had arisen, throwing Apple into dismay. She'd asked why Lady Luthrie was so very busy, hoping to hear what Alex might be up to.

"Oh, Mama likes to visit every tenant through the Christmas season. She obliges Alex to do his share with the bachelors. She likes to find out what they chiefly need so she can give an appropriate gift."

"Gracious! Do you mean she gives something to everyone?"

Georgy waved an airy hand. "Mama considers it her duty. All the servants get a gift too, and there's a ball for them on Christmas Eve. We always have a cold collation to give them time to prepare, and Mama insists we all go down to make an appearance at the ball. She won't dance these days, but I'll have to partner the butler for one turn, and Alex must take out Mrs Herbert."

A sinking sensation had crept into Apple's stomach. "And the gifts?"

"The servants get their boxes on the day after Christmas, when they are allowed to go off to visit their families once breakfast is served, and then Papa and Alex ride in the hunt. I won't be able to go in my condition, and Mama gave it up years ago."

This did not answer the question in Apple's mind, although the insight into Alex's life both alarmed and awed her. "And what of Christmas day?"

"That's a family day with us, though many choose to entertain. Mama thinks it is unfair on the servants and she refuses to burden them. There are enough parties and visitors through the following days, she says."

Apple sighed inwardly. It was no use. She was going to have to ask outright. "Do you then exchange gifts on this family day, Georgy?"

Her friend — when had she started thinking of Georgy as her friend? — wrinkled her nose as she looked at her. "What troubles you, Apple? You won't be expected to give anyone a gift."

"But if, as you say, your mother is in this habit of giving gifts to all the tenants…"

Georgy laughed. "Yes, but it will only be a token, Apple. You need feel under no obligation."

Apple could not dismiss it so lightly. Apart from the hideous possibility of receiving gifts to which she could not reciprocate, she already felt under an immense obligation to the Luthries. Not only had they accepted her presence without protest, but Lord Luthrie had taken pains to draw her out and even to provide her with entertainment.

"Do you play cards, Appoline? Or backgammon perhaps? Chess?"

"I was taught chess, but I'm afraid I am not very good."

Lord Luthrie had smiled at her, lowering his voice to a confidential murmur. "Neither am I, my dear, but I do enjoy the game. Shall we try it?"

In fact, he proved excessively good and Apple had a hard time pitting her wits against him. She could not have acquitted herself too badly, however, for he solicited her for a game on several occasions, one of which went on so long they were obliged to leave the chessmen in place and return to the game upon the following evening.

On another occasion, he'd caught her as she left the breakfast parlour with Georgy. "Do you care for plants, Appoline?"

She stared at him. "Plants?"

Georgy chimed in. "Oh, Papa, you are not going to bore poor Apple with your dratted exotic specimens, are you?"

Lord Luthrie twinkled. "Well, if she does not care for them, she has only to say so, you know."

"I don't understand."

"You exhibit intelligence enough for chess, my dear Appoline, so I supposed you might have a little more extensive interest than mere frills and furbelows."

Amused and a little intrigued, Apple agreed to it. "I'd like to see your exotic specimens, sir, if it is not too much trouble."

"No trouble at all. I am always delighted to show off my darlings."

His darlings proved to be a collection of plants of varying kinds, which appeared to Apple's untutored eye both weird and wonderful. Lord Luthrie was clearly in his element, becoming more animated than she'd before seen him, and rapidly losing her as she tried to keep up with strange Latin names and the details of the care required to encourage rare plants to grow out of their natural environment. Apple rather enjoyed herself, and the visit gave rise to her idea for overcoming the vexed question of Christmas gifts.

"Should you object to it, sir, if I came again to have a look at them?" she asked, when at last Lord Luthrie arrived at the end of his enthusiasms.

"Feel free, my dear. I am only too pleased to find someone who is actually interested enough to come again. Only don't touch, and make sure to keep the door closed."

Apple promised, resolving there and then upon creating a series of charcoal drawings as gifts for her hosts for Christmas. She'd begun by asking Georgy for paper and pencils, pretending a wish to do a little sketching.

"For it will give me something to do while you are resting."

Georgy was ready enough to oblige her. "Certainly, if you care for it. I must say I hated the drawing classes at Madame Fribourg's. I could not wait to abandon my sketching book. I still have it somewhere. You may use it if I can find it."

A hunt through the plethora of childish toys and books in a cupboard in the nursery produced the sketch book and a collection of pencils. Apple developed a habit of taking the book to the family room along with some white work and pretending to sew there, which allowed her to make surreptitious sketches of her subjects.

But for the actual drawings she needed charcoal and parchment. The latter was acquired through the kind offices of the housekeeper, who, learning why it was needed (although sworn to secrecy), rifled Mr Outram's store on her behalf. A startled chambermaid, making up the fires in the early hours, granted Apple's request to steal a couple of pieces of coal from her bucket, although she clearly supposed the guest to have taken leave of her senses.

Armed with the necessary accoutrements, Apple worked on her drawings mostly in the privacy of her bedchamber, once she'd sketched the preliminary outline. But Lord Luthrie's plants were much more difficult to copy, and she'd taken the chance of doing the drawing in situ.

She lifted the paper by its edges and held it away from her, checking it against the lush vegetation of exotic trees forming an arching shape with the glass dome just visible at the top.

"That is extraordinarily good."

Apple jumped, almost dropping the parchment, and cast a glance over her shoulder.

"Alex!"

He grinned. "Startled you, did I? Beg pardon."

Caught between dismay at his finding her engaged on this work and the flurry in her heartbeat at seeing him so unexpectedly, Apple could not speak.

His gaze was still on the drawing and he leaned close to look at it. "You've got hidden talents, young Apple."

She found her tongue. "What are you doing here?"

He straightened and his brows rose. "Why shouldn't I be here?"

"I thought you were — I don't know, visiting on your mother's behalf, Georgy said."

He eyed her, a frown gathering. "Came looking for my father. What's to do?"

Apple felt warmth rising into her cheeks. "Nothing. I just didn't expect you to come creeping up behind me like that."

His lips quirked. "Didn't expect you to be in here. Besides, I wasn't creeping. Can't think why you didn't hear me."

"Well, I was absorbed."

"I can see that." He waved a hand at the parchment she was still clutching. "You should show that to my father. He'd be even more impressed."

Apple stared up at him. "Impressed? With me?"

"Says he has the devil's own job keeping ahead of you at chess."

"He does not! Why, I can barely keep up with him."

Alex was regarding her in a quizzical fashion. "No? In any event, you ought to show him that."

"Oh, no, no, pray don't mention it to him, Alex. It's — it's a surprise."

She could not say a gift, for she did not wish him to know what she was planning. That would spoil everything, especially when she hoped to surprise him with his own portrait.

A quiver disturbed her heartbeat. "Not at all. It's you who turns me into a — a—"

"Termagant? Scolding little nag? If that's so, permit me to return the compliment. I'm never so autocratic as when you drive me up the wall."

Apple ignored this. "I'm not a scolding little nag, how can you say so?"

"Termagant then."

"Not that either! Really, Georgy is right to call you a horrid creature. I wish you will go away and let me finish this picture."

To her mingled astonishment and delight, he dropped down to his haunches and laid a hand over hers, a look half quizzical, half rueful in his face.

"If you want the truth, I've missed this, Apple. Bandying words with you. Hate being obliged to pretend you're no more than an acquaintance to me." His hand tightened on hers, and Apple could not utter a word for the pounding in her bosom. "It's odd, but I feel as if I've known you forever. Not sure I can stand to lose you when all this is over."

With which, he let go of her hand, rose to his feet and gave her cheek a light pat, leaving Apple trembling and near to tears as he walked out of the glass structure, closing the door behind him and striding away towards the house.

Chapter Eighteen

The customary mingling at the Luthrie Arms in the village before the hunt set off did not this year fill Alex with the light of anticipation. While he quaffed and responded suitably to friendly overtures of the neighbouring gentry and laughed at the Master's sallies, his attention kept straying to the carriage where Apple sat with Georgy, who had insisted on coming to see them off. He worried she might be overwhelmed and kept an uneasy eye on her, especially when one or other of the family's acquaintances went up to greet his sister.

She was honour-bound to present Apple, and Alex could not help feeling uncomfortable about the necessary deception. Difficult enough keeping up pretence before his parents. He'd nearly undone it all yesterday, when Apple presented those extraordinary gifts of hers.

She'd entered the morning room when the family assembled there after breakfast, looking considerably flustered, her arms full with a pile of beribboned tissue paper. She looked from one to the other, her eyes meeting his only fleetingly. Then she fixed her attention on his father.

"I didn't know when to do this, sir. Georgy mentioned that you exchanged family gifts on Christmas Day, and — and..."

An echo of the rush of tenderness he'd felt as he realised what she was about slid through Alex. Recalling the tentative and troubled look on her face, as if she feared to be making some dreadful faux pas, he felt all over again the urge to rush to her aid. He'd had to bite his tongue to stop himself speaking out. He must be ever grateful to his sire for taking the matter out of his hands and smoothing the moment.

"Can it be that you have taken the trouble to honour us with gifts, my dear Appoline?"

"Well, yes. It's nothing much, but — but you've been kind ... you've all been so kind. I wanted to do something, if I could."

Georgy jumped in, squeaking with protest. "Apple, I told you there was no need. Oh, you shouldn't have."

Lord Luthrie intervened, moving to relieve Apple of her burdens. "Indeed she should, if she wanted to, Georgy. How very kind of you, Appoline. What is concealed in all this tissue, I wonder? I am greatly intrigued."

The twinkle in his eyes must reassure her, Alex hoped, adding what he trusted would not give him away. "So am I, sir. Can't imagine what Apple's been up to."

As he spoke, he glanced at his mother and found her regarding Apple with a frowning look, but not with disapproval. He breathed more easily when she smiled and gestured to the card table, opened out for the occasion, where the family had each laid down their offerings for each other.

"You have chosen your moment well, my dear Appoline. We are just about to make this very exchange."

Lord Luthrie moved to the table and laid down the pile of Apple's gifts. "I think we must enjoy these first, my dear Pippa, do not you?" He held out a hand to Apple. "Appoline, my dear, will you do the honours, if you please?"

Alex glanced again at the pile and took in the shape of the gifts. Something clicked in his head, and he remembered catching Apple in the succession house the other day. Was this the drawing she'd been doing? Apple began handing out the gifts and Alex instantly found himself wondering what she'd drawn for him. Then she was before him, holding out her offering, a smile of such tantalising sweetness in her face that

Alex had much ado not to seize her up and kiss the quivering lips.

"This is yours, Alex. I haven't done you quite as I'd wish." The last was uttered in a mischievous under-voice and his lips quirked.

"Done me? God help me!"

A tiny giggle escaped her, choked off as she threw a glance over her shoulder to where the others were engaged in removing the ribbon and tissue.

"I'd best open it then," he said and proceeded to do so.

Confronted with his own face, the likeness uncannily accurate, Alex was bereft of speech. He looked from the portrait to Apple and found her watching him, so anxious an expression on her face that he broke into laughter.

"Don't look like that, Apple! I just can't believe how well you've caught me. Thought you were good, but this…"

The beam of her smile lit up her face and his heart both. Fortunately for his peace of mind, his relatives began exclaiming.

"Apple, this is unbelievable! It's me! How are you able to do that?"

Georgy was holding up a rendition of herself that caught something of her sparkling personality, not only her likeness. His mother was holding her gift with a stupefied expression in her face, her mouth at half-cock. Alex had rarely seen her so confounded. Drawn, he went across and looked over her arm.

"That's the view from across the lake. See, there's the west oak and the edge of the conservatory. Apple, this is amazing."

Lady Luthrie lowered the paper. "This, my dear child, shows extraordinary talent. Georgiana, why did you not tell us of your friend's artistic ability?"

"I didn't know!" Alex winced inwardly and Georgy flooded with colour, and desperately tried to retrieve the slip. "I mean — I mean, I knew Apple could draw, of course, but I had no notion..." She faded out, and Apple leapt in with an adroitness that commanded Alex's admiration.

"You must know, ma'am, that Georgy never pays attention to such things. And we were not schooled together. Had I been adept at style and fashion rather than drawing, of course, it would be different."

Even Georgy joined in the general laugh, and the slip was forgotten as Lord Luthrie took a hand.

"I cannot sufficiently thank you, Appoline. You could not have given a gift that meant more." He held up his parchment for all to see, and Alex was surprised to feel pride swelling in his bosom on Apple's behalf. "I shall have this framed and placed in my library, where I may refresh my eyes when Outram drags me from my darlings and forces me to attend to business." He then commanded Alex to ring the bell for a celebratory glass, and the family gifts were distributed.

Alex was grateful for his sister's warning some days before.

"I suspect Apple is planning something, Alex, so you must get her a gift."

As it chanced, he'd already purchased a pretty little brooch that caught his eye when he was on an errand for his mother in Salisbury. It was a trumpery thing, but he hoped the depiction of a coach and horses might amuse her. Apple had thankfully opened the box while his parents were engaged in admiring their own gifts, for after a single glance, she'd looked up, met his eyes, and gone off into a fit of the giggles.

On tenterhooks, and torn between delight at her appreciation of the joke and dread that an explanation would be called for, Alex inserted himself between where she sat and his mother's chair to block her view. Frowning down at Apple, he shook his head, giving her a minatory look. In a moment she had contrived to control her laughter, but her eyes sparkled up at him in the mischievous manner that had become, insensibly, a look to which Alex looked forward.

"It is only missing the pistol," she murmured.

"Even harder to explain," he returned.

That quenched any remaining amusement, and Alex regretted saying it when she glanced past him to where his parents were thankfully still in close discussion together. He went across to the tray on the sideboard and picked up the decanter, moving to top up her glass. He handed it to her. "A little more wine, Miss Greenaway?"

She sipped at it and surprised him yet again. "It's a fine Madeira, but the Douro red is better."

Alex had to laugh. "Take it you're a connoisseur?"

"I ought to be, but I'm not. Papa wouldn't allow me to join the tasters often enough to be able to judge properly."

"Seems you've an educated palate at least."

She glanced again at his parents, now clearly visible. "You oughtn't to be talking about it, Alex."

He'd cursed himself for forgetting for a moment, and had reluctantly resumed his pose of disinterest for the remainder of the day. It had been harder to hold aloof, and worse to realise how much he hated the necessity.

Alive to the consequences of falling too much under Apple's spell — for there was no denying her manifold attractions — he yet found it both galling and uncomfortable to hold back. For the first time in his adult life, he was moved in all sorts of ways by a female, and she was as ineligible as she could possibly be. And very likely more so, if his suspicions had any foundation.

The assembled huntsmen were just beginning to take to horse for the start when Alex found one of the inn's waiters at his elbow.

"A note for you, my lord."

Alex took the unsealed paper and unfolded it, reading its message with astonishment:

My lord Dymond, if you could spare me a moment, this fellow will lead you to my private parlour. Vergette.

What in the world —? The lawyer had come seeking him! Today of all days? His business must be urgent indeed.

Alex cast a glance across at the carriage. Should he alert Apple? Not yet at least, if the fellow chose rather to write to him. With rising apprehension in his chest, he nodded at the waiter. "Lead me to him, if you will."

With a word to his groom to keep his horse on the move, he followed the waiter through the oaken front door of the Luthrie Arms and up the wide ancient stair to a door on the first floor. Both intrigue and dismay mounted as his guide knocked and a voice called out, "Come."

Vergette was standing by the mantel, as urbane and avuncular in his appearance as Alex remembered. He came forward as Alex dove a hand into his pocket and bestowed a suitable douceur upon the waiter, dismissing him with a nod.

"Very good of you to give me a moment, my lord Dymond. May I wish you the compliments of the season?"

Alex shook hands, impatience rising. "Yes, never mind all that, Vergette. What the devil does this mean? Why should you come seeking me here, and at such a moment?"

The man's customary urbanity did not falter. "That, my lord, I will reveal if you will kindly consent to an appointment in this place tomorrow, since I take it that today is out of the question."

"Obviously. Hunt's just about to leave. Shouldn't think we'd be back for several hours."

"And you cannot be absent, naturally, my lord Dymond. In any event, it is no part of my desire to lend particularity to our meeting."

Alex lost patience. "What the deuce is this about, Vergette? Seems to me your coming here like this is of a piece with the rest. Dashed havey-cavey, the whole business!"

Vergette gave him one of those enigmatic looks that this time annoyed Alex almost beyond bearing. "That, my dear sir, is a more precise encapsulation than I could have made myself."

Despite himself, Alex could not help a snort of laughter. "Well, I wish you will at least give me a hint. What's to do?"

Vergette sighed. "You are an intelligent man, my lord Dymond. You must surely perceive that only the direst necessity would serve to bring me to you at this season."

"That's what I'm saying!"

A slight bow was all the acknowledgement he received to this exasperated remark. "I am here, my lord, at the behest of my client." He held up a hand, the fingers delicately poised. "I do not refer to Miss Greenaway. There is, as no doubt your keen senses will have told you, another hand upon the reins, as it were."

Feeling as much perplexed as troubled on Apple's behalf, Alex was fairly bursting with impatience. "Well, who the devil is this mysterious client?"

"That, my lord Dymond, I am not at liberty to say."

"Might have known it! Damn it, man, this is not to be borne!"

Vergette's smile went a trifle awry. "You have my sympathy, my lord, I do assure you. Yet I will tell you as much as I am able if you will honour me with your presence tomorrow. Shall we say eleven o'clock?"

There was clearly no more to be got out of the man. Baffled and a good deal more troubled than angry, Alex left him. He could hear the hunt moving off already, and wished he might cry off as he ran lightly down the stairs. Dratted fellow was right about that. It would draw precisely the attention he was anxious to avoid. And his sire would be bound to question it, even if his mother did not.

He was making for his horse when he saw Georgy had exited the carriage and was chatting with a youthful neighbour, an old friend of hers, leaving Apple alone. Without pause for thought, he strode over and jumped onto the step, leaning in and lowering his voice. "Vergette's here, Apple."

She'd smiled at his approach, but shock entered her eyes at this. "Mr Vergette? Here?"

"Just seen him in his parlour. Fellow wants me to meet him here tomorrow. God knows what it's all about, but seems highly suspicious to me, don't mind telling you." Apple's cheeks had whitened, and he at once regretted his words. He put out a hand. "Oh, Lord! Don't look like that, Apple. Shouldn't have said anything. Only the fellow's put my head in such a whirl, I can't think straight."

She looked more horrified still and Alex inwardly cursed.

"What did he say? Pray don't keep it from me, Alex!"

"Didn't say anything. Fellow's as close as ever he was. Only says there's a client in the case who ain't you. It's due to him — if it's a man as I must suppose it is — that Vergette's here, he says."

"Client?" Apple's eyes looked enormous as she stared at him. "Is it the person who set up the trust?"

"No use asking me, is there?" He put his hand on hers and gave it a reassuring squeeze. "Don't trouble your head about it, Apple. We'll know more tomorrow. Got to go, or I'll be late to the ground. Don't fret now, promise?"

She gave him a wavering smile, but those tempting lips quivered. "I'll try."

"Good girl. See you at dinner."

His groom had brought his hunter nearer to the carriage and he swung himself up into the saddle, wishing he'd held his peace. Shouldn't have worried Apple with it until he had something worthwhile to tell her. He turned for a last look and found her watching him. He smiled, saluted with his whip and trotted off with the other stragglers in the direction the hunt had taken.

Chapter Nineteen

Apple watched Alex ride away, waiting until his horse had vanished around a turn in the road. Her pulse was behaving in an unruly fashion, but she would not be deterred. Such an opportunity was not to be missed. She climbed down from the carriage and moved to confront the coachman on the box.

"Will you tell Lady Georgiana that I've gone into the inn for a moment, if you please?"

The groom standing nearby came forward. "I'll let her ladyship know, miss, if she asks."

Satisfied, Apple slipped casually through the remaining gentry who had, like Georgy, come to see the hunt away, and went into the inn, where the bustle was dying down. A little uncertain, she looked about for someone to show her the way. A waiter with a laden tray of empty jugs came through the front door, and Apple moved to intercept him.

"Pray can you direct me to Mr Vergette? I believe he is staying here?"

The waiter, evidently tired and out of temper, pointed towards an inner door. "Best ask the mistress, ma'am. She'll be in the tap."

Apple knew very well that a lone genteel female did not commonly enter a tap room, but that could not be helped. She went swiftly to the open door, from whence the sound of muted talk emanated, as well as a waft of smoke and tobacco. Peering in, she looked about for a likely female form and saw a stout woman serving at the counter.

Without hesitation, she marched up to her. "Pardon me, but would you be so kind as to direct me to Mr Vergette's parlour? I have an appointment with him."

The woman looked her up and down in an assessing way, and Apple lifted her chin, giving the woman what she hoped was an outraged stare. It had an effect, for the woman's manner altered. She wiped her hands on her apron.

"Certainly, ma'am." Raising her voice, she called across the room, "Joe! I want you!" A harassed-looking waiter came up. "Take this lady up to the gentleman in the second parlour. Mr Vergette it is."

Relieved, but with a rising feeling of nervousness, Apple followed the man up the stairs and waited while he knocked on the door. An invitation sounded from inside, and Joe opened the door and poked his head in.

"Lady to see you, sir."

Then he nodded at Apple and she strode boldly into the room.

A gentleman sat at the table, a pen in his hand poised above a sheaf of paper on which he had clearly been writing, his head turned towards the door. He was of middle years with a pleasant face, just now wearing an expression of surprise.

Apple drew a breath for courage. "I am Appoline Greenaway, sir."

Mr Vergette's brows rose. "Indeed? How fortuitous." He pushed back his chair and rose, smiling as he came forward, holding out a hand. "And how delightful. How do you do, Miss Greenaway?"

Apple took the hand, her nervousness giving way to bewilderment. "I didn't think you'd be pleased to see me."

"On the contrary. Won't you sit down?" He set a chair for her at the round table and resumed his own, turning it so that he faced her. "I take it Lord Dymond does not know you are here?"

"No, and I can't be long for Lady — I mean, his sister will start wondering what has become of me."

"Ah, that would be Lady Georgiana? The lady Charlotte, I understand, is not in residence?"

Apple blinked. "Yes, but how did you know?"

"It is my business to know, Miss Greenaway."

The smile was enigmatic, and Apple recalled Alex's "havey-cavey" designation. Which threw her at once into speech. "Mr Vergette, why have you come? Why did you want to see Alex — Lord Dymond? There is something horrid to tell him about me, isn't there?"

His eyes took on a veiled look, although his manner remained that of a kindly uncle. "My dear Miss Greenaway, you are jumping to conclusions."

Apple's instinct urged her to batter the man into revealing whatever it was he'd come to see Alex about, but if she'd learned anything in these weeks under his protection, it was to use a more cautious approach. "You will admit, sir, I have a right to know."

"I should not dream of denying it, Miss Greenaway."

"Then since I am here, you may tell me directly rather than using Alex as a go-between."

Mr Vergette eyed her in silence for a moment, and Apple waited, apprehension mounting, her instincts on sharp alert. At last he sighed. "My errand here is to Lord Dymond himself, not to you, Miss Greenaway." She opened her mouth to protest, and he held up a finger. "On balance, however, it may be more politic to open the matter to you instead."

Apple did not wait for him to come to the end of his reasoning. "You are going to tell me I am not John Greenaway's daughter, are you not?"

He was visibly taken aback. "Have you reason to think so?"

Apple let her breath go. "I've often thought so. It's not only the existence of the trust. Papa brushed it aside, but I could never understand my lack of resemblance to him or my mother. Besides Papa so often insisting I must not think of doing this or that, as if certain tasks were beneath me. And then the secrecy! How could I suppose otherwise when there was so much unsaid, such mystery about the trust? I knew it had nothing to do with the winery, and why should that be so?"

Mr Vergette was drumming his fingers where they rested on his knee. "Yes, I can see how you might arrive at your conclusion."

"Well then?"

A tiny sigh escaped the lawyer. "It is no part of my duty to inform you of these matters ahead of the time, but circumstances alter cases, my dear Miss Greenaway."

He got up and paced across to the mantel, turning there to survey her. Apple watched him, her breath tight in her chest.

"The trust was set up by your grandfather. Not a Greenaway, as you surmise, but a gentleman of, let us say, some stature in the world."

In spite of all, Apple quivered inside. She'd wanted to know so badly, but on the brink of the truth, she began to feel the shock of it seeping into her veins. The word he'd used replayed in her head. "Stature?"

He pursed his lips. "Status, rank, call it what you will."

"You mean he's an aristocrat?"

"*Was*, Miss Greenaway. Your grandfather died some years ago. My client, his son, is your father."

Apple's heart thumped. "I'm illegitimate."

Mr Vergette gave a small bow of acknowledgement.

Her mouth dry, Apple could barely get the words out. "And my — my mother?"

"Also a lady of rank, whose reputation could not be saved by marriage since the gentleman in the case — your father — was already married with a hopeful family."

"Then how did she... I mean, what happened to her?"

Mr Vergette's tone was matter of fact, no vestige of the tragedy of Apple's origins touching his story. "Naturally the matter was hushed up. I understand she waited out her time in secret and was afterwards hustled into matrimony with some eligible gentleman, perhaps less worthy than she might have hoped for under more propitious circumstances."

"And I was given up for adoption?"

For the first time, a measure of sympathy came into Mr Vergette's eyes as he returned to his chair and sat down again. "Your grandfather, Miss Greenaway, was a man of integrity. Not wishing you to suffer for his son's misdemeanour, he set up the trust and arranged for John Greenaway, with whom I believe he had business interests, to take you into his household."

Apple's head was whirling, but her heart was cold. She must not lose her senses. "Papa thought I might be a boy, didn't he? He wanted an heir for the winery."

"It may have been so. I am not privy to Mr Greenaway's reasons. Certainly he did not balk at taking you for his daughter when the time came."

Curiously, Apple found she was less affected by the deception, the necessity for which she could appreciate, than the immediate consequences in her present situation. To know about the trust became imperative.

"Is it money, Mr Vergette?" She saw his brows draw together and threw up a hand. "You must not think me mercenary, sir. I would have been content to labour in the business, but Papa would not have it so. And when he died ... well, you know what happened for I wrote as much to you."

Mr Vergette inclined his head. "I acquit you of wishing to do more than escape the bonds of matrimony, Miss Greenaway."

A shaft of misery went through Apple and she was obliged to clasp her fingers tightly together, for it had come to her in a flash that the notion of matrimony in another guise had become, all unknowingly, a secret hope. An impossible, foolish notion, which must be slain at birth.

Gathering her courage, she looked again at the lawyer. "You are my trustee?"

"I am, Miss Greenaway."

"Then tell me, if you please, if my — my grandfather's generosity will give me enough independence for a scheme I have in mind."

His brows lifted. "You seem to be a lady of decided resource, Miss Greenaway. What is your scheme?"

Apple drew a breath. "I will tell you, but I must first have your promise that you won't reveal it to — to Lord Dymond."

"You begin to interest me extraordinarily, Miss Greenaway."

A tiny laugh escaped Apple. "Well, I know he won't like it, and he is bound to try to stop me, if — if he does not altogether…"

Her voice failed. Had Alex guessed? But he could not know the true circumstances. And when he did —! Her mind balked, refusing the possibility that Alex would repudiate her. He never would. It was not in his nature.

She discovered Mr Vergette was holding out a handkerchief. Apple took it, the tears spilling over as she glanced at him, her voice husky. "Thank you. I did not think you would be so kind."

Mr Vergette's manner became even more avuncular, and his tone softened as he leaned a little towards her. "I am not a monster, Miss Greenaway. And if I am not very much mistaken, you are the more to be pitied for my Lord Dymond having crossed your path."

"Oh, no, never! And it was I who crossed his, you know." She blew her nose and wiped her eyes. "I could not regret having met Alex, however much I might miss..." She faded out, having recourse to the handkerchief again. This would not do. She must control herself, or she would infallibly give herself away. There was a whole day to be got through before she could carry out the plan revolving in her head.

It had materialised almost immediately upon hearing of her background, curling into life at the back of her mind. Which was why the grief was coursing through her. With determination, she turned again to Mr Vergette. "I fear I must ask for your help, sir. May I rely upon your discretion?"

Chapter Twenty

The morning found Alex in a mood of dismayed anticipation. The brief encounter with Vergette had thrown up so much speculation in his head he'd been unable to keep his attention on the hunt, and almost came to grief across one of the jumps. His father had noticed, accusing him of being distrait at the post-hunt gathering in the Talbot Inn at Berwick St John, close to where the hunt had ended when the fox went to ground.

"Sitting in a brown study, my boy, with all around you breaking into song. It's not like you, Alex. What's to do?"

He'd evaded the question. "Got something on my mind, sir, that's all."

His father's penetrating glance had rested on him for several minutes. But he thankfully refrained from question. And since Alex made an effort to join in thereafter, nothing more was said.

They arrived back at Dymond Garth only in time to change for dinner, and Alex had no chance to exchange a word with Apple. He was a little surprised that she did not seek a snatched interview. Indeed, she appeared rather to avoid him, challenging his father to a game of chess which kept them both occupied until the tea tray was brought in.

As she and Georgy were about to retire, she did come up to him, briefly smiling. "Alex, I haven't thanked you for all you've done for me."

He was seized with an odd sense of finality and broke into instant speech. "Why should you be saying that now?"

A flush crept into her cheeks and she lowered her voice. "Well, because — because there is no knowing what may happen when you see Mr Vergette tomorrow, and…"

Alex eyed her with a sliver of dismay. "Was wondering why you hadn't asked about that."

"What was the point? I've been trying not to worry about it."

"Any success?"

She gave a tiny laugh. "Not much. But I'm learning, Alex."

"Learning what?"

"To be a bit more patient."

He was betrayed into a snort. "That'll be the day." To his consternation, a stricken look flashed across her face. Remorse gripped him. "I didn't mean that, Apple!"

"I know." A smile wavered on her lips, and the conviction that she was on the verge of tears seized him. "Goodnight, Alex."

Then she was gone before he could say anything else, leaving him as much perturbed about her upset as the coming interview with Vergette. He slept ill, disturbed by dreams of chasing Apple into unknown destinations, and waking so many times that he felt little rested by morning. By the time he came down to breakfast, he was chafing and wishing the hours away to his meeting with the lawyer at eleven o'clock.

The usual quiet prevailed at the breakfast table, which relieved him of the necessity to make polite conversation. His mother always read her correspondence while his father perused the morning paper. But when Georgy came in unattended, the brief peace was at an end.

"Where's Apple?"

His sister halted in her way to the table, looking about. "I thought she must have come down before me. Usually she waits, you know."

A horrid presentiment attacked Alex. "Is she in her room?"

Georgy stared at him. "I must suppose so."

"Go and look! Or no, I'll go myself."

By this time, both his parents had laid down their morning occupations.

"What is amiss, Alexander? Why are you so jumpy?"

Alex paused as he made for the door. "Tell you later, Mama. First things first."

Wholly forgetting the masquerade under which he'd brought Apple to his home, his mind alive with apprehensive conjecture, Alex sped up the stairs, taking them two at a time, and made the best of his way to the room next to Georgy's.

He tapped on the door, calling out at the same time. "Apple? Apple, are you in there?"

There was no response.

His heart dropping, Alex turned the handle and opened the door, flinging it wide.

Apple's room was empty, but the bed had clearly been slept in. Did that mean she was still here? He would soon find out. He crossed to the bell-pull and tugged at it hard, knowing Georgy's girl Nelly would come in answer. He was just wondering in which place to search first when a light footstep sounded outside and Georgy tripped into the room.

"Goodness, isn't she here?"

"No. But if she's gone off, it wasn't last night. She can't be far."

Georgy stared. "Gone off? But why, Alex? She wouldn't run away. Not now!"

He wasted no time in refuting this. "Where would she keep her clothes? And that bandbox or valise, whatever she had?"

Clucking with distress, Georgy ran to the press. Flinging open the doors, she began hunting through the drawers. "Well, the newest gowns are still here. Oh, but I don't see the ones she first got at Emmeline's. No, and look, Alex! Her undergarments are missing!"

Alex declined to inspect Apple's clothing. "What did she pack her things in then?"

At this point, the maid tapped on the open door, coming in on the echo of her knock.

"Oh, Nelly, where did Miss Apple keep her valise and the bandbox she had?"

Nelly blinked at her in some confusion, but on being urged not to stand like a stock, she moved towards the free-standing mirror in the corner. Stopping in her tracks, she pointed. "The bandbox is there, my lady."

Alex went across and looked behind the mirror. Sure enough, the bandbox from Emmeline's was set neatly against the wall. Nelly joined him, and let out a gasp, putting her hands to her mouth.

"Oh, but the valise ain't there! It were down beside the bandbox, for I set it there myself."

That was enough for Alex. With a brief word of thanks to the maid, he seized Georgy's hand and dragged her willy-nilly from the room, beginning his questions the moment they were out of earshot.

"Yesterday at the Luthrie Arms, Georgy. What happened after I left with the hunt?"

Georgy, hurrying along beside him, protested. "Stop rushing me, Alex! I'm in a delicate situation, remember."

Alex cursed and let her go, slowing his pace as they approached the stairs. "Very well, but answer me!"

"Nothing happened, for goodness' sake! I was talking with Maria Ambleside for a while, and then we got into the carriage and —" She broke off, halting in the middle of the stairway.

Alex stopped, taking in vaguely that both his parents were standing in the hall below, watching them. "Well?"

"Apple went into the inn for a bit. I thought she'd gone to use the facilities."

"Vergette! Damn it, she must have seen him!"

He left his sister on the stair and hurtled down the remainder of the steps, shouting for Meech.

"Alexander, what does this mean? What has happened? Where is Appoline?"

Alex turned to confront his mother, but before he could speak, his father intervened.

"Has she left us, my boy? Run away perhaps? Now, why?"

Alex drew a huge breath and let it out. "No point in concealing it from you any longer. Come into the breakfast parlour." With which, he strode towards the parlour door and met the butler coming out. "Meech, has there been any note left for me?"

"Not that I am aware, my lord, but I will enquire."

"Do so with all speed, if you please."

Striding into the breakfast parlour, he found the rest of the family crowding in. His father came up and laid a hand on his shoulder.

"Sit down, my boy. Let us all take a cup of coffee and calm ourselves. There is nothing to be gained by panic."

Alex allowed himself to be pushed into his recently vacated chair, reflecting that panic was the least of his problems. Churning deep inside him was the hideous certainty he'd lost

Apple as surely as if she'd died. Her flight, on the heels of Vergette's arrival, confirmed the suspicion he'd nurtured for weeks.

To his abiding gratitude, Lord Luthrie busied himself with replenishing cups and keeping his wife and daughter from bothering Alex with questions. Though Georgy looked distressed, he had no room to spare to comfort her for the desolation in his own heart. He was glad of the butler's return, hope reviving as he saw the man held a slip of paper in his fingers.

"This arrived but a few moments ago, my lord. The messenger came from the Luthrie Arms."

"Vergette!"

Alex tore open the note.

I regret I am obliged to return with all speed to London, my lord Dymond. Our meeting must be postponed. I will write to apprise you of my movements.

Alex read this last with rage burning in his chest. "Oh, will you? I think not, my buck! I'll be after you before you know it!"

Georgy exploded. "For goodness' sake, Alex! Don't keep us all in suspense!"

"It's from Vergette. He was staying at the Luthrie Arms yesterday. Sent for me to arrange to meet today. Like a fool, I mentioned it to Apple before I went. And now you say she went into the inn."

"Then she saw him?" demanded Georgy.

"You may wager your diamonds she saw him! What do you suppose when the fellow sends to cancel our arrangement and Apple has left me — us?"

He glanced from one parent to the other as he realised his own slip, and found his father watching him with an attentive frown. Lady Luthrie, on the other hand, was looking decidedly displeased. She seized the moment. "Alexander, what is this? Explain yourself at once!"

Georgy threw him a look of panic and buried her face in her coffee cup.

Lord Luthrie glanced at the butler. "Be so good as to enquire if anyone has seen Miss Greenaway this morning. Discreetly, Meech."

"Certainly, my lord." The butler bowed and withdrew, and Lord Luthrie turned to Alex. "Now, my dear boy." The tone was gentle, but with that hint of steel he knew so well. "Cut line. The truth, if you please."

Alex drew a heavy breath. "Apple ain't a friend of Georgy's. I came upon her by accident. Or rather, the other way about."

His mother's measured voice cut in. "By accident? She sustained an accident or you did?"

To Alex's relief, his father put out a hand. "My dear, let us allow Alex to tell it in his own way, or we shall all become hopelessly muddled."

There was no point in prevarication. As succinctly as he could, Alex gave an account of Apple's eruption into his life and the subsequent events leading up to his deciding to bring her to Dymond Garth. He was permitted to tell his story without interruption, but the growing thundercloud in his mother's features and the frown on his sire's brow were more unpleasant than a deal of exclamatory comment. Georgy kept her head down, not much to his surprise, no doubt afraid of incurring a scold. He did his best to avert that.

"You must not blame Georgy. She only did what I asked of her."

Lady Luthrie took a fortifying sip of her coffee and laid the cup down. "So, Alexander. You say Appoline would have gone to Mrs Reddicliffe, yet you chose instead to bring her here."

He winced. "I insisted. It's not Apple's fault. She didn't want to come."

"My dear Alexander, I am far from laying any blame upon the child. It is evident to me that your conduct has been throughout reprehensible, if well-meaning. You should have taken her at once to her home."

"No, I shouldn't," snapped Alex, firing up. "Not when I'd heard what those vultures intended."

"From all I have been able to make out, you did not then know they were vultures, as you put it. How if it had been Georgiana or Charlotte in such a case? For all you knew, Appoline had parents or guardians who were perfectly frantic at her loss."

"Cases aren't the same, ma'am. Besides, Apple would have run away again if I'd tried to take her home. Couldn't, in all honour, leave her to her own devices. Chit's hot at hand, can't you see? Look what's she's done now, and without a word to me. Cozened Vergette into taking her with him, I'll be bound."

He realised, with a sense of shock, that his fury was concentrated more on Apple than Vergette. Fury, and hurt. He'd believed she trusted him, and now look. First hint of trouble and she was off.

His father spoke for the first time. "What do you intend to do, Alex?"

Alex looked across, frowning. "Go after her, of course. What else?"

"To what purpose?"

The question brought him up short. He gazed at his sire, anger dropping out. There was nothing in his head but the urgent need to fetch Apple back. Because he couldn't bear to live without her. But he couldn't say so, not to his father. He fell back on the excuse he'd been using all along. "Made myself responsible for her, sir. Can't renege on that."

Lord Luthrie eyed him in silence. His helpmeet, having waited for him to finish whatever he was going to say — as was her practice — now took a hand.

"It is evident, Alexander, that Appoline does not wish for your intervention."

It struck him like a blow, and Alex could not speak for a moment.

"And an excellent thing that is," pursued his mother, "since you have taken her out of her natural sphere and subjected her to embarrassment."

Alex hit back. "Nothing of the kind, ma'am. She'd settled nicely. And I meant only to keep her here until her birthday, when we'd have gone to Vergette in any event."

"But she has pre-empted you," said his father before she could answer this. "Do you have any notion what Vergette may have told her? I may say, the fact that he is involved in the matter at all gives one furiously to think."

Diverted, Alex eyed him with suspicion. "You know the fellow?"

"I know of him. He is legendary in certain circles."

"So Wintringham said. And Vergette told me it's due to his client he came to see me here."

"Charles, what is this? Pray enlighten me, for I am all at sea."

His father turned to his wife. "My dear, it is apparent that Appoline's natural sphere is not perhaps as clear as you may have thought. However, until Alex has the full story from

Vergette, I'm afraid there is little to be gained from discussing the matter."

"But why should he go and see this lawyer fellow in any event? The sooner he extracts himself from this debacle, the better."

At this point, Georgy entered the lists. "Oh, Mama, pray don't be so horrid! Poor little Apple must be dreadfully unhappy. Of course Alex must find her."

"Dreadfully unhappy? What in the world do you mean, Georgiana?"

"Oh, you don't know her, Mama. If she wasn't in distress, she would have told Alex what she meant to do."

"No, she wouldn't," Alex cut in. "It's typical of her, if you want to know. She knew I wouldn't stand for it if she meant to run off. What's more, she knows I'll come after her, for I've told her so enough times." Abruptly, he recalled Apple's last words to him on the previous evening, and his heart lurched. "But you're right. She was distressed."

He rose from his chair, turning to look at his father. "Beg your pardon if you don't like it, sir, but I've no choice. Got to find her."

"More to the point, my boy, you must find out what Vergette told her to make her leave your protection."

"Luthrie, have you run mad? You are encouraging him in this?"

Once again, his sire, rising also, turned to his wife. "My dear Pippa, whatever comes of this, I should be sorry to think any son of mine would be so callous as to abandon the child who has been, to all intents and purposes, under his care."

Gratified, Alex thanked him, braving his mother's obviously rising wrath.

"Besides," added Lord Luthrie with a smile that embraced both his wife and son, "I like the girl. Intelligent little thing."

"Because she plays chess and admires your infernal plants?"

"That too, my dear Pippa. But if you had taken the trouble to draw her out as I did, you would know there is a deal more to her than one might at first suppose."

The door opened at this moment to admit the butler. Alex looked across with eagerness. "Anything, Meech?"

"One of the gardeners reports having seen Miss Greenaway approaching his lordship's principal greenhouse." He turned to Lord Luthrie, holding out a twisted screw of paper. "I took the liberty of investigating, my lord, and found this note. It is addressed to your lordship."

Alex started forward, but his father held up a hand as he took the note and straightened it. A tattoo started up in Alex's chest as his sire's lips quirked. He looked up, compassion in his gaze.

"Your courageous little protégée regrets leaving us thus precipitately, Alex."

Impatient, Alex twitched the paper out of his father's hand. His sister ran to look over his arm. "What does she say?"

"*I am sorry to depart without a word,*" he read, "*but I can no longer trespass upon your hospitality under false pretences. Thank you, sir, for your kindness. Appoline.*"

Alex gazed at the childish hand, his heart bleeding for the pain he detected underneath the conventional phrases. He felt his father's hand on his shoulder.

"Do your duty, my dear Alex. Bring her back, if she will come. If not, at least bring news of her and do not allow Vergette to put you off. Find out the whole, and let us see what may be done to mend matters for the child."

Alex thanked him, but was obliged privately to acknowledge that if his suspicions proved true, there was nothing in the world possible to mend what fate had decreed.

With his father at his back, the dismay Alex had been experiencing dissipated to some degree. Whether Lord Luthrie had surmised what he himself suspected about Apple's birth, he could not tell. He did not ask, having no wish to introduce the subject unnecessarily. But Apple's flight was a sure indication of the potential truth, assuming Vergette had told her. His best hope lay in the probability the lawyer had taken Apple up with him and meant to convey her to London.

Despite the cold, he elected to drive himself in his curricle. He would make better time, and Carver could take the reins to give him a rest from driving.

Both warmly wrapped in greatcoats and mufflers, with blankets over their knees, he and the groom set off within an hour of discovering Apple's absence. He nourished a hope of catching up with his quarry on the road, since he could not be more than two or three hours behind. Assuming Vergette was travelling by coach and must make several stops, he might reasonably expect to overtake the man.

With this in mind, he pressed on after the change at Salisbury, resolving to take a late luncheon at the Dragon at Winchester if there was no sign of the travellers before.

His luck held. Carver was driving, which was why Alex was able to give his attention to the unhorsed carriages standing in the yard as the curricle swung through the arched entrance.

A sense of déjà vu attacked him, throwing him back to the moment of his very first meeting with Apple. An image surfaced: of her face, half-concealed under the hood of her cloak, her gloved hand holding the useless pistol steadily aimed at him. A swooping sensation within took him unawares, and he was obliged to grip the side of the curricle even as it came to a standstill.

Lord, how he missed her! She'd been gone, what? A matter of hours? And it felt like a lifetime! How had she insinuated herself so thoroughly into his mind and heart in the short time he'd known her? Indeed, he could hardly remember a time when he hadn't known Apple, so embedded was she in the fabric of his life.

With renewed energy, he leapt down from the curricle. "Stable 'em, Carver. We'll bait here, no matter what."

Leaving the groom to his duties, he strode into the inn through the busy back entrance. A couple of maids and waiters made room for his passage, and he came to the hallway just as the landlord came bustling out of the tap. His brows rose in recognition.

"My lord, is it you again?"

"On my way to London and I'll take a late luncheon, if you can accommodate me."

The man assured him he could and proceeded to a list of the viands on offer. Alex approved a meal of cold meats and pie, washed down with ale.

"Stay, though. Was hoping to run into a friend of mine who's on the road. Fellow of middle years, a trifle portly, name of Vergette. Seen him?"

The landlord beamed. "Mr Vergette? Why, he's a regular with us, my lord. Indeed, he's but just stopped for the change and came in for a quick bite."

Hope soared. "You mean he's here?"

"He left but a moment ago."

"Good God! Then his coach may be still here."

Striding to the door through which he'd just entered, Alex dragged it open and flung out into the wind. A coach and four, the horses clearly fresh and restive, stood in the yard, the groom just about to take his place behind.

"Hi, you! Wait a bit!"

Alex leapt forward as he yelled. The groom paused with his foot on the step up to the box and looked back.

"Me, sir?"

Reaching him, Alex seized his arm. "Is this Vergette's coach?"

The man pulled his arm away, his expression turning surly. "Who wants to know?"

"I'm Lord Dymond. Is he within?"

The groom hesitated. Cursing, Alex left him and went to the coach door. He seized the handle and wrenched it open.

"Vergette!"

The dim figure within leaned forward and Alex found himself looking into the lawyer's features, exasperation for once overlaying the fellow's customary urbanity.

"My lord Dymond! I suppose I should have anticipated this."

Alex wasted no time, but pushed his head through the doorway, searching the coach. There was no other occupant.

He glared at Vergette. "Where's Apple?"

The lawyer sat back. "My dear Lord Dymond, you are her keeper, not I."

"Don't play games with me! If she ain't with you, then you've a deal of explaining to do."

Vergette sighed as Alex got into the coach and plonked down on the opposite seat. "Really, my lord, it is quite unnecessary to waylay me in this fashion."

He ignored this. "She saw you yesterday, didn't she? What did you tell her?"

He could see the lawyer watching him, his expression hard to fathom in the uncertain light within the interior of the coach. Alex guessed he was assessing the odds and promptly raised them. "I ain't leaving until you satisfy me, Vergette, so you may as well cut line."

He saw the fellow's shoulders relax, and his anxiety reduced a trifle.

"Since my errand was to you, my lord Dymond, it can do no harm to give you the facts. Whether it will do the slightest good, however, I strongly doubt."

"Talking in riddles, man. Did you or did you not burden Miss Greenaway with some tale or other to make her fly from me?"

The lawyer's head went back. "What an extraordinary way of putting it, my lord Dymond. Yes, if you must have it, I told Miss Greenaway what she wanted to know. I did, as you suppose, surmise that it would have the effect my client hoped for. More so than if I had told you, I now perceive."

Alex began to cherish a wish to plant the man a facer. "For the Lord's sake, speak plainly man! What's the tale?"

Vergette gave another of his resigned sighs. "Miss Greenaway is the natural daughter of my client. She was adopted by Greenaway at the behest of my client's father, who also set up the trust."

"Apple's grandfather then?"

"Just so."

Alex was a little surprised at his own lack of reaction. He'd known it, or guessed it, almost from the first. "Who is this client of yours? Some duke or marquis?"

The inevitable conclusion, given Vergette's involvement. But the lawyer refused to be drawn. "That, my lord Dymond, I may not disclose."

A bitter note entered Alex's voice. "Fellow wanted you to warn me off. Afraid of scandal, eh?"

"I think, my lord Dymond, you must see his point of view."

Possibly, but that made it no better. A niggle surfaced and he gave it voice. "Yes, but this don't add up, Vergette. If this duke or marquis of yours gave some girl a slip on the shoulder, why should his father take the trouble to set up a trust? Only have to pay off the female to be rid of the business."

Vergette's urbanity was fully back in place. "My dear Lord Dymond, I am sure your keen intelligence must give you the answer. The lady in the case was of genteel birth, and my client was already married at the time."

Fury scorched Alex. "Scoundrel!"

"Just so. Fortunately, his sire, who is no longer with us to my regret, was a man of integrity and vision."

"He made provision for Apple."

"Or, should the outcome have been different, for a young fellow who needed to make his way in the world."

"And you told her all this?"

"The bare bones, I do assure you."

Which was enough. Alex remembered his last glimpse of Apple's face when she'd left him last night and almost ground his teeth. "Now we have that straight, where is Apple, Vergette? Did she head for Portsmouth? Back to those vultures? And don't pretend you don't know."

His eyes had adjusted to the gloom and he saw the lawyer smile.

"My dear Lord Dymond, I should not dream of pretending anything, but the fact remains that I do not know." He held up a gloved finger. "Except that she was adamant she would not return to the Greenaways."

Worse yet! Where the deuce was she then?

"And you left her to her own devices? Don't believe that for a moment. I know her too well."

"Then you are better placed to locate her whereabouts than I."

"Are you telling me she didn't beg a lift from you? Or that you weren't careful enough of her reputation to offer to bring her with you to London?"

"I would have done so, but Miss Greenaway assured me she had a safe refuge where she might wait out the time to her birthday."

Impatience gnawed at Alex, combined with a rise of dread. Had Apple gone off on some mad scheme? "What refuge?"

"Miss Greenaway would not divulge it. I did press her to tell me, my dear Lord Dymond. However, as is now seen, I believe she was anxious to avoid your coming up with her."

Alex's heart dropped. Yes, she would be over-anxious on that score. After what she'd heard about her birth, what the devil else was one to expect? Not that it would deter him in the slightest.

"You took her up, didn't you?" The lawyer hesitated and Alex lost all patience. "Look, man, I don't care what your damned client wants! That chit was under my care and I ain't about to ditch responsibility for her, no matter if I have to search the length and breadth of the country. What's more, Apple knows I'll come after her. I told her often enough." He leaned towards the man. "I'm no fool, Vergette. I'm an earl's heir, as you well know, and I ain't one to bring shame and scandal down on anyone. Least of all Apple herself. But I won't leave her to fend for herself. I'll see she's safe and bring her to you to get this damned trust sorted out. And then it's down to what she wants. Do you understand me?"

The lawyer held out his hand and Alex took it, receiving a strongly gripped handshake.

"You're a man after my own heart, my lord Dymond. And, I may add, one who would gladden the heart of my former client."

Released, Alex sat back. "Well?"

The lawyer smiled. "I dropped her at Romsey. I dare say you know the address."

Chapter Twenty-one

Clutching a large basket, now somewhat heavy with provisions, Apple trotted briskly out of Market Place and walked down the Hundreds. The cold bit through the gap in her cloak, despite all efforts to hold it together with her free hand.

In a way, she welcomed the wind in her eyes, raw from crying, and a spatter of light rain that refreshed her reddened cheeks. Mrs Reddicliffe had tutted and cooed while she wept on the nurse's ample bosom as she husked out her story.

Reddy had let her have her cry out and then recommended her to dry her tears and went off to prepare a tisane in the little kitchen. By the time Apple had drunk it and been chided for thinking she must beg to stay in the cottage when the nurse declared she was only too ready to help any friend of Lady Georgiana's, Apple's spirits had lifted enough to enable her to run Reddy's errand.

"I've baking on the go, my dear, and a rabbit to make ready for the pot, but there are one or two little things we'll need to augment the meal now there's two of us."

It was a deal easier to bear the nagging distress when she had something to do, and Apple set about her task with energy, if not much enthusiasm. Even as she dropped into Herbert's the grocer, where Reddy had said she might purchase the needed spices along with a small measure of tea and another of cocoa, her mind was never far removed from the lawyer's revelations. Since she was certain Alex would try to find her, she expended a deal of cogitation on what she would say to him. It was largely fruitless, since her thoughts obstinately centred on the dismal future stretching ahead of her without him.

It was both odd and inconvenient to think how so short a time ago she would by now have been lost in growing excitement and anticipation of her long-held plans coming to fruition. Except she'd never been certain they could or would, since the contents of the trust remained a mystery. Yet now the prospect of journeying along with the hired companion she'd envisioned was bleak beyond words. Oh, she could still conjure a modicum of enthusiasm for the places she'd hoped to see, the artefacts she'd only known in pictures and descriptions that she had hoped to witness in person. Only, what she saw in her mind's eye was the big Alex-shaped empty gap at her side.

It was ridiculous, futile and utterly presumptuous even to imagine him there, but his absence yawned like a wound, an actual physical hurt in the region of her heart.

She supposed that time must dull the ache. But first she must find the courage and strength to withstand any attempt he might make to resume control of her life. Now that she knew what she was, it would not do. No amount of chivalry on his part was going to change that. And if, as in a corner of her secret bosom she suspected, he'd grown a little fond, Apple could not allow him to jeopardise his reputation by association with a female in her situation. No, it simply would not do.

This dogged determination buoyed her spirits. Of all things, he must not see how much it hurt. Once more on the move, she turned left into Latimer Street and then right into Love Lane where the cottage inhabited by Georgy's old nurse was situated.

Arriving at the door, she knocked. It opened, and all her careful thinking vanished at a stroke.

"Alex!"

The grim look on his face relaxed into a grin. "Didn't expect me this quickly, eh?"

"No, and I wish you hadn't come," she lied, struggling against the flurry in her pulse.

Alex took the basket from her and drew her into the living room of the cottage, which opened directly onto the street. "Come in out of the cold. Mrs Reddicliffe is making coffee."

Apple rubbed her hands together to still their trembling as she moved into the small room, shifting as far from Alex as the space would allow. His presence dwarfed the place, filling the emptiness like a whirling hurricane of energy.

"Mr Vergette betrayed me then?"

He came to her and helped her remove the cloak. "Most unwillingly, I assure you. Practically had to shake it out of the fellow."

Apple took the cloak from his hands and went to lay it aside on one of the straight chairs at the table set near the front window. She gripped the back of the chair. "Did he tell you…?"

"Yes, I made him tell me." Alex's voice came from behind, and his hands on her shoulders turned her to face him. "And it don't make a particle of difference to me, Apple. Guessed it ages ago, if you want the truth."

She gazed up into his face, fighting the urge to sink into his embrace and lay her head and her troubles on his broad shoulder. "It does to me, Alex."

"So I should suppose, but you were a victim of circumstance, Apple. Not your fault."

"Unfortunately, that does not change the facts, does it?" She slipped out of his hold, unable to bear the intensity of his gaze. He'd set the basket on the table and she went to pick it up. "I must take this to Reddy."

But at that moment, the nurse came bustling into the living room. "Is that you, my dearie? Did you find the spices we need?"

Apple turned with relief to the elderly dame, handing over the basket. "Yes, along with tea and cocoa, and also the greens and a fresh loaf. Oh, and I got cheese and butter from that little dairy in Market Place as I was passing."

The nurse's plump features brightened. "That would be Dumper's. Well, that was a kind thought, my dear, thank you. Now, I'll just pop back to the kitchen with these. The coffee won't be but a moment."

Apple took a step or two after her. "Shall I come and bring it in?"

Mrs Reddicliffe turned at the door. "No, no. You stay and talk to Master Alex." She wagged a finger at him. "And don't you go upsetting the poor mite, Master Alex!"

He was watching Apple, much to her dismay, but he turned his head at that. "Last thing I wish to do, Reddy."

"Well, see you don't. She's had enough to bear and that's a fact." With which, she stomped through to the rear of the cottage, leaving Apple decidedly embarrassed.

She tried to avoid Alex's gaze, making a business of shaking out her petticoats and taking a seat in one of the two comfy old armchairs either side of the fire.

Alex perched on the arm of the other, his eyes still on her, his expression hard to read. For this, the gloom of the late afternoon was responsible. Mrs Reddicliffe had lit candles in a wall sconce and a three-pronged candelabrum on the mantelpiece, but the fading daylight outside the window had not yet grown dark enough for the candlelight to prevail.

"You look sick as a cat, and no wonder," he said at last.

Apple sighed and brushed at her cheeks, cold still from the wind and rain. "I feel like a drowned rat."

His explosive laugh sounded, and a pang smote Apple for the familiarity of it. She covered her face with her hands.

"Don't, Apple. Please don't cry." She dropped her hands and looked up to find his expression gentler than she'd before seen. "Can't bear to see you upset."

She managed a wavering smile. "I'm not crying. I'm all cried out if you want the truth."

He leaned a little towards her, his tone becoming earnest. "Listen, Apple, it's not the end of the world. At least your grandfather made provision for you. You ain't dependent on those vultures, and you can choose your own path."

"I know." Her voice was stronger now. "It was just the shock, finding it was true after all. Silly of me, because it's not as if I wasn't expecting it. Only I didn't suppose he would turn out to be someone so — so high up in the world. Mr Vergette said a man of stature. He meant rank, of course."

"Yes."

The monosyllable shot suspicion into Apple's mind and she frowned at Alex. "Did he tell you who it was? *Is*, I mean?"

Alex put out a hand. "Of course not. I'd tell you if I knew. Only I guessed, Apple."

"How?"

"When I went to see the fellow in London, a friend told me he only serves men as high as dukes or marquises. My father said the same."

Apple gazed at him, dazed. "Dukes or marquises?"

His sudden grin lightened her heart. "Got to admit it don't sound like you, young Apple."

A laugh escaped her. "Not in the least. In fact, I don't think I believe it."

"Dare say we'll never know. It's obvious Vergette is sworn to secrecy on the identity of the fellow. But that need not concern you, as long as he hands over the dibs."

The underlying gloom resurfaced. "Why did you chase after me, Alex?"

"Well, you know why, don't be a hen-wit. Might as well ask you why you went off without a word to me, but I know you too well to need telling."

Apple clasped her fingers together rather tightly, looking down at them. "I knew you would stop me if I told you."

"Well, you're right there. But that don't mean I don't understand. Knew the moment Georgy said you'd been into the inn that you'd seen Vergette and heard enough to make you fly the coop."

She looked up again. "I couldn't stay, Alex. How could I accept your parents' hospitality, knowing what I was? We'd been deceitful already."

"Well, they know now."

Her heart sank. "You told them everything?"

He nodded. "And my father said he'd help us if he could. Help *you*, I mean."

"How can he? What can anyone do? The facts can't be changed, Alex."

"No, but you don't deserve to be shunned, Apple. What kind of people do you think we are?"

She caught her breath and smiled at him. "No, I know you would never do so. You're much too kind."

Even in the candle glow, she could see his cheeks darken. To her amusement, he spluttered with embarrassment.

"Balderdash! Kind? Nothing of the sort. And that ain't what you said when I insisted on keeping you with me."

She had to laugh. "No, I thought you were horridly autocratic."

He grimaced. "Suppose I was a bit. But you needn't think I regret it, for I don't."

"Nor I." She drew a quick breath on a half-sob. "I'll always be glad I held you up, Alex. It's been a — a mad ride, but one I would not have missed for the world."

He was silent for a moment, and Apple began to fidget under his gaze. At last he spoke, and something in his voice touched her to the core.

"You talk as if it's over between us. Is that what you want? I promised I'd see you safe and take you to Vergette."

Apple gripped her fingers together, hurting with the effort to keep her voice as natural as she could. "I'm safe here. And — and Mr Vergette advanced me some money so I could travel post. Reddy says she'll go with me."

"But that doesn't answer my question."

At this excessively awkward moment, Mrs Reddicliffe came in with a laden tray. "The coffee's boiled, my dears. And I've brought in the fresh baked scones."

Apple jumped up to take the tray and set it on the table, taking refuge in helping Reddy to set out the accoutrements for the coffee, together with plates and a large dish of hot scones.

"I've put a morsel of that butter you brought in the dish, my dearie, and I've the damson jam made last year, if Master Alex should fancy it." She did not seem to notice the prevailing atmosphere of disquiet, but ushered them to the table and proceeded to pour the coffee. "Give his lordship a scone, dear, and take one yourself. That's it."

Apple set a plate before Alex and offered the dish of scones. He took one, and seemed visibly to pull himself together.

"These look good, Reddy. Took a mouthful at Winchester, but feels like hours ago."

"Then you'd best stay and dine with us, Master Alex."

He hesitated, glancing at Apple, who quickly dropped her eyes to her plate and took a scone for herself.

"Can't do that. Already bespoke dinner at the White Horse. Besides, wouldn't dream of incommoding you."

Apple was beset by a horrid fear and could not withstand the question. "Are you staying the night?"

He looked at her. "Planned to, yes. Hoped I could persuade you to accompany me back to Dymond Garth tomorrow."

Oh, no. She'd hoped this purgatory could not last more than an hour or two. The less she saw of Alex the better for her peace of mind, despite the dreadful hollow engendered by the thought of his going.

"You'll be setting off straight after breakfast then, I dare say."

She glanced at him as she spoke, and a shaft went through her at the look in his face. She'd hurt him! Instinct urged Apple to retract, put out a hand to seize his and tell him she hadn't meant it and beg him to stay with her forever. But it could not be. It was better if he thought her indifferent. Better for him at least. She must bear the very different knowledge of her own heart.

Trying for a cheerful note, she buttered a scone with energy. "This is very cosy, Reddy. I do like being here."

The old lady's hand stopped with the coffee pot poised over Alex's cup. "Do you, my dearie? That's nice. But you've to learn to live a bigger life than this. It's not fit for the likes of you, now, is it?"

"The likes of me?"

She warmed at Alex's sudden grin. "She don't know you very well, Apple, that's the trouble." He pointed his half-eaten scone at the nurse. "One of a kind is this chit, Reddy. She won't fit in any box you care to name."

A breathless giggle escaped Apple, releasing a little of her despair. "I do try to conform."

"And make a pretty poor job of it."

Miss Reddicliffe tutted at him, but Apple, her mouth full of scone, was hard put to it not to spray the lot out again. She swallowed it down and took a gulp of coffee to clear her mouth and throat.

"It's too bad of you, Alex. I was perfectly well-behaved at your parents' house."

"Yes, because you were such a scaredy-cat you couldn't help it."

Was he trying to provoke her deliberately? She eyed him, and he caught her looking. A faint smile and a wink came her way. Apple's heart lifted and she spoke without thinking. "Well, if you want to know, I'm about to be even more unconventional. Eccentric even, some might say."

His brows rose. "Holding me up with a pistol wasn't eccentric enough?"

She giggled. "Stop it, Alex. You know I had good reason for that."

His smile embraced her and her heart turned over. "Go on, then. Shock me."

Abruptly realising what she was doing, Apple hesitated. She'd avoided telling him what she meant to do because she'd been convinced he'd say it was hen-witted and find a way to stop her. But of course, it no longer mattered. He couldn't stop her, because of what she was, not just because she was not of his world. Sooner or later, he must step back and let her go her own way. "It won't shock you because you always supposed I had a crazy scheme afoot."

His gaze narrowed. "Are you talking about this secret notion you have when Vergette hands over the dibs? Something you need a companion for?"

"Yes, and Reddy knows of just such a one as will suit, so I don't even need to advertise." A little of her original enthusiasm was filtering back. If she could not have Alex, at least she could realise her dream. She looked him boldly in the face. "I am going to travel the world."

No explosion greeted this announcement. Alex simply stared at her.

She waited, noting that Reddy was watching Alex in a puzzled way. At last he spoke, with an effort, as it seemed to Apple. "How much of the world? Just Europe? Or do you mean to venture as far as India?"

A flood of heat enveloped Apple, and she had to stop herself lifting her hands to her burning cheeks. "I don't know. I hadn't thought of India. I just — I just dreamed of the arts, the paintings to be found in Florence and Venice. Paris too, but whether one can venture there in these times I don't know. And then there is the scenery. I used to pore over Papa's prints of all the places where his wines came from and wish I might visit Lisbon and Lombardy, or Cirò in Calabria. I wanted adventure…"

Alex was watching her, an expression hard to read in his face, but there was warmth in his eyes and involuntarily she smiled at him.

"It's all the fault of *Robinson Crusoe*, you must know."

His brows drew together. "*Robinson Crusoe?*"

"I read it over and over when I was a child. That, and later, I read the adventures of Peregrine Pickle and Roderick Random.

Yes, I know I should not have done, so you need not tell me so. I used to wish I was a boy so that I might do as they did."

"How did all that turn into this notion you might travel the world, as you put it, since you aren't a boy?"

Apple took a fortifying drink of her coffee. He was taking this too well. At any moment, he might burst into one of his explosive snorts and pour derision all over her dream.

"I read Mrs Hester Piozzi's book of her travels through France, Italy and Germany. If she could do it, why should I not? If I was properly chaperoned, and if there was money enough in the trust, I could at least see the places and things I'd read about and seen in etchings."

She stopped, looking across at the old nurse, who was wearing a comfortable smile, just as if she'd not exclaimed with horror when Apple had mentioned the scheme. She'd only done so because she was in such a state of upset at the time she hadn't thought about what she was saying. But as soon as she'd told the nurse she didn't mean to go alone, Reddy had changed her tune, suggesting a widow she knew who lived here in Romsey might be the very person.

Alex set down his cup. "Well, I knew it would turn out to be hare-brained. Bound to be, coming from you, young Apple."

He sounded more resigned than shocked.

"You don't object to it?"

His brows shot up. "Object to it? I said it's hare-brained, didn't I? Feather-headed, that's what you are. Of all the bird-witted notions you've had, that one takes the crown."

Apple swallowed her disappointment. Ridiculous to miss him berating her in his usual fashion. She could not prevent the burning question. "You won't try to stop me?"

He shrugged. "Not much use if I did. You'd only be off the moment my back was turned."

"Yes, I should," she said, goaded.

"There you are then."

Apple finished her scone in silence. Had she convinced him of her indifference? Or did he really not care? She found that hard to believe, but his ready acquiescence was puzzling. And unwelcome, if she must be truthful.

Within a few moments, Reddy stood up and began to gather the empty plates and cups onto the tray. Apple went to help her and was waved away.

"You've to settle matters with Master Alex, my dearie, before he goes off. Sit you both down now while I clear this lot away."

Thus adjured, Apple moved back to the chair by the fire and watched Alex follow suit. He did not speak for several minutes, staring into the fire in a way that began to prey upon Apple's nerves. What was he thinking? A resurgence of the grief lodged in her bosom startled her.

"I wish you weren't going."

It was out before she could think and heat flew in her cheeks as his head turned, a frown between his brows.

"Yet you won't come with me."

"I can't, Alex."

Her throat was tight all over again, and she cursed her own slip.

He leaned forward and held out his hand in an imperative way. Without even thinking about it, Apple put hers into it and his touch sent a flitter down her veins. Her heart began to beat a little faster.

"Won't you trust me, Apple?"

She could barely speak. "How trust you?"

"Made you a promise, didn't I? Said I'd take you to Vergette. You didn't think I wouldn't come for you when the time came, did you?"

"But, Alex…"

"No buts. If you won't come back, you won't. Can understand that. But if you think I can walk out of this cottage and never see you again, you must have windmills in your head."

His hand tightened on hers as he spoke, and Apple's eyes pricked. She knew her voice was husky, but it must be said. "You'll have to, Alex, in the end."

"Don't know that." He grinned. "Might decide to go to perdition myself and come adventuring with you."

She gave a watery chuckle. "What, and make me the one to bring madness into your life?"

"You did that already, my — young Apple. My life changed from the moment you hid yourself in my coach. And the devil of it is, I don't want it changed back."

Apple could not speak. If she said anything at all, she'd end by weeping into his coat. His hold had loosened and she gently withdrew her hand, sitting back in the chair. He didn't move, just sat where he was, regarding her in a way that made the rhythm of her pulse uneven. Apple struggled to contain the sob rising in her throat. She forced it down, swallowing hard.

With a brisk movement, Alex rose from his chair and moved away to the centre of the little room. "I've got to go." He went to the door through which Reddy had disappeared with the tray a few moments since and called through it. "Reddy, I'm off." He came back and looked down at Apple. "Don't go anywhere. I'll be back for you." He raised a finger. "You know I mean it. Disappear and I'll come after you."

Apple managed a tiny smile. "I know you will."

He came a step closer, dropped to his haunches and found her hand, raising it briefly to his lips. The tiny kiss sang through her veins.

Then Reddy was in the room, and her voice and Alex's mingled briefly in the fog in her mind. Next instant, he was gone, leaving only the imprint of his lips upon her fingers.

Chapter Twenty-two

Much as he wished to see Apple again before leaving Romsey, Alex chose instead to make an early start. If he went to Reddy's cottage, he knew he would find it hard to tear himself away. Because the devil of it was, Apple had it down with an accuracy that gave him a restless night. His wishes aside, there was no overcoming the obstacle of her birth.

He toyed with the notion of consigning duty and common sense to the devil, but it would not do. Even could he subject himself and his family to the scandal, he could not do it to Apple herself. He knew his world too well. What, throw her to the lions to endure the slights and snubs of the ton? She'd be a sight more miserable than if he were to let her go.

He spared little thought on the possibility of persuading her to find some other scheme than this crazy notion of going off to foreign parts, with no more protection and help than some widow who'd spent her life within the shores of England and very likely never stepped far outside her own home town. The thought of the trouble Apple would inevitably get into stood his hair on end. But she was such a stubborn little thing there'd be no stopping her when he couldn't be at hand.

The best he could hope for was that this trust proved generous enough to allow her to hire a courier as well. He'd oversee the finding of a suitable fellow, one who would be useful in a fight besides paving her way and, most importantly, who could be depended upon to scotch any nonsensical flights of fancy Apple might take into her head. He was still trying vainly to think of such a person, other than himself, when he drifted into sleep.

Arriving at Dymond Garth close on noon upon the following day, Alex entered his ancestral home to a scene of noisy chaos.

Both his parents were in the hall, along with a number of other persons not all immediately recognizable, and his sister's shrill voice was the first that smote his ears as the butler shut the door behind him.

"What the devil is going on, Meech?"

Before the butler had a chance to enlighten him, one of the individuals, heavily cloaked against the cold, happened to turn. Alex cursed.

"Miss Greenaway? Oh, good God!"

Apple's arch wife of a guardian whirled towards him, grabbing the arm of a stocky fellow in a rough serge coat and corduroy breeches and dragging him forward as she pointed an accusing finger at Alex.

"There he is! That is the man who kidnapped my cousin! Arrest him at once!"

The effect of this outburst brought everyone present into play.

Walter Greenaway pushed past his sister to confront Alex. "Ha! Thought you'd seen the last of us, did you, Lord Dymond? You see how mistaken you were? This here's a Bow Street Runner, and he's come to take you into custody!"

"How dare you?" shrieked Georgy. "My brother is not a kidnapper!"

"Where is my cousin?" demanded Marjorie Greenaway. "Tell him to produce her, Mr Benjamin!"

The stocky individual spoke for the first time. "Give me leave, madam. I'll do any asking as is needed. Nor I don't need no help in choosing what to ask."

Lady Luthrie's arctic tones cut across the hubbub. "Alexander, who are these people?"

"My dear, I think we had best retire and leave Alex to handle the business."

"Yes, but where —?"

"Enough, Pippa! Georgy, come!"

To Alex's relief, his family began to mount the stairs. He turned to the butler. "Meech, escort these visitors to the library, will you?"

Marjorie blocked his way. "While you escape again?"

Alex ignored her, instead addressing the runner. "I'm Dymond, and I'm not going anywhere, except to put off my coat. Be so good as to follow the butler and I will join you directly. Refreshments to the library as well, if you please, Meech."

The fellow Benjamin perked up at this. "I take that kind in you, me lord. Happy to await your convenience."

Miss Greenaway exploded. "Await his convenience? And pray will you say it's convenient when you're giving him time to conceal my cousin?"

Alex eyed the woman with dislike. "She's no longer with me, Miss Greenaway. You're wasting your time."

Her brother leapt in. "What have you done with her, villain?"

"I will tell you, but I ain't discussing it in the hall. You'll go into the library or go away. I don't care which."

He nodded to the butler, rigid with disapproval. Meech gave a slight bow towards Marjorie. "If you please, madam."

She huffed, but as the runner chose to follow, she had little choice but to accept the invitation.

Walter hesitated. "We won't be leaving without our girl, so don't think to pull the wool over our eyes."

Alex regarded him with disdain. "I repeat, I ain't discussing it here."

The fellow drew a breath and puffed it out. "Very well then. But don't be long."

With relief, Alex saw him turn and follow the others. Unbuttoning his coat, he ran up the stairs and found his father waiting for him.

"Well done, Alex. I take it Appoline wouldn't come back with you?"

Alex shook his head. "How did you know I'd found her?"

Lord Luthrie smiled. "You wouldn't be back if you hadn't." He slung a comforting arm about Alex's shoulder. "I'm sorry she wouldn't come, but it's fortunate as it turns out."

"Seems so, sir."

Releasing him, his father patted him on the back. "Get rid of them, my boy, and then come into the morning room. Your mother's had a notion you might be glad to hear."

Too preoccupied to enquire what this might be, Alex merely nodded and passed on to his own rooms. Pendell was waiting, and as he allowed the man to divest him of his outer garments and mud-spattered boots, he ran over in his mind which facts he was prepared to supply to the minion of the law. Preferable to have dealt with them then and there, but he'd advocated the library and refreshments to give himself a breather. No point in confronting this hideous situation without giving himself time to think.

It had never seriously occurred to him that they would carry out the threat to have him up for kidnapping. How in the world they'd persuaded one of the Bow Street magistrates to send a man to look into the matter, he could not imagine. No doubt they'd twisted the story to suit themselves. In which case, nothing but the bald truth would serve. Or as much of it as might be needed to make Bow Street understand Apple left the Greenaways of her own free will. Under no circumstances was he going to divulge her whereabouts.

Thus determined, he donned the polished boots his valet produced, tugged his coat back into place and made to leave the room.

"Your hair, my lord."

Pendell was holding out a comb. With a muttered exclamation of impatience, Alex grabbed the thing and looked in his dressing-room mirror as he dragged it through his dark locks. Then he flung it down.

"That'll do. Good enough for this lot, in any event."

His valet permitted himself a tiny smirk. "I suspected your lordship was not best pleased."

"I'm damned annoyed, if you want to know. Disturbing my parents like this. I'll give them snuff!"

The fury sprang full-blown into his head, as if the shock of the arrival had held it back. Kidnapping indeed! When those damned rogues knew full well what had happened. And how they'd treated poor little Apple. Thank the Lord she'd refused to come with him. At least she was spared this.

The dangerous mood held him as he sped back along the corridors, down the stairs and strode along the hall, flinging open the library door without ceremony and marching in.

His gaze swept the room, fixing upon the Bow Street Runner, who was standing by one of the tall windows. The woman Marjorie was sitting in one of the armchairs by the fire, her brother taking a stance at the mantelpiece. All three were armed with glasses, and Alex was glad to note the butler had seen fit to remain in the room.

"Thank you, Meech. You can leave us now."

Bowing, the butler removed himself and Alex went directly up to the runner. "Mr Benjamin, is it?"

"That's right, sir — er, me lord."

"Be good enough to tell me exactly what brings you here."

An explosive snort came from Greenaway and his sister broke in at once.

"You know perfectly well why he's here, my lord Dymond."

Alex turned on her, letting the full force of his rage show. "Hold your tongue, madam! Or I'll have my butler throw you out of the house."

She turned purple, either with rage or chagrin, glaring at him. Greenaway's jaw dropped open. Neither ventured a word. Satisfied, Alex returned his attention to the runner, who gave him a look compound of respect and smugness. Alex raised his brows. "Had a deal to bear from those two, I dare say?"

Benjamin let his breath go. "You could say as that's so, me lord."

"Yes, they seem to delight in causing scenes. Had 'em at my sister's not long ago, prating of kidnapping then, as if they didn't know just why their cousin took the chance to escape from their clutches."

The runner frowned. "You do know the young lady then, me lord?"

"Oh, yes, I know her all right. Helped her find somewhere to stay while she waited for her birthday."

The man's eyes narrowed. "Why would you do that, me lord?"

"Because she was hiding in my coach and begged me to take her to a posting stage where she might pick up the stagecoach to London."

"He's lying!"

"Ask him why he didn't return her at once to her home!"

The Greenaways were in again.

This time Benjamin took a hand, moving a step or two in their direction. "I've to ask as you'll allow me to be pursuing of my investigations without interruption, sir and madam. You've been and laid your information, and it weren't by my wish as you chose to accompany me on me duty."

Marjorie was up now. "To see this wretch didn't try to cozen you with his nonsense and lies, of course."

Benjamin held up a hand. "I'm a runner, madam. We ain't in the habit of being cozened. Nor we don't allow no one to give us no Canterbury tale. But I can't be asking questions if you keep butting in, and that's a fact."

The woman reddened again and Walter pushed forward. "Don't you speak to my sister like that!"

Benjamin remained stolid, but polite. "If you'll remove her from this here room, sir, while I settle with his lordship here, I won't have to speak to her at all."

Walter pulled his sister back to the chair and whispered in her ear.

"Oh, very well," she said in a disgruntled tone and sat back down, retrieving the glass she'd left on a side table and taking a gulp of whatever it was Meech had served them.

Alex watched Greenaway take the other chair, similarly resuming his drink, and waited for the runner to return to him. The fellow gave a nod of satisfaction and came back.

"Now then, me lord, if you please."

Alex began to entertain the hope it might be easier than he'd supposed to be rid of the business. "It's as I told you. Young Miss Greenaway was looking to get to London and escaped from these two into my coach."

The runner eyed him with obvious doubt. "Begging your pardon, me lord, seems to me as a well-behaved young lady wouldn't go accosting no stranger for help."

Alex seethed at the implication but kept his voice even. "She's a very unusual young lady."

"Seems to me as it'd be a dangerous undertaking, me lord."

"So it was. Damned dangerous. Told her as much myself. What's more, told her I'd take her back to her guardians."

Alex knew what was coming and mentally revised his story.

"But you didn't go for to take her back, me lord. Why was that then?"

"Because she told me these guardians of hers were constraining her to marry Greenaway's partner, so they could get hold of the money she has in trust." The runner blinked, and it was plain this part of the tale was new to him. Alex curled his lip, glancing back at the two by the fire. "Didn't see fit to divulge that to your magistrate, I dare say."

Greenaway was red in the face and Marjorie looked furious.

Benjamin went across, addressing himself to the brother. "Is this true, sir?"

"Nothing to do with the case. What business was it of his if my cousin was betrothed or not?"

"Betrothed, sir? To whom?"

"None of your damned business!"

To Alex's admiration, Benjamin, stolid before the man, merely looked him in the eye. Greenaway began to bluster.

"Look, man, this ain't to the point. I mean, the girl's my ward — for another week at least. Naught to do with anyone if I choose to give her hand to —"

"Be quiet, Walter!" Setting down her glass, Marjorie rose, bosom heaving with wrath. Ignoring the runner, she turned on Alex. "I knew you'd try to cozen your way out of it. Oh, I knew." Her glare returned to the minion of the Law. "Tell me this. By what right does he aid and abet my cousin, who was in my care, mark you, to flout her guardian's authority?"

Benjamin's glance came back to Alex and he stepped forward, his tone redolent with scorn. "I claim no rights, ma'am. Pure fellow feeling, that's all. Besides," he added, turning to Benjamin, "it was plain to me young Miss Greenaway would only run away if I attempted to take her back. Thought she was safer with me than blundering about on her own." He held up a finger as Marjorie opened her mouth to protest. "What's more, I had every care to her reputation and took her to stay with my sister. Which is where these — these guardians of hers caught up with us and started bleating about having me up on a charge of kidnapping. And that was only because I refused to give her up to them."

Benjamin held up a ham-like hand. "Just a moment, me lord. If they was her guardians, I'm bound to state you didn't have no right to hold on to the lady when they come to fetch her."

"Ha! There's for you!"

"What have you to say to that, my lord girl-stealing Dymond?"

Inwardly cursing, Alex struggled to control his rising temper. "I have this to say. Apple didn't want to go back with you, and —"

Walter Greenaway sprang forward. "That's a lie! She even said she'd come and you wouldn't let her."

"That's so," said Marjorie in an eager tone, turning to Benjamin. "Apple was ready to return. I'm telling you, the whole thing was a concerted plot. That sister of his pretended she didn't even know her, but then he arrived —" pointing an accusing finger at Alex — "and Apple emerged from hiding and said she'd come home."

"Only this monster refused to allow it. Said we'd take her over his dead body or some such thing. Threatened to have us chucked out of the house and all!"

"And I'll have you chucked out of this one if you don't stop yelling in my father's library!"

Two fulminating faces turned on him. Glancing at the runner, Alex found him enviably unmoved by the kerfuffle surrounding him. The hiatus enabled him to take a hand.

"When you've quite finished, sir and madam, maybe you'll let me do the job as you've wished me to do."

Alex could not but admire the fellow's stolidity. Did nothing shake him?

"Now then, me lord. What you're telling me is, I take it, as the young lady was wishful of remaining with you of her own free will?"

Consigning a twinge of conscience to perdition, Alex closed with this promising avenue with alacrity. "That's it. Knew she'd be off on her own if I let her go. Managed to persuade her she'd be a deal better off remaining with my family here until her birthday, when I'd take her to London as she wished."

Benjamin eyed him in a ruminating way that Alex found distinctly unsettling. The Greenaways, for once refraining from interference, looked poised for what the runner might say. "You ain't going to deny as she was here then, me lord?"

"Wouldn't dream of denying it."

Guessing what was coming, Alex braced for the inevitable.

"Then where is she now, me lord, if she ain't here?"

Here it was. The question he couldn't and wouldn't answer. Evasion would only increase the fellow's suspicion. "Can't tell you that."

"Oh? And why not, me lord?"

Alex cast a glance at the Greenaways, both of whom were showing signs of believing in their triumph. "Because I won't allow these so-called guardians of hers to trouble her."

"Ha!"

"You see? You see!"

Benjamin held up his hand again to silence them, but his eyes remained on Alex. "I'm bound to state, me lord, that it don't look good."

"I'm aware of that."

The runner ruminated for a space. Alex waited. No point in precipitating anything. Besides, his best defence lay in silence.

"What I don't see, me lord," said the fellow at length, "is what's significant about this here birthday. Would I be right in thinking the young lady comes of age?"

"You would."

"And would I be right in thinking as this trust you spoke of comes into play here?"

"You would," said Alex again.

Another glance at the Greenaways found them tight-lipped and glowering. Afraid he'd spill the beans?

"Then I'll take leave to say, me lord, as I can't accept your word for it that the young lady ain't being constrained against her will."

"Ha, there's for you, Dymond!"

"At last!"

The ham-like hand of the runner was once again raised, accompanied by a severe look. The Greenaways subsided. Wondering if this was where he was removed from the premises with gyves about his wrists, Alex set his teeth as Benjamin's steady gaze returned to his face.

"Be that as it may, me lord, there ain't no evidence neither to suggest as you stole the young lady by force." Alex breathed again, ignoring the muttering behind the runner. "The only thing as will serve, me lord, is for me to see the young lady for meself and ask her straight."

Stymied, Alex stared at the man. Nothing was further from his wishes than to haul poor Apple here to confront her ghastly guardians and a Bow Street Runner. But if he was to keep her hidey-hole secret from the Greenaways, it began to seem as if he must do so.

Searching his mind for alternatives, he hit upon sacrificing Vergette. "There is one other option, Benjamin."

The fellow's brows rose. "There is, me lord?"

At least he'd surprised the man. "You could go to see the lawyer in the case. He can corroborate what I've said about the trust. Moreover, he's seen Miss Greenaway lately, and —"

"What's that you say?" Exploding all over again, Walter Greenaway leapt forward. "Apple's seen him? How? When?"

"Be quiet, Walter!" Marjorie surged in, her cheeks suffused as she pushed past Benjamin to confront Alex. "Tell me this, Lord Dymond. If Mr Vergette has seen Apple, why should she stay away? You claim that was her purpose in leaving us, but if she's done that, there's no occasion for her to remain in your custody, is there?"

A snorting laugh escaped Alex. "My custody? That's how you see it?"

She ignored him, turning on Benjamin. "You see? He's lying. I'm willing to wager my cousin hasn't seen hide nor hair of this Vergette fellow."

But Benjamin, to Alex's amazement, was looking dazed. He fixed his gaze on Alex.

"Mr Vergette? You're sure of that, me lord? It's Mr Vergette as is the young lady's lawyer?"

"He is. Why, do you know the fellow?"

Benjamin gave a harsh laugh. "There ain't no one in the business of the law don't know Mr Vergette, me lord." A dire look came Alex's way. "Is he ... is he acting for you too, sir?"

"Good Lord, no! Ain't enough of a high-flyer for Vergette myself."

Benjamin drew an audible breath and let it out again. "I'm bound to state, if it's true as Mr Vergette is indeed acting for the young lady, as that puts a vastly different complexion on the matter."

Marjorie cut in again. "Why should it? You're afraid of him, are you?"

"Afraid?" Walter thrust his portly bulk back into the fray. "Afraid of Vergette? Why should you be?"

The runner squared his jaw at the man, stolid once more. "I never said as I was afraid of him, did I? Only when you've Mr Vergette in the firing line, you're leery, see? Ain't no law officer as don't tread with caution around Mr Vergette."

Alex could have cheered. Never had he thought to be grateful to the lawyer, puzzling though it was. How the fellow came to have such an intimidating reputation at Bow Street was a mystery. Unless he did in fact serve other than high-ranking aristocracy, as was rumoured.

"You're not going to let yourself be bubbled, are you?" demanded Walter, in a disgusted sort of tone.

Benjamin drew himself up. "Bubbled, sir? I ain't in the habit of allowing meself to be bubbled. But nor I ain't in the habit of running afoul of one of the niftiest lawyers this world ever did see."

Marjorie glared at the man. "You're going to let him go?"

"Weren't never no question of taking him into custody, madam, so it's no manner of use your railing at me." He held up his hand again to stem any further protest. "But I've me duty just the same." He turned to Alex again, this time with a note of apology in his voice. "Truth to tell, me lord, it don't make no happorth of difference if the young lady seen Mr Vergette or she ain't seen him. What I say and what I stick to is, without the young lady's corroborating your story, I ain't to be shifted from me purpose."

"Which is?"

"To have a sight of the young lady and hear it from her own lips as she ain't been kidnapped nor held captive against her will. Do you take me, me lord?"

With another inward sigh, Alex nodded. "Then I've no other recourse than to fetch her back here. However, I've been journeying all morning and I've no intention of taking off again until tomorrow."

The Greenaways became voluble again.

"Ha! Think we're going to hang about waiting upon your convenience?"

"And what if you don't come back? Who's to say he won't take off with her again? Mr Benjamin, you can't let him go off alone."

Alex eyed them with dislike. To his annoyance, it appeared the runner was not suited with his solution either.

"I'm bound to state, me lord, as there's something in what the lady says."

"That I'll go off somewhere? Are you off your head? This is my home. Bound to return, aren't I?"

"Ah, but when, me lord? I don't have no orders to be kicking me heels neither. Bow Street won't take it kind if I've took more time than needed to settle the business."

Clutching at straws, Alex tried again. "What if I bring Miss Greenaway to London, to Bow Street?"

Benjamin eyed him, waving down the mutterings starting up from behind. "The problem with that, me lord, is I can't be certain as you'll come, can I? Seems to me as I had ought to accompany you to wherever the young lady is."

"And have those two follow you and start badgering her again? No, I thank you."

The fellow began to ruminate all over again, and Alex breathed a little more easily. It was plain he had the upper hand. Vergette's name had fortuitously acted as a powerful deterrent, for which he was mightily relieved. For no consideration would he trust the Greenaways not to nose their way in if he was to consent to take the runner with him to Romsey.

At last Benjamin spoke. "I'm bound to ask you for a written undertaking, me lord, as you'll bring the young lady to Bow Street within a day or two."

"Three. Three days." Alex was ready enough to set his signature to such a thing if he could bargain for more time. "I've to allow Miss Greenaway a chance to prepare and I ain't setting off before the morning. It'll take us a day to get to London and I've to find accommodation."

"I will say that's reasonable, me lord."

"Reasonable? You're letting him off scot-free!"

"If you'll allow me to finish, madam? I'll be glad if you'll write that undertaking, me lord, and I'll take it with me afore I leave this house. After which, sir and madam, you may do as you please, but I'll be off to London by the night mail."

Ignoring the outbreak of hostilities, Alex sat down at once at his father's desk and hunted in the drawers for paper. Selecting a pen with a reasonably sharp point at its end, and with a passing instant of gratitude for Outram's efficiency in ensuring the inkwells in the standish were kept freshly filled, he set about the task of writing what was needed. It did not take long. He signed it with a flourish and shook sand over it. Giving the ink a moment to dry, he again took to the drawers, looking for the Luthrie seal. He was not yet entitled to use it, but it would serve better than his own.

Using a flint to light the candle kept with the stick of sealing wax, he heated the end and dropped a splodge on the folded note. As he stamped it with the seal, he found the runner waiting by the desk.

Alex held out the letter. "I've addressed it to your magistrates. Trust that'll serve?"

"Nicely, me lord," said Benjamin, taking the note and carefully tucking it into a pocket book he unearthed from within his voluminous great-coat. He nodded at the Greenaways, still arguing near the fire, and lowered his voice. "Doubt you'll be troubled by 'em, me lord. They've taken the notion to post down to Bow Street to be sure and catch the young lady there."

"As long as they don't try to follow me."

"They won't do that, me lord." Benjamin laid a finger to the side of his nose and winked, a ghost of a smile on his lips. "Tipped 'em off as it'd hurt their case if they took it into their heads to do any such thing. Hindering an officer of the law in the execution of his duty is that, me lord."

Alex grinned. "Do you mean to say they believe you?"

The fellow raised his brows. "And why wouldn't they, me lord? Who'd know the law better than me?"

Thanking his stars for the influence of Vergette's name, Alex got up and went across to the bell-pull to summon the butler.

The front door shut behind the unwelcome visitors, and Alex let his breath go. He'd seen them off himself, along with the butler. There was no trusting the Greenaways not to start something, and he wanted to make sure they were gone before re-joining the family.

"Thank the Lord for that, Meech. Don't let them back in, will you?"

"Certainly not, my lord. I must beg your pardon for their having entered the house at all. Had it not been for the individual from Bow Street, Matthew would not have been overborne."

"Oh, it was Matthew let them in, was it?"

"Unfortunately I was not at hand at the time, my lord."

"Then for the Lord's sake instruct Matthew to refuse them entrance if they should dare to show their faces again."

"I have already done so, my lord." The butler gave a little bow, as urbane as if his day had not been disturbed by the late commotion. "There will be a light collation set out in the small dining parlour within the half hour, my lord."

"Excellent. I'm hungry as a hunter."

It did not take Alex long to mount the stairs and make his way along the gallery to the family room. He entered to find his parents in earnest discussion and Georgy at the window, presumably watching the departure of the Greenaways.

She turned as he closed the door. "Alex! Thank goodness! I was afraid that horrid man would have arrested you."

"My dear Georgiana, don't be ridiculous," said his mother before he had a chance to respond. "I am astonished the Bow Street magistrates paid any mind to such a nonsensical charge."

"They must at least investigate, my dear, since an information had been laid." Lord Luthrie was on his feet, moving to the side table where a tray with a decanter and glasses stood. "Madeira, my dear boy? I imagine you stand in crying need of a restorative."

Alex laughed. "I do, sir." He glanced at his mother. "Don't mind telling you, ma'am, there was a moment when I thought the fellow was going to haul me off to Bow Street."

Georgy uttered a shriek. "See? Did I not say so, Mama?"

"Nonsense! Your father would have had something to say about that."

Lord Luthrie did not bother to enter into the discussion, only smiling as he held out a glass full of red liquid. Alex took it and fortified himself with a couple of sips.

"By good fortune, Vergette was mentioned. Seems he has something of a reputation with Bow Street, and this Benjamin fellow wasn't keen to run afoul of the man."

His father laughed. "I can't say I'm surprised."

"Yes, but I am. Mean to say, if he don't serve any but the highest ranks, can't see how he'd have anything to do with Bow Street."

"I doubt he does personally," said his father. "But I set Outram to make a couple of discreet enquiries and from his report, Vergette advises his fellow lawyers. His reputation is fearsome."

"Well, thank the Lord for it, sir, because even though I've got to produce Apple at Bow Street within three days, I was able to keep her whereabouts secret."

"And where is she in fact?"

Alex sighed. "With Mrs Reddicliffe."

Georgy clapped her hands. "Oh, famous! Did you take her there?"

"No, Vergette dropped her at Romsey. Caught up with him at Winchester, and what he had to tell me ain't pretty."

Lord Luthrie laid a hand on his shoulder. "No, I imagine not. We've been discussing the matter, my boy, and I'm afraid our conclusions are decidedly unwelcome."

Alex's heart dropped, but his sister chimed in, indignant.

"Yes, but I refuse to believe such a thing of poor Apple. Alex, they will have it that she is someone's natural daughter and only adopted by Mr Greenaway. So horrid of you, Papa!"

Their father ignored this, his eyes fixed on Alex. "Is it so?"

The nagging ache within him started up again, and Alex was hard put to it to answer without giving himself away. He nodded, clearing his throat. "Vergette told me as much of the tale as he could."

"Which is?"

Alex looked across at his mother, and found her remarkably calm, although her beak of a nose was pointed in his direction in the way that still on occasion had the power to intimidate him.

"It is of no use to conceal anything from us, Alexander."

"No intention of doing that, ma'am. Apple's real father was a man of high rank, but so was her mother. Or genteel, at least. He was already married, so the thing was hushed up. It was the grandfather who settled the trust on Apple and arranged for Greenaway to adopt her."

He'd told it in as matter of fact a fashion as he could, stripped of the implications, the soiled background that rendered Appoline Greenaway unfit for the future he'd have given anything in the world to offer her.

Georgy burst into tears and buried her face in her handkerchief. Had his distress shown after all? Or was she upset for Apple?

Lord Luthrie rubbed a hand along his back and the touch of sympathy very nearly overset Alex. He swung his mind away from remembrance of Apple's tortured little face and, lifting his glass, tossed off the remainder of his wine.

His father took his glass and set it down. Another one appeared in front of Alex, this time with a measure of golden liquid in the bottom.

"Here, my dear boy. Sit down and sip this."

Pushed into the chair opposite his mother's, Alex took a sip of the fiery liquid and realised his sire had given him the more potent restorative of brandy.

"That's better." Lord Luthrie looked at his daughter. "You sit down too, my pet, and try not to interrupt."

Georgy, still sniffling, sank into a chair by her mother. Lord Luthrie, evidently satisfied, drew a chair up near Alex's and laid a hand on his son's arm.

"I dare say you've forgotten in all the excitement, Alex, but did I not say that your mother has had a notion?"

A vague recollection filtered through the hollow in Alex's head. "When I came up earlier?"

"Just so." His sire looked across at his wife. "Now, my dear Pippa, if you will."

Alex eyed his mother's face with a rising sense of apprehension. She did not look disapproving, rather to his surprise. Instead, she wore an expression in which he recognised the signs of the managing disposition which had frequently resulted in the complaint that she was an interfering busybody. The apprehension deepened. Had his mother got her teeth into this? If she had, woe betide him. Once she was set on a course, nothing deterred her.

The thought that his father evidently approved flitted through his mind, and the worry lightened a trifle. He trusted Lord Luthrie to have his interests at heart.

"It was this business of your keeping Appoline safe until her birthday that made me think of it, Alexander."

"Think of what, ma'am?"

"Her age, my dear boy. If she is almost one and twenty, it fits in very nicely."

Impatience began to ride Alex. "What in the world are you talking of, ma'am? Wish you won't talk in riddles."

"If you will have the courtesy to listen, Alexander, you will understand directly."

The sharp tone irritated, but his father's hand was once again on his arm and he refrained from retort.

"Do be quiet, Alex," his sister chimed in. "Much as I dislike Mama's notion, you do need to hear it."

"I thank you, Georgiana, but I can dispense with your assistance." Georgy subsided, flushing, and Lady Luthrie returned her gaze to Alex. "An old scandal, Alexander. I have as yet no proof, but the coincidence is much too close to discount."

Alex set down his glass on the little table beside his chair and sat up. "Do you mean to say you know who Apple really is?"

His mother tutted. "I cannot know until I hear back from Lady Mere. But if I do not miss my guess, Appoline is the Duke of Melkesham's daughter."

Dumbfounded, it took a moment for Alex to find his voice. "I don't believe it! But the fellow's a stickler. You're saying Apple is a skeleton in his closet?"

"As I say, I cannot yet be certain, but the facts fit."

"Well, what are they? And how do you know if it was hushed up?"

"It happens that Lady Mere, who is the duke's sister, you must know —"

"I didn't, but let that pass." Alex was feeling stunned and not a little bewildered.

"Lady Mere," pursued his mother in the measured tone she always used when she was obliged to repeat herself, "was a friend of my girlhood, which is how I became privy to the facts of the case. She was still Lady Oriana Damerham at that time and thus witnessed the entirety of the scandalous proceedings at first hand. She was distressed and confided in me, and I may say I have never opened my lips upon the subject from that day until now."

A riot of tangled emotion was churning in Alex, along with the crushing of the tiny hope he'd not even realised existed somewhere deep inside. But the extraordinary adjustment he must make about Apple's heritage took precedence at this moment.

"What were the facts, ma'am? I hope you mean to tell me."

"Naturally I must do so, if, as I surmise, Appoline is the offspring of that debacle."

"But are you only making this assumption on the point of her age, ma'am? Bit of a blind leap, ain't it?"

"Not when one considers the details, which you obviously cannot do if you will not permit me to state them."

Alex flushed at the tart note and begged pardon.

Lady Luthrie inclined her head. "In addition, since you have just told us who made the arrangements on Appoline's behalf, I am the more inclined to the likelihood of her proving to be the late Duke of Melkesham's grand-daughter. It is conduct typical of him, unlike that of his feckless son."

Alex could not let this pass. "But the fellow's reputation goes before him. He's known to be punctilious and correct to a fault."

"Not to those of us who knew him in his youth, my dear Alexander. Be that as it may, the fact is Melkesham, or rather Trubridge as he was then styled, saw fit to seduce the sixteen-year-old daughter of his neighbour, Lord Keevil. When the child's condition was discovered, it all came out. Lord Keevil arrived at Trubridge Castle armed with a horsewhip —"

"Good God! Don't tell me he set about the fellow?"

"Fortunately, it seems he did not get the chance," Lord Luthrie cut in. "Hard to keep it secret if the man had received a lashing."

"Indeed, Charles. As it was, the then-duke's servants succeeded in subduing Keevil, and the duke took him off to his library where a good deal of shouting went on, so Oriana told me. I regret to say she was so lost to all sense of propriety as to listen at the door, but it did put her in possession of the facts. Trubridge was sent for and the ensuing row, as Oriana reported to me, was worthy of one of these dramas at Drury Lane."

Lord Luthrie was softly laughing, Georgy sat in wide-eyed attention, but Alex was appalled. If this was indeed the story of Apple's beginning, she would be the most hurt by a revival of it.

His mother's brows lifted as she glanced at her husband. "Yes, it is well to be entertained at this distance in time, Luthrie, but if you remember, poor Oriana was utterly cast down. The announcement of her betrothal to Mere was imminent, and she had a great fear the scandal might cause him to sheer off. I felt obliged to insist upon her remaining with us for a se'ennight."

"Yes, I recall it, my dear, and you proved yourself a true friend." He glanced at Georgy and then at Alex. "Your mother would never tell me the cause of Lady Mere's distress. Until now, I had no knowledge of the matter, although I gather the repercussions did not end there, did they, my dear Pippa?"

"By no means, Charles. Suffice to say that with Trubridge claiming to love the girl, his wife choosing to behave like a tragedy queen — for which one must have some sympathy — and quarrelling mightily with her husband and anyone else who tried to remonstrate with her, it was not wonderful that whispers spread about the county in no time."

Alex blenched. "Then there was a scandal? I thought you said it was hushed up."

"It was, for Melkesham acted with a speed and efficiency one can only admire. Trubridge and his wife were despatched to the continent on the pretext of a long planned visit to some relative. The wronged child was taken to a spinster aunt who was living at Keevil's expense, along with a nurse to see to her comfort. Melkesham closed with a vicar under his patronage to marry the girl once she had been brought to bed, no doubt with pecuniary inducements attached. In short, he managed to avert public knowledge beyond vague rumours that none dared openly question, and the matter was in time forgotten."

"Not entirely," said Lord Luthrie on a dry note, "if Vergette's descent upon Alex is anything to go by."

"Naturally, Trubridge — or rather Melkesham as he now is — will not have forgotten. Nor will Oriana, which is why I have written to her. I am in hopes she will respond by return."

Alex found himself hoping instead that Lady Mere would prove to be away or incapacitated and incapable of corroborating this hideous tale. Or, if she could, to refute any possibility that the unfortunate child of its making and his little Apple Greenaway would prove to be one and the same.

He broke into rapid protest. "But this is not to say Apple's trust has anything to do with the late Duke of Melkesham.

You've not said, Mama, that he made any provision for the child born of this union."

His mother regarded him with an expression he could not penetrate. "Did I not say that this matter of the trust was the more persuasive?"

"Yes, but —"

"I do not know what arrangements Melkesham may have made, for Oriana did not tell me. It is probable she did not know either. But what I do say is it is just what one might have expected of the old duke."

Lord Luthrie set his hand on Alex's arm, his tone one of sympathy. "Considering the provisions he made for the rest, my dear Alex, can one suppose he ignored the claims of the infant?"

No, one could not. That was just the trouble. He took another sip of brandy and found it unpleasant to his palate. There was no remedy for the affliction under which he now laboured. No remedy for the killing of all hope. Only one thought surfaced and he gave it voice. "Can't burden Apple with all this."

Georgy was in tears again. "Oh, no, don't tell the poor thing, Alex. It would be too dreadful for her."

Lady Luthrie glanced at her lord. "It would be premature to do so in any event. Until I hear from Lady Mere, this is pure speculation."

Alex was tempted to demand why, in that case, she'd told him. Futile. He knew why. His mother, as downy a woman as any he'd met, had somehow divined his growing tenderness towards Apple. Typical of her to throw such a bar in his way, rather than attempt to appeal to his reason. She was aware he had too much respect for the family name to dishonour it.

Unlike Apple's putative father — if it was Melkesham — he could not put desire before duty.

He set down his glass and stood up. "You need have no fear, ma'am. This duke of yours must take me for as much of a rogue as he is himself, to be sending Vergette to warn me off. Honour aside, I'd not drag Apple through the mire for all the world."

Lady Luthrie gave him one of her rare and lightning smiles. "No, my dear Alexander, I know you would not. I am very sorry for Appoline. She is a sweet and talented girl, and one with whom I would have been glad to become better acquainted."

By which measured pronouncement, Alex understood her to dismiss Appoline Greenaway from their collective lives. He balked.

"I've given my word, ma'am. If this is your mind, I'll keep her in London, suitably chaperoned, until her birthday."

Lady Luthrie flushed, and his father was on his feet. "There is no necessity to take that tone with your mother, Alex. Nor has she said she will not welcome Appoline's presence. I make every allowance for your lacerated feelings, my boy, but that is going too far."

Alex set his teeth, struggling with himself. His sire had ever been able to curb him with a word, but never had he felt so inclined to rebellion. With a sense of shock, he realised that his loyalties had altered. Apple now came first with him. On her behalf, he was ready to fight all comers.

Something of his thoughts must have shown in his face, for his father's stern countenance relaxed and his smile was rueful. "I see how it is, my boy, and I sympathise. I had not recognised how badly you've been hit."

A snort escaped Alex. "Much good may it do me, sir!"

"An unfortunate choice, as it turns out. But a worthy one, Alex."

A lump lodged in Alex's throat and he could not speak. Turning away, he crossed to the window, struggling to master his emotion. Difficult, when the image of Apple's piquant little face with its large candid eyes and those kissable lips persisted in his head.

The butler saved him, entering at this inauspicious moment to announce that refreshments had been laid out in the small dining parlour. The prosaic announcement served to dissipate his distress sufficiently to enable Alex to follow the rest of the family out of the morning room.

He caught up with his mother in the gallery. "Beg your pardon, ma'am. Spoke out of turn."

Lady Luthrie gave him a measured glance. "It is of no consequence, Alexander. I am not wholly ignorant of your distresses, my son, and can only wish for your sake that matters had turned out otherwise."

"I wish so too, Mama, but it ain't a particle of use wishing, is it?"

She laughed at that. "You must have forgotten how my wishes for your cousin came to fruition. Wish away by all means."

Recalling how his mother's intervention had been instrumental, though in a roundabout way, in securing the happiness of his cousin Justin and his wife Marianne, a faint thread of optimism lightened Alex's gloom. He knew it to be futile, but he needed something if he must somehow hold his countenance in Apple's company.

Chapter Twenty-three

The coach lurched over a rut, throwing Apple sideways so that she almost fell against Alex beside her. He turned in his seat, at the same time catching his arm about her shoulders to steady her. He set her back in her place.

"All right, Apple?"

"Thank you, yes."

His arm fell away, and Apple felt an immediate sense of loss. In that brief instant, his strength protecting her from harm, she'd felt a flash of the erstwhile warmth there had been between them.

The cold penetrated more deeply with realisation and she huddled into her cloak, pulling the fur rug more securely about her legs. Weary and heart-sore, she turned her gaze upon the greyness beyond the window, where the passing scenery was becoming increasingly urban. "Are we nearing London?"

"It'll be another hour yet."

It was that distant tone again, and Apple all but shivered. Alex was changed in a way she could scarcely define. Oh, he laughed and smiled still, but it seemed forced. He'd not teased or barked at her either in his usual fashion. In fact, from the moment of his sudden arrival at Reddy's cottage, with the horrid intelligence about Walter and Marjorie and his promise to take her off to Bow Street, Apple had felt a difference in his manner towards her. She recalled his baffled look when Reddy had said she could not make the journey.

"I'm sorry to disoblige you, Master Alex, and if weren't for the rheumaticks taking hold, I'd do it. I'd be more of a hindrance than a help, for I can scarce take a step outside without my old bones aching fit to lay me low for a se'ennight."

Apple had added her mite. "She can't possibly come, Alex, and I wouldn't dream of asking her. Besides which, I don't know how Reddy will manage without me at this moment."

The nurse had tutted. "There's no call to worrit yourself about me, dearie. I've got young Joyce who comes in to clean, as you know. I can easy ask her to do those tasks you've kindly taken on, and Master Alex has no choice but to take you, that's clear."

Alex sat silent for a space, staring at Reddy. His gaze did not even stray to Apple, until his brow cleared. "What's that you were saying last time, about some widow Reddy knew who might suit for your companion?"

"Mrs Tinkler?"

He turned instantly back to Reddy. "What's her direction? I'll go at once to ask if she can accompany us to London."

Apple entered a protest. "But she'll want paying, Alex."

"Not a problem. I'll stand the nonsense."

"But —"

"No buts."

The curt tone had dismayed Apple, but worse was to come. Having secured Mrs Tinkler's services, he returned to the cottage only briefly to warn Apple to be ready to set off at an early hour upon the following morning.

"No point in starting today, for you and this Mrs Tinkler can't be expected to scramble to be ready soon enough if we're to avoid spending a night on the road."

He'd refused Reddy's invitation to dine with them, saying he had too many arrangements on hand, and Apple had not seen him again until the coach turned up at six that morning, with

Mrs Tinkler already installed inside on the forward seat. Which had made any conversation other than the trivial impossible.

The widow, a talkative woman, had beguiled the first part of the journey with a flood of reminiscences about travels she'd undertaken in the past, interlarded with her gratitude and willingness to serve his lordship in this way.

Apple struggled to make conversation, beset as she was with apprehension. It was rooted more in the aloofness she detected under Alex's insouciant manner than in the thought of confronting the magistrates at Bow Street. She yearned to talk to him in private, but the opportunity had not yet offered.

Every mile increased the distance she felt between them, and it hurt. The absence of the camaraderie, the companionship she'd always felt in his company, distressed her, even though common sense dictated it was better this way. When this was all over, as it must be in a matter of days now, she would likely never see him again.

This melancholy thought had the effect of suspending the breath in her chest as she fought to restrain the instant rise of grief. She must not weep. Whatever it was that had caused Alex to withdraw a little — for that was precisely how it felt — she must not appear conscious.

But no amount of chiding in her own head served to settle her mind. At last she could endure it no longer. Glancing across the carriage, she saw that Mrs Tinkler's head was nodding. Had she fallen asleep?

"Alex!" A hushed whisper.

He turned his head. "What is it?"

She was grateful for the instant understanding that made him use a similar murmur in response. "Alex…" Her voice stuck in her throat. She could not ask him! How to say that his manner was <u>killing her</u>? How to tell him that in spite of all her careful reasoning, the inevitable approaching farewell sat in her breast like an open wound?

She saw him shift slightly, his face little more than a shadow in the dim interior. Then his fingers found her hand, and the warmth of them closed around it. He did not speak. Only kept her hand imprisoned within his own, turning his head away again.

Apple swallowed down the choking lump in her throat as silent tears seeped from her eyes and trickled down her cheeks. She made no move to wipe them away, trying not to sniff or make a sound. Her heart felt as if it was breaking. Alex knew. He understood. He was not aloof after all. But his silent acceptance of her grief told its own tale. The tiny thread of hope she had not been able to conquer snapped in two.

For an endless moment Apple struggled, but the exigencies of her situation forced the tears back and the worst effects subsided. At any moment Mrs Tinkler would wake. If she was to say anything at all, it must be now.

Alex's hold had relaxed a little, and she gently withdrew her hand. He looked round. Apple drew a breath for courage. "You know something, don't you?"

"Not now, Apple. Not here."

She persisted. "But do you?"

He hesitated, seemingly searching her face in the gloom. Then he sighed. "Yes. Or at least, I think so."

She caught her breath on a last sob. "That explains it."

"Explains what?"

"Why you've been aloof."

Another hesitation. Another sigh. "Forgive me, Apple. Can't endure the thought of... Well, you know what I mean. Don't need to say it."

Apple sniffed. "Can you lend me a handkerchief?"

At that he laughed, and her heart lifted to the spontaneous sound.

"Here." She took the glow of white from his hand. "Have to buy you a supply of the things, since I won't be there to hand one over on your travels."

The hollow opened up again, but Apple made a determined effort to sound cheerful. She kept her voice low and gestured across the coach. "I think Mrs Tinkler is well travelled enough to manage, don't you?"

"Seems so from her discourse." He dropped his tone to a murmur. "If you can stand her chit-chat."

"I'll welcome it, I think."

Anything to keep her mind from dwelling on Alex once he was out of her reach.

The coach hit cobble, and the resulting noise and bouncing under a pace necessarily slow woke Mrs Tinkler. She sat up and yawned behind her hand, looking towards the window. "Oh, dear, did I drop off? Goodness, I do believe we are nearing journey's end."

She was right. Leaning forward, Apple saw the coach was passing through streets still busy even as dusk settled over the capital. Never having been to London before, she found her upset dissipating under a rise of interest. She could not see a great deal through the fuggy atmosphere outside, despite the prevalence of lanterns bobbing along and lamp posts at intervals which threw a pool of light on frosty surfaces and eerie faces hanging about in odd corners. Presently the road became smoother, the lamp posts more frequent and there were fewer stragglers.

"Ah, we are entering the more genteel part of the town, my dear Miss Greenaway," piped up her chaperon.

Apple looked round at her. "You've been before?"

A complacent note entered the woman's voice. "Indeed, yes, my dear. Upon several occasions. Though I'm sure I cannot claim as great an acquaintance with the place as Lord Dymond must enjoy?"

The sycophantic note irritated Apple, and she sighed at the thought of being obliged to have this woman's company instead of Alex's robust energy.

All too soon, she was alighting in the yard of the Bristol Hotel, of Alex's choosing, in Cork Street. "Not one of the most fashionable places," he murmured, leaning in as he gave her his hand to help her down the step, "but best not to draw attention to ourselves."

Apple had reached terra firma and she paused. "Are you staying here too, then?"

He shook his head. "Wouldn't do, Apple. Don't want to set the town talking. Not that we're likely to run into anyone I know in this place. Too early in the year besides. But no sense in running the risk. I'll take a room at Stephen's in Bond Street."

The reminder of her unacceptable status threw Apple's senses back into disorder, and by the time she had mastered herself she was surrounded by the bustle of the hotel, and Alex was engaged with a woman who, she supposed from the modest gown of blue bombazine, must be the concierge. Within a very short time, she was ushered up the stairs and into a welcoming apartment with a cheerful fire burning, a comfortable chair to either side and dominated by a four-poster.

"This is very nice indeed, dear Miss Greenaway," said Mrs Tinkler. "We will be cosy enough in here, I dare say."

Shock swept through Apple. Was she to share the room with her chaperon? For the first time for what seemed an age, her heart rose up in rebellion against Alex. What was he thinking? Did he suppose she would not wish for a modicum of privacy?

She looked round, half expecting to see him in the doorway. But there was only a servant, burdened with her valise and a small portmanteau which must belong to Mrs Tinkler.

Without thought, she accosted the landlady. "Is Lord Dymond waiting for us downstairs?"

The woman paused in the catalogue she was reciting to her chaperon of services available in the hotel. "I don't know, ma'am. Would you wish me to —?"

But Apple did not wait for her to finish. In seconds, she was out of the door and hurrying back along the corridor towards the stairs, glad she'd taken note of the way. Halfway down she saw Alex in the hall below, in conversation with a stout fellow who had the appearance of a butler. She hurried down the remainder of the stairs.

"Alex!"

He turned his head, his brows drawing together. With a brief word to the other man, he came across the hall. "What's to do?"

Apple went straight into the attack, her voice low so as not to be overheard. "What do you mean by arranging for me to share a bed with that woman?"

His brows flew up. "Why not? Thought you'd be more comfortable if you weren't alone."

"With a woman I scarcely know?"

He grimaced. "Suppose there is that."

"Of course there is that! What's more, I much dislike sharing a bed with anyone. It reminds me of school."

"That's as may be, but I'd feel a deal happier if I knew you were safely ensconced with your chaperon."

Apple glared at him. "You'd feel happier? I suppose it's of no consequence if I don't."

"Well, of all the stupid things to say! You know I want you to be happy."

"Then you have a peculiar way of showing it. Why in the world didn't you ask me? Of all the high-handed autocrats, you're the worst, Alex Dymond!"

For a moment he stared down at her in a fulminating way. Then a grin split his face. "Should have known it wouldn't be long before you broke out of that unnatural submissiveness. Do you want me to ask for a second room?"

Apple's fury dropped right out as a giggle escaped her. "You are quite abominable, Alex. You know I can't possibly ask that now. It would hurt Mrs Tinkler's feelings."

An odd expression flitted across his face. "Why should you care? As you said, you scarcely know the woman."

Her mouth dropped open. "Have you run mad? What does that matter? Besides, if she is going to travel with me, I shall have to get to know her."

Alex began to laugh. "Incorrigible, that's what you are, Apple. First you ring a peal over me for making you share her bed. Next you're berating me for suggesting I change the arrangements."

Apple eyed him frostily, waiting for his laughter to subside. He stopped, but the amusement was still visible in his eyes.

"The point," she began in a careful tone, "is that —"

"I should have consulted with you in the first place," Alex supplied.

"Yes! It's too late now."

He gave a mock little bow. "As your ladyship pleases." And then, to her astonishment, his cheeks darkened and consternation entered his eyes.

Apple gazed at him, a horrid suspicion curling inside her. "Why did you say that?"

"What?"

"Your ladyship."

His shoulders shifted. "I was jesting, Apple."

"No, you weren't. At least, perhaps you were, but you look conscious, Alex. Why?"

He threw back his head and a sigh escaped him. "Wish to God you weren't so cursed acute!"

A memory stole into Apple's mind. He knew something about her past! How could she have forgotten?

"You weren't going to tell me," she accused.

A rueful look swept across his face. "No, I wasn't. Not yet."

"Well, you'll have to now or I shan't sleep."

Alex glanced around the hall, and Apple followed his lead. The man who looked like a butler had gone, but there were a couple of gentlemen conversing near an open door from which emanated the sound of general conversation.

She allowed Alex to steer her to a small sofa set against the wall to one side.

"Sit here. If we look to be talking, we won't be disturbed."

"We are talking," Apple pointed out as she sat down.

He took a seat beside her. "You know what I mean."

"Oh, stop prevaricating, Alex, and tell me what you know!"

"Give me a chance, will you?"

Apple gripped her fingers together. "Please, Alex!"

The light from a massive chandelier above them did not fully reach the sofa, instead throwing shadows onto his face. Apple found herself hoping it was that which made him look grim.

"My mother thinks she knows the particular scandal that may have involved you."

A hush settled in Apple's mind. "She knows who I am?"

"Keep telling you, no. She can't know until she's heard back from Lady Mere, and perhaps not even then."

"Who is Lady Mere?"

"An old school friend of my mother's. Seems she's the sister of this duke and —"

"*Duke?*"

It came out as a squeak, and Apple threw a hand to her mouth.

Alex cursed. "Didn't mean to say that."

"It's too late now," said Apple with a good deal of asperity. "What do you mean, duke? What duke? You don't mean to say Lady Luthrie thinks my real father is actually a duke? How can she be so mad, Alex?"

"It ain't as mad as it seems."

He sounded resigned, and a thudding started up in Apple's chest. Could it possibly be true?

"Why isn't it mad?" Alex eyed her in a troubled kind of way and did not answer. Apple let out an exasperated breath. "It's of no use to look at me like that. Tell me what you meant."

He threw up his hands. "Very well, if you must have it. Even before I saw Vergette that first time, I'd learned he only served men of the highest rank. Been worrying me ever since."

"Because you suspected this? Why didn't you tell me?"

"Well, you know why, Apple. Try not to be more of a hen-wit than you can help."

"I'm not a hen-wit, and I shall be obliged if you will answer my questions without so much roundaboutation."

Alex's brows shot up. "Phew! Now you even *sound* like a duke's daughter."

Apple's little spurt of anger deserted her, and she let out an involuntary giggle. Not that the horrid notion was in the least bit funny, but a hideous sense of disorientation was overtaking her mind and she felt much inclined to throw herself to the floor and drum her heels on the carpet, screaming the while.

Instead, she took several deep breaths, looking about the spacious hall in a bid to re-orient herself. To her consternation, she caught sight of Mrs Tinkler descending the stairs.

She turned to Alex, dropping her voice to a whisper. "What is this horrible duke's name, Alex? Quick!"

"Melkesham. Which, if you'd been other than his natural daughter, would make you Lady Appoline Damerham."

Apple stared at him, only half aware of the twittering voice of her chaperon approaching. Lady Appoline Damerham! The daughter of a duke! Of higher rank even than Lady Georgiana Dymond! The absurdity of it overtook the apprehension, and Apple broke into helpless giggles.

"Good gracious, what in the world is the matter, Miss Greenaway?"

Alex had risen on Mrs Tinkler's approach, and the look on his face as he gazed down at her only succeeded in redoubling her laughter. Aware in a corner of her mind that this was an expression of the hysterical fit she'd wanted to indulge in, Apple tried vainly to control herself and offer a suitably innocuous explanation.

"It's — it's n-nothing… Lord Dymond t-told me a — a joke."

Except that it was anything but a joke. If it was true, she was effectively barred from any association with the gentry. The realisation arrested her amusement, and she hiccupped into silence. She looked up at Alex and found him regarding her, an unreadable expression in his eyes.

"That's why Mr Vergette came to find you at Dymond Garth? He'd been instructed to tell you to have nothing to do with me."

Alex's brows drew together and he flicked a glance at Mrs Tinkler, who was looking bewildered, as well she might. Apple's cheeks warmed.

"Mrs Tinkler, would you be so kind as to bespeak dinner? Lord Dymond will not be joining us."

"Oh, dear, won't he?"

A worried look went to Alex, who smiled. With an effort, Apple thought.

"Got to arrange my own accommodation, ma'am. I'll return for Miss Greenaway in the morning."

Her chaperon's brow cleared. "Ah, I see. Very well, I'll go and speak with Mrs Pearcey. A most obliging woman. I feel sure she will set an excellent repast before us. Pray do not go until I return, my lord. I should not wish Miss Greenaway to be sitting here unchaperoned."

With which, she twittered off towards the noisy room across the hall, leaving Apple to confront the intimidating look on Alex's face. She did not wait for the storm to break. "Why are you looking like a thundercloud, Alex? What have I said?"

"Do you think I care for what this damned duke wants? Do you imagine I'd let you go at his bidding?"

Apple drew in a tight breath. "I know you wouldn't and you didn't, or you would not have followed me to Reddy's. But, Alex, does it matter at whose bidding? If it is true, you know as well I do there is no remedy. You can have nothing to do with a woman in my situation."

Alex sat down beside her again and seized her hands, holding them so strongly that she winced. The intensity in both eyes and voice struck deep into her soul.

"Don't talk like that! Do you think I care who or what you are in the eyes of Society? You're my Apple, and that's all I care for."

"Then I must care for you."

"No, you don't understand! I know I can't keep you, Apple. Can't throw duty to the four winds. And I can't drag you through the mud, because it would stick and I can't have that. But I won't have you believing I think any the less of you for all that."

Apple's heart squeezed painfully in her chest. "Do you suppose I think so little of you as to believe such a thing? After all we've been through? My Alex is just Alex, not Lord Dymond."

His grip tightened and the dark of his eyes deepened, but he did not speak.

And then Mrs Tinkler was back and the moment was gone. Alex released her hands and stood up, but the impression of his grip remained in Apple's tingling fingers.

Chapter Twenty-four

The magistrate was polite, but it was plain to Alex the man's patience was wearing thin. For this the inevitable presence of Walter and Marjorie Greenaway was undoubtedly to blame.

"Took you long enough," was the accusation with which Walter Greenaway greeted Alex within seconds of his entering the busy premises of Bow Street Magistrates Court with Apple on his arm.

She'd been subdued and jumpy when he went to fetch her after yet another restless night. He'd dined alone at Stephen's hotel where he'd taken a room, beset by a plethora of demons urging him to throw his cap over the windmill like a moonstruck girl.

He recalled the luck of his cousin Justin who, after years of putting duty before the promptings of his heart had unexpectedly found the happiness he'd yearned for. Yet even he had not faced the sheer impossibility confronting Alex. If Lady Luthrie's theory proved sound — and even if it didn't as was the brutal truth — there could be no reprieve. He even found himself wishing Apple had chosen some other coach than his in which to hide, except that the thought of never having known her was unbearable.

The singularly pointless question of whether it was worse not to have known her or to have known her only to be obliged to give her up kept him tossing on his pillows. Until it occurred to him Apple would berate him or laugh at him for being so ridiculous, and the memory of her giggles made him smile into the darkness.

He slept but fitfully and woke little refreshed, and felt worse on discovering Apple's nervous state. As a result, he was anything but in a mood to tolerate the impertinence of the Greenaways.

Walter pounced on them before Alex had a chance to ask for the runner Benjamin or a magistrate. "Ha! So you've come at last. Took you long enough."

Before Alex could respond, Marjorie accosted Apple.

"Where has he been hiding you? You'll be sorry you started this, Apple Greenaway, I promise you!"

Alex pulled Apple away. "Stand off from her! Leave her alone!"

"Let her go, you monster! You kidnapper, you!"

"I'm still her guardian," announced Walter, making a spirited attempt to grab Apple.

Alex put her behind him. "Don't dare touch her, you fiends! Haven't you harmed her enough?"

"That's a loud one, coming from you, my lord girl-stealing Dymond!"

To Alex's chagrin, Apple popped out from behind him, fury on her lips.

"How dare you call him that? He's been kinder to me than you ever were, Marjorie! And he didn't steal me, and so I shall tell the magistrates here."

Marjorie went red in the face and Walter clenched his fists. But before either could say anything more, a stout individual inserted himself between the warring parties, and Alex was obliged to give way.

"Now then, now then, we'll have no argy-bargy in here, ladies and gents," said this stalwart, holding up a pudgy flat hand towards each side. "If so be as you've business here, you'd best state it to me."

Alex let out a quick breath. "In good time. I'm Dymond and I'm here to present Miss Greenaway to make a statement. Is the runner Benjamin here?"

The fellow's manner became a touch more deferent. "No, yer honour, he'll be about his duties. But I'll see if Justice Armitage is free." He turned to the Greenaways. "Do I take it as this here gent and lady is who you've been waiting for, coming in and out two days running and making a nuisance of yerselves?"

Marjorie's nose was in the air. "Impertinence! What's it to you, my man?"

Walter waved her down. "Yes, it is, and we demand to see the Justice along with them."

The fellow rubbed his chin. "As I recall you already seen him yesterday."

"Yes, but they are here now and we insist upon being present."

"That's up to his honour, that is. I'll arst him, but I don't reckon he'll take kindly to your nagging at him all over again."

Triumph lit in Alex. If the Greenaways, in their inimitable fashion, had already managed to alienate the magistrate, Apple's case looked a deal more hopeful. The enemy were clearly not yet routed, but the fellow directed them to a bench and bid them wait while he consulted with Justice Armitage. Grudgingly, the Greenaways did as they were told and the fellow turned back to Alex, his gaze shifting to Apple.

"If you and the young lady will accompany me, sir, I'll lead you to his honour."

Alex began to follow, but felt Apple's fingers grab his arm and found her hanging back. She leaned up to whisper, "Alex, what if he won't believe me? There's no denying Walter is my guardian still."

"Not for long. Don't fret, Apple. Let's see what the fellow asks."

He ushered her in the wake of their guide, who led them through into a corridor and up a set of stairs which came out into a bright gallery.

"This here's Justice Armitage's office, yer honour." The fellow knocked on a nearby door, and a voice within bade him enter. "What's the name again, yer honour?"

"Dymond." Feeling his status would not go amiss in this situation, he clarified this. "Lord Dymond, and Miss Greenaway."

The stout man put a finger to his forelock. "Begging your pardon, me lord, but I weren't to know."

"Of course not."

Opening the door, he preceded them into the room, addressing the gentleman seated at a desk set to catch the light from a large window behind him.

"It's the lady as was expected by them two as have been plaguing you these two days, sir."

The magistrate rose and came around the desk. A man of middle years, spare of both figure and face, with a peevish look about him, he came forward, brows raised in enquiry. His minion waved at Apple.

"Miss Greenaway, sir. And this gentleman is Lord Dymond, who asked for Mr Benjamin, sir."

Alex elected to take a high hand. "Justice Armitage?"

The gentleman pursed his lips. "I am he, my lord." He then gave a small bow towards Apple, indicating one of the chairs set in front of his desk. "Would you care to sit, ma'am?"

Apple glanced up at Alex, and he gave her a reassuring smile, urging her into the chair.

The magistrate nodded dismissal to his minion and came around the desk. He waited, looking at Alex, who was reminded of nothing so much as his master at school. But then the fellow gave a thin smile.

"Pray be seated, my lord."

Breathing a little more easily, Alex took the chair next to Apple and watched Justice Armitage reseat himself, setting aside the paper on which he'd been engaged and drawing a fresh sheet towards him from a stack on one side of his crowded desk. Laying it down on the blotter in a precise fashion, he replaced his spectacles on his nose and picked up a pen from the standish, dipping it into the inkpot.

Alex watched him write Apple's name at the head of the paper, and impatience got the better of him. "Don't you wish to hear what Miss Greenaway has to say, sir?"

Justice Armitage looked up. "All in good time, my lord." He directed his spare smile towards Apple. "Will you be kind enough to confirm your identity, ma'am?"

Apple opened her mouth, shot an anguished look at Alex, and shut it again. It wasn't difficult to divine what troubled her. The last thing in the world she was able to do at this moment was to say exactly who she was.

The magistrate looked up in clear question and Alex thought fast. She'd been Appoline Greenaway for long enough to satisfy Bow Street. The legality of it was another matter. Who knew whether John Greenaway had some sort of certificate of adoption?

He leaned a little towards her. "Give him your name, Apple."

As might have been expected, the fellow's eyebrows shot up. "Apple?"

"It's a pet name, sir."

At last Apple spoke up. "I am Appoline Greenaway, sir."

Again came the smile that did not reach the fellow's eyes. "I see. Then the matter becomes comprehensible. I thank you, Miss Greenaway."

Turning aside, he opened a drawer in his desk, rummaged for a moment, and drew out a roll of papers tied with red tape. Setting them on the desk, he removed the tape, unrolled the sheets and riffled through them, reading here and there.

Resisting the temptation to lean across the desk to try to read what was written there, Alex looked instead at Apple and found her frowning deeply as she watched the man across the desk. He was about to put out a hand to draw her attention, when she spoke, her tone much more like her usual self.

"What have you there, Mr Armitage? More of Marjorie's lies?"

The magistrate ceased his labours and peered over his spectacles, a startled look in his eyes. "Lies, Miss Greenaway?"

"Yes, if she claims Alex — I mean, Lord Dymond — kidnapped me. It is quite untrue."

The magistrate set lightly clasped hands on his blotter, steepling two fingers. "Indeed? Then what is the true story, Miss Greenaway? Did you in fact escape into his company?"

"Escape? Nothing of the sort!"

"Ran away then?"

"I did not run away. I was going to London to see my trustee."

The magistrate set his spectacles more firmly on his nose and consulted his notes again, running a finger down the page. It stopped and he looked up.

"Mr Vergette?"

Quick to spot the distinct note of distaste in the fellow's voice, Alex entered the lists. "That's right. As I told your man

Benjamin, you may seek corroboration from Vergette any time you care to."

Justice Armitage held up a hand. "If you please, my lord, it will better serve your purpose if you allow Miss Greenaway to speak for herself."

All too true. Alex subsided, fulminating nevertheless. But Apple's hackles were clearly up.

"I will speak for myself, sir, and I will tell you that if my guardians say I ran away, they have it wrong."

"But you admit they are your guardians?"

"Yes." She bit her lip and Alex longed to seize her hand for comfort. "At least, I have always believed so. But in any event, it makes no matter, for I will come of age in a matter of days."

The magistrate tapped his fingers on the blotter. "That, Miss Greenaway, is not germane, if you will forgive me. The matter before me is a charge of unlawful abduction on the part of Lord Dymond here."

"What?"

"Abduction! That's what they told you? How dare they? Alex has not laid a finger on me. Nor would he dream of doing so. He's a gentleman!"

Shock held Alex silent for the moment, and the magistrate came back strongly.

"That, ma'am, is no guarantee against unlawful conduct."

Apple was on her feet. "But I won't have this! It's quite untrue!"

"Apple, calm down," said Alex, finding his voice and rising also. "Won't serve us to be flying into a temper."

She turned on him. "I've every right to be in a temper! The notion of kidnapping was bad enough. But abduction? Only wait until I get hold of Marjorie!"

"Sit down, Miss Greenaway!"

The sharp tone evidently cut through Apple's rising choler, for her head whipped round and she stared at the magistrate, her eyes wild.

Alex would have seized her shoulders and dragged her back to her seat, but the thought of how it might look stayed him. Things were bad enough. If he showed himself capable of manhandling her, he would only pile up evidence against himself.

Thankfully, Apple plonked back down into the chair, gripping her fingers together in the way she had when she was overwrought. Alex resumed his own seat, wishing he had the right to seize her out of this and to the devil with all of them.

"Perhaps, Miss Greenaway, you will be kind enough to relate the circumstances which led to your being in Lord Dymond's company."

Apple raised her head at that, shooting a dagger look at the man. "If you think I was in his company without a chaperon, you are fair and far off. We were alone together only for a matter of hours, and even then his servants were present."

The magistrate did not bat an eyelid. "Very well, Miss Greenaway, but that does not answer my question."

Apple drew an audible breath and her voice was unsteady. "If you must know, I hid myself in his coach and asked him — at pistol point — to take me to the next stage."

That flurried the fellow's complacency, Alex thought with satisfaction. The magistrate's startled look almost caused him to laugh out.

"So you see he had no choice," Apple resumed. "After that, Lord Dymond acted purely out of chivalry. He could not approve of my travelling alone when I told him my story, and he did not try to take me home because he supposed I should only take off again, which is perfectly true. So instead, he took me to his sister's house and left me there while he went to consult with Mr Vergette on my behalf. Then we went to stay with his parents at Dymond Garth for Christmas. There, sir. Does that sound like an abduction to you?"

She flung the last words at the man in a way so typical of his Apple, Alex was obliged to hide a smile.

Justice Armitage pursed his lips. "I must concede that it does not. However, there is no gainsaying that Lord Dymond had no right to hold you against the express wishes of your guardians, who claim that he refused to release your person into their charge."

"At my sister's house, yes," Alex put in. "And so would you have done, my dear sir, had you heard the manner in which they chose to speak to her."

Before the man could respond to this, an altercation could be heard outside the door. Voices were raised, including the familiar shrill one. The magistrate half rose from his seat as the door crashed open, admitting a tumble of Marjorie, Walter and the individual trying to prevent their entry.

"I will be heard!"

"You'll not stop us, that you won't!"

"Jackson!" roared the magistrate. "What the deuce are you doing?"

Panting, the stout fellow threw his hands in the air, turning to address his superior. "Couldn't stop them — sir! Did — my best!"

"Get that man out of my office!"

Alex had leapt up and turned, as had Apple, who gripped his arm, dismay in her face.

Justice Armitage strode around the desk to confront the intruders, as Jackson made a valiant attempt to eject Walter from the room.

"What is the meaning of this?"

Marjorie, righting herself from a near fall, waded in, arms akimbo. "I'll tell you, my good sir, with pleasure! I'm here to see this precious Lord Dymond of hers don't cozen you into believing his nonsense, that's what."

Outraged, the magistrate glared at her. "Madam, you do yourself no good by this interference, I assure you."

"I'll be the judge of that." Pushing past him, she came up to Alex, wagging a finger in his face. "I'll go bail you've told him a pack of lies!"

Walter, still grappling with the stout Jackson, made himself heard. "Hoy! Let go, will you, man?" Then yelling across the fellow's form, "Don't you be fooled, Justice, sir! Smooth-tongued rascal he is, and all!"

The magistrate, evidently feeling that further remonstrance was useless, addressed himself to his minion. "All right, Jackson, let him go."

Released, Walter staggered a little, righted himself, and tugged at his disarranged clothing.

The magistrate regarded him with a look of loathing. "Mr Greenaway, if you do not cease, you will find yourself up on a charge of hindering an officer of the law in the execution of his duty." Swinging on Marjorie, he added, "And that applies equally to you, madam. Do I make myself clear?"

Both parties muttered what might have been agreement, though Marjorie's flushed countenance told Alex she was by no means acquiescent.

"Jackson, you will remain by the door in case I need you."

The unfortunate minion, already a good deal mauled by the look of him, took up his stance in a manner rather resigned than eager, and remained there, stolid before the door.

"You, and you! On the bench there."

Such was the power of the magistrate's eye that Walter, pulling his recalcitrant sister along with him, retired to the short bench at one side of the room, from where they were perfectly well able, Alex surmised, to observe both himself and Apple as well as Justice Armitage.

Inwardly cursing, he whispered to Apple to sit down again and retook his own seat as the magistrate once again came around the desk. Before reseating himself, he directed a final glare at the interlopers.

"You will remain silent unless I ask you a question."

Walter nodded, but a returning glare was the only response Marjorie made. Ignoring this, the magistrate sat down with an air of finality and turned his gaze upon Apple once again. "You were saying?"

Apple blinked at him. "Yes, but I don't think I was."

Suspecting the fellow was trying to appear more in control than he actually was, and in fact had no recollection himself of where they had got to in the previous discussion, Alex cut in swiftly. "You were going to tell Justice Armitage how Mr Vergette came to see you after Christmas."

She was not about to do any such thing, but the introduction of Vergette's name had been productive of a satisfactory effect the last time. Besides which, with an audience consisting of the Greenaways, it was likely the best ploy. To his relief, Apple seized the notion.

"Yes, that's right, he did."

"Why?"

Damnation! Alex began to see why this man was employed in the capacity of magistrate. Apple threw him a look, and on impulse he opted for the truth.

"Came to see me, if you must have it, sir. Had something to tell me. But Miss Greenaway saw him in my stead."

Justice Armitage looked from him to Apple and back again. "I have a strong feeling that you are keeping something from me, my lord. Both of you."

Warmth rose into Alex's cheeks, and he shot a brief look across to the bench where Walter was looking puzzled. Marjorie's suspicious eyes went from one to the other, and Alex thought it would not be long before she broke out again. A quick look at Apple found her tight-lipped and white of face. Alex gathered his forces.

"The intelligence conveyed to Miss Greenaway by Vergette is confidential, sir. Nothing to do, moreover, with this trumped up charge these persons have brought against me."

The magistrate inclined his head. "Very well, I will accept that for the time being. However, there is still the matter of your refusing to allow Mr Greenaway to remove his ward from your custody."

"Ha! What have you to say to that?"

Justice Armitage turned his head. "I will not tell you again, Mr Greenaway."

Walter pouted, muttering. But it was obvious to Alex that Marjorie was bursting to speak and would not maintain silence for long. He was about to answer when he was forestalled.

"Custody? You call it that?" Apple's fury was palpable. "Alex was protecting me! He knew I didn't wish to marry Mr Cumberledge and that they would force me to do so if he let them drag me away."

For the first time, the magistrate looked bewildered. "Cumberledge? Who the deuce is Mr Cumberledge?"

"He is Walter's partner, and they want me to marry him so that they may get at my trust. That's why I wanted to see Mr Vergette, to beg for his support against them. But the truth is that my trust has nothing whatsoever to do with the winery, only they refuse to believe it."

It was plain that all this was new to the magistrate, for he cast a deeply reproachful glance at the couple on the bench. Walter looked a trifle confounded, but Marjorie, once more red in the face, was clearly raging.

"It seems to me," the magistrate said heavily, "there is a great deal more to this matter than I have been privileged to understand." To Alex's chagrin, he turned back again and fixed him with a beady eye. "However, none of this alters the facts, Lord Dymond. You do not deny, whether for reasons of chivalry or otherwise, that you held Miss Greenaway against her guardian's expressed wish?"

"Of course I don't deny it. Obvious that I did so, ain't it?"

"But not against my will, which is the point, isn't it? And he didn't steal me or abduct me or kidnap me!"

With difficulty, Alex refrained from putting out a restraining hand, so inimical was the glare Apple directed at her guardians. To his mind, the whole affair began to assume the aspect of a Drury Lane farce. If he wasn't so incensed on Apple's behalf, he'd be convulsed.

Unfortunately, it did not appear that Justice Armitage was similarly affected. The silence grew tense as he tapped his fingers on his blotter, his eyes running down the notes in the file on his desk. He turned a page with deliberation, and Alex could almost feel Apple's rising anxiety. He flicked a glance at her and gave an infinitesimal shake of his head. To his relief, she remained silent. The less said the better at this juncture.

The magistrate read through to the end of his notes and then set them aside and looked up. "I believe we have covered all the queries I had, and it does not appear to me that there are grounds for the charge against you to stand, Lord Dymond."

The outbreak from the bench was inevitable, dissipating the instant relief in Alex's breast.

"What? You're letting him go?"

"This is outrageous!"

Both Greenaways were on their feet, and the fellow Jackson at once thundered across the room, intercepting himself between them and the desk.

"No, you don't!"

Marjorie ducked under his arm. Reaching Apple, she seized her by the elbow, addressing herself to the magistrate before Alex could do anything. "If you won't throw him in prison, as he deserves, you'll at least release my brother's ward back into our charge."

Apple tried to pull away. "Let me go, Marjorie! I won't go with you!"

Alex was on his feet. "You see, sir? This is why I wouldn't let them take her."

"Miss Greenaway, unhand the girl at once!"

"She's coming with us!"

"I said unhand her! Jackson!"

The burly minion released Walter, whom he'd been holding back, and took up a threatening stance beside Marjorie. She let go and Apple shot out of her seat and took refuge behind Alex, grabbing onto his coat. He eyed Marjorie with disfavour, but he saw the magistrate take note of Apple's manoeuvre, brows raised. An explanation was clearly called for.

"Miss Greenaway trusts me to keep her safe, sir. Gave her my word I would do so until she comes of age and is able to take control of her own future."

"Take control of her future, is it?" Arms akimbo, Marjorie went into the attack. "What sort of future, I should like to know?" She flung a hand in his direction, turning to Justice

Armitage. "Ask him what he intends! If she don't come home with us, a carte blanche is all she'll be fit for!"

Alex very nearly hit her. "How dare you? Nothing of the kind! She's been chaperoned throughout. As if I'd so insult her!"

"Will you sit down and be quiet, Miss Greenaway?"

The unexpected thunder from the prissy little magistrate shocked Alex out of his fury, and he was not much surprised to see Marjorie drop into the chair vacated by Apple.

But Walter was swiftly in again, his tone more wheedling than bombastic. "She's in the right of it, sir. All very well to say Lord Dymond here has had my ward chaperoned. The fact is, no one of our acquaintance will believe it. Only thing is to get her married off as quick as we can."

The magistrate turned on him. "To this Cumberledge fellow, I take it?"

"Over my dead body!"

Justice Armitage turned his head. "Patience, Lord Dymond, if you please."

But Alex had had enough. "I'm out of all patience, sir! If you think I'm going to stand here and allow these vultures to claim Apple after all we've been through to keep her safe from their schemes, you can think again."

"And in any event, I won't go with them," declared Apple, entering the lists.

The magistrate held up his hands for silence, his tone biting. "I am not concerned with the wishes of anyone present. My interest is purely with the legality of the proceedings."

The threat of losing Apple at this point drove Alex to throw caution to the winds. "Then I suggest you send for Vergette, sir, if you want legality. Truth is, Apple ain't this fellow's ward."

"Alex!"

Ignoring Apple's plea, he directed a look of triumph at the vultures. "She ain't even your cousin. She's not a Greenaway at all. You've no rights over her whatsoever. Put that in your pipe and smoke it!"

Both Greenaways were gazing at him in a dumbfounded fashion, but the magistrate was not similarly affected.

"I trust you have proof of these allegations?"

"I don't, but Vergette knows the truth. Let them go and badger him if they choose. But Apple don't belong to them, and she ain't theirs to dispose of."

Chapter Twenty-five

The coffee house was far from fashionable, situated as it was within a stone's throw of Bow Street, but the very nature of its clientele was soothing to Apple's lacerated sensibilities. Hidden away in a booth, with the murmur of conversations, clinking cups and curling smoke from a pipe or two, she sipped gratefully at the hot chocolate Alex had procured for her.

He had seated himself opposite and was drinking coffee poured from the pot with a look of slight distaste on his face.

"Are you thinking of the fracas back there?"

He grimaced. "No. Thinking this coffee ain't up to much. Old grains re-boiled, if you ask me."

Apple took another sip of her drink. "You should have had the chocolate."

His lips quirked. "Glad you're enjoying it at least."

"It's very welcome after all that, thank you."

A small sigh escaped Alex. "For a hideous moment, didn't think the magistrate was going to let me take you away."

"I know." Apple all but shuddered. "I was in dread he would insist on my going with Walter and Marjorie until Mr Vergette should have been consulted."

"He probably would have done, if they hadn't queered their own pitch. Fellow was thoroughly ruffled by their conduct, and I don't blame him."

Apple let out an unsteady breath. "I wish you had not been obliged to say it, Alex."

His dark gaze held on her face. "Didn't mean to. Only those two made me so mad I couldn't help myself."

He drank again, with another grimace that made Apple laugh despite her tension.

"Is that the coffee, or are you regretting having said it?"

A faint smile creased his mouth. "I don't regret it, except for embarrassing you. To my mind, it's the only thing likely to get those two off your back."

"Do you suppose Mr Vergette will tell them?"

"Doubt he'll betray you. But I'd guess he'll say enough to satisfy Justice Armitage. Gave the fellow my word I'd return tomorrow to hear his verdict, but there's no need for you to appear."

"But what if he decides in favour of Marjorie and Walter?"

The look of concern on his face struck at Apple's heart, bringing back the unwelcome reflection that this cosy moment between them was but a passing interlude.

"That's what troubles you? Don't fret. I've no intention of letting them find you again until you've come of age."

"Perhaps we should find somewhere else for me to hide. I'm persuaded it won't take them long to find the hotel, if they set their minds to it."

"This ain't the country, Apple. Nor are we leaving a trail as we did on the road the last time. They'd be hard put to it to scour every hotel in the capital, even if they guessed you'd be staying at a hotel in the first place. More likely to try to run you to earth in Berkeley Square, and that'll get them nowhere because the place is shut up."

Apple could not be satisfied. Marjorie's dogged determination had been well demonstrated. "I would never have believed she would go to such lengths."

"Marjorie? Woman's a human bloodhound!"

"You see? You've just said it yourself, Alex. What in the world are we going to do?"

"If it comes to it," he said forcefully, "I'll just have to remain with you and stand guard."

Apple let out an overwrought giggle. "You can't do that, you know you can't. We've got to be circumspect, Alex. Especially if Marjorie learns the truth about me. I wouldn't put it past her to spread the tale about."

Alex looked quite thunderous and her heart warmed. "Makes no matter if she does. You'll be leaving the country."

"But you won't, Alex. And your parents and poor Georgy will be pilloried too, all for giving me shelter. It isn't fair."

Alex leaned across the table between them and laid a hand over hers, sending a flitter through her veins. "Stop fretting, you little goose. No such thing. Marjorie don't move in the kind of circles where she could hurt my family."

"She's quite capable of sending the story to one of those horrid scandal sheets."

"Well, they won't dare name names for fear of a suit at law. And Vergette won't even disclose the name of this infernal duke of yours to you, let alone giving ammunition of that kind to those vultures."

"He's not *my* duke," Apple protested, fastening on to the one thing that rankled above all else. "Besides, it's pure speculation on your mother's part that he is a duke at all."

"Whoever he is, Marjorie won't know any more than you, so that's quite enough fretting and fuming about that."

He sounded quite as autocratic as his old self, and a wave of nostalgia overtook Apple. She buried herself in the cup of chocolate and took balm from the hot, sweet liquid as it slithered across her tongue, which caught a stray drip from her lip.

"I'd best get you back to the hotel."

The rough tone startled Apple and she looked up, unable to help the question. "Why?"

Alex's colour deepened and he looked away. "Because I'm hanged if I can stand to be in your company without forgetting myself."

It was a savage mutter, and a tide of warmth rushed through Apple as she realised what he meant. Taking a firmer hold of the cup, she drank down the chocolate, unable to withstand an instant vision of being clutched in Alex's arms, his lips on hers. She'd not been plagued by such images for days, having schooled herself to banish them at the first hint. The danger in his company had been dissipated by the turbulent events of the morning, but at this instant, when she felt again all the certainty of his finding her desirable, she was quite unable to bring her recalcitrant mind under control.

With a determined air, she set down the fancy tall cup in its saucer. "I'm ready."

No words were exchanged as they left the coffee house and Alex called up a hack. But once inside, with the dim interior concealing the colour she was sure must be flying in her cheeks, Apple forced herself to speak in as normal a tone as she could.

"I dare say Mrs Tinkler will be wondering how we fared. Oh, I have not told her the whole, be sure," she added as Alex's head turned towards her, "but I had to give her the gist of our adventures."

"*Our* adventures?"

The amusement in Alex's voice made her giggle again. "Well, you can't deny I've provided you with a degree of adventure."

"A *great* deal, as it chances."

"You weren't so pleased about it that first day."

"I didn't know you then."

A certain quality in his tone could not but affect her. She adopted a rallying tone. "No, and if you had, I dare say you would not have hesitated to take me back at once."

He did laugh at that. "Thank the Lord I didn't."

She drew a tight breath. "Alex."

There was a tiny hesitation before he answered. "What's to do?"

"I might not get the opportunity again to say this, but — but I…" Her voice died, the impossibility of what she wanted to say stopping her tongue.

"But you —?"

The prompt was urgent, and out it all came in a rush.

"I'm so glad I held you up. I'm so glad you refused to take me back, and that you thought I was too feather-brained to be left to my own devices and wouldn't let me go. I can't imagine now never having known you, never having this time to — to cherish and remember…"

Her voice became suspended and she turned her head away, gripping her gloved fingers tightly together. For an eon he did not speak, and the sound of the horse's hooves on the cobbled streets battered at her ears.

At last his voice came, low and vibrant. "Can't in honour say what I want to say, Apple. Glad ain't a good enough word for me. Dare say you can furnish one that fits without me saying it."

Yes, she could, and would savour it at a more convenient time, when her heart didn't feel as if it was splitting in two.

The silence was too painful to tolerate. Apple made a valiant effort to overcome the atmosphere she had herself evoked. "Can you imagine poor Mr Vergette's face when the lot of them descend upon him?"

To her relief, Alex burst into laughter. "Oh, Apple, you're incorrigible!"

"So you've said before."

"Should think I must have said it a dozen times. You're right, though. I'd give a monkey to be in the fellow's office at this moment."

The hackney was slowing as they turned into Cork Street. The imminent parting hung heavy on Apple's breast. She'd agreed with Alex that she should remain hidden in the hotel with Mrs Tinkler until her birthday. At her insistence, he'd consented to stay away, providing less chance of anyone finding them out. A precaution which was much more pertinent now the Greenaways were so much in evidence.

The coach stopped and Alex jumped out and let down the steps, giving her his hand. She took it and climbed down, reaching terra firma just as Alex was accosted by a fellow heavily coated against the cold.

"Your pardon, my lord!"

Alex turned. "Carver? What the devil are you doing here?"

Only then did Apple recognise Alex's groom. The slouch hat he wore had half hidden his face, but she now saw an expression of anxiety there.

"I didn't think you'd wish me to look for you at Bow Street, my lord, so I came here instead." He touched his forelock towards Apple. "Morning, miss."

Alex was frowning. "But why should you look for me at all? Told you I'd not need you today."

The groom's look of anxiety increased. "Thing is, my lord, as I thought you'd wish to know straight."

"Lord, what now?"

Foreboding was in his voice and the rhythm of Apple's pulse increased.

"It's her ladyship, my lord. In fact, it's all of 'em, sir. His lordship, her ladyship and Lady Georgiana and all."

Alex was looking thunderstruck. "What, here? They've come down?"

"That's right, my lord. Her ladyship sent Matthew and John ahead to open up the house, and the whole party arrived not an hour since. Spent a night on the road, according to his lordship's coachman. Seems as her ladyship were in a mighty hurry to get here."

On tenterhooks, Apple paced the private parlour Alex had bespoken, unable to sit quietly as Mrs Tinkler urged her to do.

"You'll not bring him back any the quicker, Miss Greenaway, for wearing a hole in the carpet."

Irritation got the better of Apple. "I wish you will not call me that!"

The elder lady tutted. "What am I to call you, my dear, if not by your name?"

"It isn't my name! Lord knows what my name may be, and this descent upon the capital of the Luthries makes it almost certain there is no bearing it, whatever it is."

Mrs Tinkler's bewilderment was plain. "My dear Appoline — if you insist upon it — I cannot make head nor tail of what you say. Can you not be a trifle more specific?"

"No!"

Apple paced back to the window that looked out into the busy yard, peering down in the vain hope of seeing Alex jump out of one of the coaches. Ridiculous. He would come by a hack again. She'd be better listening at the door for a knock. She felt a gentle touch on her arm and found Mrs Tinkler beside her.

"My dear child, you do yourself no good by all this agitation. I gather there is some unfortunate mystery afoot, but recollect that you succeeded very well at Bow Street."

"Yes, and that's another thing. Alex was confident Marjorie and Walter could not again accost his parents, but if they've come to town…"

Mrs Tinkler was drawing her towards a chair by the fire. She was pushed into it willy-nilly. "I am going to ring for some refreshment. Would you prefer coffee or wine? I dare say the latter might revive you."

"I don't care," Apple said, suddenly listless. "Either will do. Oh, make it tea, Mrs Tinkler, if you please."

Her chaperon picked up the hand bell set upon the table and rang it with vigour. Then she came to sit in the chair opposite, adopting a determined air of cheerfulness.

"There, that is more comfortable."

Apple did not feel in the least comfortable, but she was seized by a qualm of conscience. "I beg your pardon, ma'am. I've been abominably rude."

The widow tutted again. "I quite understand. I only wish I might ease your mind."

Before she could say more, a servant appeared. Mrs Tinkler put in her order for tea and resumed her seat, regarding Apple in concern. "Would it not help to talk about it?"

"I don't know if I can."

She let out a slow breath, trying to ease the tightness in her chest. She'd never fully believed in the notion concocted by Lady Luthrie, but Alex's reaction had filled her with dread.

"My mother must have heard from Lady Mere. Can't think what else would bring her hotfoot to the capital. And if it ain't true, she wouldn't have come." He'd promised to return as soon as he'd found out what was going forward. Seeing her instant dismay, he'd offered a sop. "Might be something else entirely, Apple, so don't go fretting and fuming until I'm able to get back to you."

She'd been in no mood to accept that. "How can I not? And you know very well it isn't anything else. Your mother would not subject Georgy to the jolting of the coach in her condition unless she was determined to wrest you from my clutches."

"Don't be a hen-wit, Apple. Wrest me from your clutches indeed! She knows I've no intention of ... well, you know what I mean."

"Yes, but she must know how quixotic you are, Alex. She will suppose you may take some foolish notion into your head of having compromised me or some such thing."

"Balderdash!"

"It isn't balderdash! And the way you keep going on about taking responsibility for me is enough to cause any cautious mother to take fright. You should never have followed me after I went away with Mr Vergette."

The exchange had been taking place in this very parlour, and Apple recalled how he'd not hesitated to seize her by the shoulders and give her a little shake.

"That's enough, Apple! Stop it at once!"

The autocratic tone was back and it caught at her rising hysteria. She gazed up into his stern features and a kaleidoscope of memories flashed through her brain. She drew in an unsteady breath and hazarded a small smile.

"Oh, dear, I'm being perfectly bird-witted again, aren't I?"

His grin dispelled the stern look. "Feather-headed little monkey!"

A giggle escaped her and he laughed. "That's better." He caught her into a rough hug and let her go immediately. "I'll be back before you know it."

With which, he was gone, replaced soon after by Mrs Tinkler, who fluttered in full of question and interest. "Lord Dymond requested me to keep you company until he returns." She looked appreciatively about the little parlour. "This is cosy indeed, Miss Greenaway. How very thoughtful of Lord Dymond."

Apple had replied suitably, but without Alex's sustaining presence, her nerves rapidly shredded and her fears became ever more lurid. Her chaperon's invitation to share her troubles was tempting, but she hesitated to reveal the awful truth.

The arrival of the tea provided a welcome delay, allowing her time to think how much she felt able to reveal as Mrs Tinkler busied herself with dispensing the brew.

Sipping a little of the hot liquid reminded Apple of the earlier excursion to the coffee house with Alex, and how she'd felt impelled to speak as if it was goodbye. With the threat of confirmation hanging over her head, she was seized with an urge to rush to a coach office and buy a ticket that might take her away from here. To where she had no notion, but anywhere was preferable than sitting in this parlour waiting for the blow to fall.

On impulse, she looked up. "Mrs Tinkler, would you go with me if I am obliged to leave the country?"

In the act of taking a sip of tea, her chaperon all but choked. Recovering, she gazed at Apple as if she had taken leave of her senses. "Good gracious, is it as bad as that? What in the world have you done, Miss Greenaway?"

"It's not what *I* have done," said Apple, indignant. "It's what my father has done. If he *is* my father."

Mrs Tinkler was looking perfectly bewildered. "Gracious, whatever do you mean?"

Apple capitulated. "It's of no use to keep it from you, I suppose. You are bound to know it all, should you choose to come with me."

"Come with you where, my dear Miss Greenaway? I do wish you would strive to be more coherent."

A somewhat hysterical giggle escaped Apple. "I feel as though I'll never be coherent again. Oh, I can't explain it to you. It's much too complicated."

The elder lady took a fortifying sip of her tea and set down the cup and saucer on a convenient side table. "My dear Miss Greenaway, or Appoline if you prefer it, perhaps I should tell you I am not wholly ignorant of your circumstances. Mrs Reddicliffe told me a little before you came to stay with her, which is why she was kind enough to suggest I might be of service to you."

Apple eyed her with a good deal of suspicion. "Why did you not say so before?"

"I would not for the world embarrass you, my dear. Besides, it was not for me to interfere. But when I see you such a bundle of nerves as you are at this moment, I cannot reconcile it with my conscience not to speak."

"How much do you know?"

"Only that my lord Dymond came upon you on the road and rescued you from these guardians. Mrs Reddicliffe heard something of your story, I believe, while she was at Merrivale House."

"Georgy! I might have guessed she could not refrain from chattering."

Feeling a little less fraught, Apple drank more tea and gave Mrs Tinkler a somewhat expurgated account of what had transpired to induce her to seek refuge with Georgy's old nurse.

"Only I did not then know that Lady Luthrie had recalled an old scandal which she supposed might involve me."

"And does it?"

Her chaperon's sympathetic mien served to loosen Apple's tongue. "That is just what I suspect by her coming to town in this precipitate fashion. And if she has confirmation of the circumstances of my birth, there will be nothing for it but to go abroad as quickly as I can manage it."

"Go abroad?"

"Yes, if the trust allows."

Mrs Tinkler was looking quite baffled. "But, my dear Appoline, where would you go?"

"Anywhere. Travelling. I've always wished to see the world, you must know. There are places I've dreamed of visiting. Different cultures. So much art."

She spoke without a vestige of the excitement she'd felt whenever she'd thought of it in the past. Before her life had been turned upside down by the entrance into it of a certain gentleman. And she was determined not to ruin his life as well as her own.

A look of deep foreboding overlay Mrs Tinkler's usually comfortable expression. "Am I to understand you would wish me to accompany you on this ... this extraordinary expedition?"

"Well, yes. Of course I can't go unchaperoned, and Mrs Reddicliffe suggested you."

"Then Mrs Reddicliffe was off her head! Good gracious, Miss Greenaway, what can you be thinking of? Two lone females to be wandering about the continent unescorted?"

Apple was conscious of a twinge of irritation. "Why not?"

"Why not? My dear Appoline, I can think of a dozen reasons why not. It is not to be thought of! Good gracious me! And we have been so lately at war over there. It is not safe, my dear child. Why, Mrs Reddicliffe informed me that Lady Georgiana's husband has been recalled, for the papers are full of it, you know. There is every possibility that this fragile peace will not last."

Apple grew impatient. "Then we will go somewhere where there is no war. There can be no difficulty."

"There I am unable to agree with you, Miss Greenaway. The whole enterprise seems to me so fraught with difficulty that I could not entertain it for an instant."

"Alex does not think so. At least," Apple amended, recalling certain pronouncements he'd made on the subject, "he did say it was hare-brained, but —"

"Hare-brained? He might well say so! Gracious, Appoline, I do most earnestly beg of you to think again. As for myself, I must tell you here and now that Mrs Reddicliffe was perfectly mistaken. I can think of nothing I should dislike more than to be junketing about the continent in such a manner. Dear me, the very thought of it is enough to prostrate one with exhaustion."

Apple gazed at her, dismayed. "You mean you won't come?"

"Emphatically, no!" The elder lady puffed out an overwrought breath. "I am sorry to disoblige you, my dear Miss Greenaway, but really I could not. London is one thing. But the continent, and with no notion of when to return? Gracious me, no indeed!"

Seeing her quite overcome, Apple had the greatest difficulty preventing herself from bursting into laughter. Not that it was in the least little bit amusing. She would have to remake all her plans. Or at least, discover another lady who might go with her. Which likely meant she must advertise after all. Which again meant there was no possibility of setting off in a bang as she wanted to do, once the horrid truth was out.

This reflection threw her back into agitation, and she said no more of her proposed trip. Mrs Tinkler, however, said a great deal. Apparently horrified by the scheme, she applied herself assiduously to the task of discouraging Apple from continuing in it, and kept up her discourse all through the luncheon served to the ladies in the parlour.

Apple answered suitably, and was even grateful for the lecture her chaperon read her since it helped to keep her mind off Alex's continued absence.

He did not reappear until midway through the afternoon, by which time Apple was so wound up she greeted him with a furious demand to know why he had kept her waiting for such an age.

"Did you think I would not be anxious?"

"Devil a bit. Knew you were as anxious as bedamned. Came as soon as I could, Apple."

"Not soon enough!"

He cocked an eyebrow, eyeing her. "Want to hear what's afoot, or would you prefer to carry on ringing a peal over me?"

Apple threw her hands over her face. "I don't want to hear it!"

She heard Mrs Tinkler bustle up. "I'm afraid she's been in this state the whole time, my lord. Apart from this reckless nonsense about going abroad."

"Told you about that, did she?"

"Yes, and I am afraid I cannot possibly oblige you, if you had it in mind for me to accompany her."

Apple dropped her hands. "It makes no matter. I'll advertise." She found Alex regarding her with a sober look on his face. All her fears rushed up again, and the suspense became unendurable. "Tell me! It's true, isn't it?"

His face became grimmer than ever. "Lady Mere is in town. She wants to see you."

Chapter Twenty-six

The Luthrie town house, situated in Berkeley Square, was one of those slim, tall and imposing mansions that appeared, in Apple's overwrought state, as sinister as Bow Street. Although Alex's presence enabled her to stay reasonably calm on the surface, he'd been unable to enlighten her as to the truth of her origins.

"Lady Mere sent me for Vergette. Didn't want to send a servant on the errand because of its delicate nature, she said. So my mother ordered me to go."

An errand that had accounted for his late return, since he'd had to chase about the town to locate the lawyer.

"But she must suppose it's true, Alex, or she wouldn't have come."

"Well, of course she does, Apple. But she ain't going to commit herself until she's spoken to Vergette and seen you."

Another thought struck Apple. "Had Mr Vergette seen Walter and Marjorie? And the magistrate?"

"Ran him to earth at last at Bow Street. Seems he said enough to put those vultures off. Don't know what he told Justice Armitage, but he ain't pressing charges, and he refused to hand you over to the Greenaways, so that's one worry off your list."

A measure of relief entered Apple's breast. "Thank goodness!"

But the reprieve came too late to be wholly appreciated when the shadow of her fate was hanging over her head. She managed to refrain from bursting out through the short journey to the Luthrie's town house in Berkeley Square, and was glad of it when Alex smiled at her as he gave her his hand to help her down from the hackney coach.

"Good girl! That's more like my plucky Apple."

She returned the smile, aware her lips trembled as much as her hands. "I don't feel very plucky."

"I know."

He said no more, turning to pay off the hack while she gazed up at the building, her heart thrumming in her chest.

Alex guided her up the shallow steps and knocked on the door. It was opened almost at once by a servant she vaguely recognised from Dymond Garth.

"Her ladyship is in the Green Saloon, my lord."

"Where's Lady Mere?"

"With her ladyship, my lord."

"And my father and sister?"

"They are all in the Green Saloon, my lord."

Apple seized Alex's arm and leaned up with a frantic whisper. "I can't face them!"

He glanced down, his look reassuring and turned back to the servant. "Tell Lady Mere we'll await her in the Little Parlour, Matthew."

"Very good, my lord."

Breathing more easily, Apple allowed herself to be ushered, following the servant, up a wide stairway to the gallery above. The fellow Matthew turned right and Alex steered her left, along a short corridor and into a pretty room furnished with a sofa and chairs in faded and worn chintz, which had clearly seen much use.

"This was the girls' parlour when they were young 'uns and not allowed in company. My mother preferred them under her eye and wouldn't leave them at the Garth."

Apple thought of Georgy's exuberance and felt a little cheered. The room was much more the style of thing in which she felt comfortable. Not that there was any comfort in the thought of Lady Mere joining them. She sat down at Alex's bidding on the sofa, which was turned to face the fire. He took a seat beside her and picked up one of her unquiet hands, holding it strongly.

"Dash it, you're like ice! Here, give me the other one too."

Possessing himself of it on the words, he rubbed her fingers with all the vigour that characterised him.

"Ouch!"

He grinned and lessened his touch. "Too rough? That's me all over, ain't it?"

"No, it isn't. You can be gentle too."

Apple met his eyes and her breath caught as his hands stilled on hers. He seemed about to speak. Then footsteps sounded outside and he released her, standing up to face the door.

Lady Luthrie entered, accompanied by another lady, elegant in a blue gown trimmed with frogging around the neckline and all down the buttoned front. She was much shorter than her hostess and looked surprisingly youthful if a trifle weighty, possibly from the onset of her middle years, but a pair of bright eyes surveyed Apple as she paused on the threshold.

Riveted, Apple stared back, wholly forgetting both her manners and her fright. The lady's face, framed with a fall of dark hair escaping from under a frivolous feathered and lacy cap, was at once alien and familiar. A slight plumpness imperfectly hid a pair of high cheekbones, a straight nose and an odd little chin that Apple knew only too well.

In the background of her dazed mind, she heard Alex exclaim. "Good God!"

And then Lady Luthrie's voice. "Good day to you, Appoline."

"Where's Lady Mere?"

"Alexander, you will accompany me to the Green Saloon."

"Yes, but —"

"Do not argue, if you please."

Apple glanced up, her breath now coming short and fast. "Alex…"

He put a hand to her shoulder and eyed his mother. "She don't want me to leave her."

The stranger's eyes left Apple and she came into the room. Lady Luthrie flanked her, her gaze leaving her son and shifting back to Apple.

"Appoline, this is the Duchess of Melkesham, who wishes to speak with you. *Alone*, if you will be so good."

Apple hardly heard Alex's muttered expletive. Her ears were buzzing, and she had to grip her fingers tightly together as her head swam.

"Hang it, she's going to swoon! Apple! Apple, look at me!"

She focused her eyes on Alex's face and found him down on his haunches before her. His hands caught the sides of her face so that she had no choice but to look at him.

"You're not to faint! I forbid you to faint, do you understand? Take deep breaths."

Apple drew in a breath and let it out.

"Again."

The compelling voice kept her at it until the mists began to clear and the faintness receded. She discovered that Alex had released her face and was holding her shoulders instead.

"Better?" She nodded, keeping her gaze on his. He let her go and stood up. "Might have warned her, ma'am. And me, come to that." He turned to the duchess, who had taken a seat in the chair opposite the sofa. "Beg your pardon, your grace, but I ain't leaving her."

"Alexander!"

He turned to his mother. "She's had a deal to bear, ma'am, and now this. Won't do, I tell you."

At last the other lady spoke, her tone flat and unemotional. "I won't distress the child more than I can help."

It was a mellow voice, and Apple was conscious of an odd flitter of recognition. But that was impossible. Her tongue loosened and she spoke without thinking. "I can't know you, can I?"

A flicker of surprise showed in the lady's eyes, and her lips moved in an uncertain fashion before she spoke. "I hardly think so."

Lady Luthrie cut in. "Alexander, I must beg you to accompany me. Surely you can see the need for privacy on this occasion?"

Alex took a seat beside Apple and reached for her hand. She looked round.

"What do you wish, Apple? Want me to stay?"

She drew a steadying breath. "Yes, but I quite see I must talk to this lady alone."

"You sure? I'll not have you badgered." He threw a minatory look at the duchess as he spoke. "Don't know what the devil's afoot and I don't like it."

The stranger — for so Apple thought of her still — turned her eyes on him. "You need have no apprehension, Lord Dymond."

"For heaven's sake, Alexander! What harm do you suppose could possibly befall Appoline?"

Alex's tone of suspicion did not abate. "Don't know, ma'am. But I tell you now, if she's upset by this, there'll be the devil to pay!"

"Alexander, how dare you speak so?"

But a faint smile crossed the duchess's lips and she glanced at Apple. "You have a fierce protector, my dear. I can promise you, Lord Dymond, that I mean no harm to your protégée."

Warming to that mellow voice, Apple squeezed Alex's fingers. "Go, Alex. I'll be all right."

With obvious reluctance, he released her and stood up. Lady Luthrie was already at the door, but she waited for him to join her. He turned there, again looking at Apple. She'd never seen him so uncertain, and a wave of tenderness swept through her. She smiled and his countenance relaxed a little. The door closed and Apple was left confronting the Duchess of Melkesham. She felt immediately bereft, and a fleeting regret passed through her. She should not have dismissed Alex.

To her astonishment, the lady before her changed in a bang. The dignity she'd been wearing dropped off as if it had been a cloak, and she leapt up from the chair and came to sit beside Apple on the sofa, grasping her hands and holding them tightly.

"My poor, poor little girl! Oh, I am so very sorry!"

Her eyes, large and grey like Apple's own, became luminous. Apple gazed into them, shock enveloping her all over again.

"You're my mother!"

The tears spilled over. "It cannot be otherwise! When Oriana came to me with your story, such a presentiment overtook me, I very nearly fainted clean away." She shook Apple's hands. "As you almost did, poor child, only moments ago."

Dazed, Apple could only stare at her. "But … but you are the Duchess of Melkesham. How can you be my mother?"

"I have only lately become the duchess, you must know." She sniffed and released Apple's hands, digging instead into her sleeve and producing a pocket handkerchief. An entirely irrelevant memory slipped into Apple's mind of the first time Alex had given her his handkerchief.

Having made use of hers, the duchess became a little more composed. She retrieved one of Apple's hands and held it as she resumed. "You see now why I desired to be private with you, dear child. Or may I call you Apple?"

"Yes, if you wish. It's for Appoline."

A fluttery laugh escaped the duchess. "I know. I chose it. The moment Oriana said it, I knew it must be you. Oh, my dearest child, you don't know how many times I've thought of you — and wondered … and worried. Had my father not acquainted me with all the duke's plans, I must have lost my reason."

To Apple, the whole scene began to assume the aspect of a dream. "This can't be happening. It feels so unreal."

The duchess smiled, her voice still tremulous. "It seems so to me too." It appeared to Apple as if those large eyes devoured her. "You have grown up delightfully, my dear Appoline. No, Apple, for that is what you like, is it not? Little Apple! Oh, you were the sweetest babe! Covered in dark curls!"

Her free fingers touched at Apple's hair, catching at a curl, then stroking the strands away from her forehead. The fingers strayed and Apple, quite tongue-tied, felt them gentle on her cheeks and then pinching her chin. A laugh escaped the woman's lips.

"You have my little chin. Isn't that odd? It's a family trait. You can see it in portraits."

"Do I — do I look like you?"

The duchess sat back, as if to observe her better. "The hair, yes. And your eyes are of my colour. I think there must be a general resemblance, but to me you look much more like your father."

Apple's heart dropped and she could not help a hostile note. "The duke?"

The duchess's face changed. "You blame him. They all did so, and I must confess his conduct was reprehensible. But we loved one another. We still do."

The significance of her title struck Apple all at once. Why in the world had she not realised before? "You've married him!"

"Yes. We never thought to marry, for all was at an end after you came. But fortune favours the brave, they say. Godfrey lost his wife several years ago, and my husband — an estimable man of God who was very kind to me, so young as I was when we married and so dreadfully guilty — yes, about you, my poor girl… Where was I?"

A crack of laughter escaped Apple. "Oh, dear, I am afraid we are more alike than you know. I chatter quite as much as you do."

Her mother — how odd to think of this strange woman as her mother! — broke into a girlish giggle.

"Dear me, do you drive Lord Dymond demented?"

"Yes! He tells me I am feather-brained."

"And Godfrey calls me scatter-brained!"

The shared laughter did much to soothe Apple's lacerated feelings, and the shock of discovery began to subside. "How came it about that you married the duke then?"

The duchess hesitated. Then a grimace passed across her face. "No, I will conceal nothing from you, my little Apple. Will you think badly of me if I tell you that our liaison was never severed?"

Apple blinked. She and the duke had continued their affair through both their marriages? She could not think of such outrageous conduct without deep disapproval, and struggled not to show it — in vain.

"Ah, you are shocked, are you not?"

Apple drew a breath. "I'm afraid I am. But I have no right to judge you."

"Oh, my child, if anyone has that right, it is you. I could wish I might plead mitigation, but truth to tell, there is none. I threw my cap over the windmill for love and I was rescued from my own folly. To your cost."

"No!" This at least she could say with honesty. "Papa gave me a life I would never wish undone. He never once allowed me to think I was not his daughter, even when I had my suspicions. And I was his daughter, in everything but name, as I now learn."

"Alas!" The duchess's eyes grew pitiful. "I see you will never accept poor Godfrey in his place."

"No, I shan't!"

She regretted the vehemence the moment it was out, but the duchess merely sighed. "Perhaps you may find it in your heart to forgive him one day."

Apple's tongue got the better of her, all the repressed bitterness rising up. "When he's made it impossible for me to be with Alex? It was he who sent Mr Vergette to warn him off, was it not? Had he not done that I need never have known. I may have suspected, but…"

Her voice died as she recalled there had never been the slightest chance of a life with Alex. The suspicion was enough. And if she'd been who she purported to be, who her grandfather had made her to save her face, she would still not have been good enough for the heir to an earldom.

The duchess had not spoken, only eyeing her in an odd fashion that Apple could not interpret. She caught her breath.

"Not that it matters. Either way, I am utterly unsuitable." Her hand was still reposing in that of the duchess and it felt wrong. Apple withdrew it, trying for a lighter note. "When did you marry?"

"A little over a year since my widowhood. Last November it was. When you, as I apprehend, ran off with your Alex."

"I did not run off with him! Where had you that? I just happened to hide in his coach. I had never met him before that day."

The duchess threw up her hands. "Don't eat me, dear child. Evidently I misunderstood. You shall tell me it all presently." She eyed Apple again. "But tell me this, if you please."

Feeling begrudging still, Apple met her eyes boldly. "Tell you what?"

"Do you love him?"

Apple's heart cracked. For the life of her she could not prevent the sob that leapt from her chest into her throat.

A pair of soft arms caught about her, and the velvet cheek of her mother was set against her own. "Hush, my poor girl! Oh, hush, my darling child! I know. Oh, I know how much it hurts."

The spurt of tears did not last long. Insensibly comforted by a feminine touch she'd never before experienced, Apple let the gentle rocking soothe her into quiet. At length she was able to draw away and the duchess released her. Apple sniffed and groped unavailingly for a handkerchief.

"Here, take mine."

She accepted the little square of linen and let out a giggle. "Alex is always having to give me one of his."

A mellow laugh greeted this. "Fortunately, I always keep several about me." Apple dried her cheeks and blew her nose, and then proffered the crumpled object. "Keep it. A memento."

Apple crumpled it even more as her fist closed over it. She looked at the youthful countenance beside her. "I hardly remember my mother. I mean, my adoptive mother."

"Then may I hope you will take me in that capacity?"

The words were uttered in a soft, tentative voice, a hopeful note within it.

"I don't know. I dare say we shall never meet again after today."

An astonished look greeted this. "Why in the world should you think so?"

"Well, I supposed you only wished to satisfy yourself that I truly am your daughter. And now that I know it for the truth…"

"You believe you must hide yourself away in shame?" Her mother sighed. "Sometimes I almost wish I had been sent away to make a life with you. It happens, you know. A young widow with a small child appears in a new area, with a new married name and an inexplicable allowance. We might have been very happy together."

Apple quashed this notion without hesitation. "It's of no use to think of that now, is it?"

The duchess laughed out. "Heavens, but you are so like your father! In character at least. Do you fly into rages?"

Apple flushed. "Now and then."

"You have his temperament and my rebellious nature. You poor child, what a dreadful combination."

An irrepressible giggle escaped Apple. "I must tell Alex. He will be perfectly in agreement."

Then remembrance hit and her spirits plummeted. She forgot to compose her features and the duchess clucked at her.

"Oh, you are certain you must lose him, are you not?" She gathered Apple's hands into her own and held them fast. "My dear little Appoline, cannot you tell I am determined you shall not be made unhappy? You shall not suffer for my sins any more, I promise you."

Apple returned the pressure of her mother's fingers, but her heart did not lift. "You can't change the past. There is nothing you can do."

"Oh, but there is." To Apple's utter astonishment, her eyes danced. "I may be a duchess, but I am at heart nothing more than a giddy girl in love, just as I was all those years ago. I care no more for the world's opinion now than I did then, my child."

"But you did care. Or you would not have given me up."

"My dearest Appoline, I was but sixteen years old. I was forced to do as my parents dictated. But that is all at an end. There is only one difficult task before me, and that is to persuade my dear Godfrey."

Mystified, Apple blinked. "Persuade him of what?"

Chapter Twenty-seven

Only slightly acquainted with Lady Mere, Alex remembered her vaguely from his childhood. She had been apt to live retired, unlike her old friend his mother, an active member of the social whirl. But that did not prevent him from taking her to task the moment he arrived in the Green Saloon.

"Why did you not tell me of the duchess's presence, ma'am?"

Lady Luthrie uttered a protest at his tone, but Lady Mere, a willowy female, waved her down. "My sister-in-law was insistent upon remaining incognito until I had spoken with Vergette."

Alex stared at her, feeling baffled. "Incognito? But she's the Duchess of Melkesham."

"The second duchess, and only very lately married to my brother."

Alex turned on his mother. "Why didn't you tell me, ma'am?"

Lady Luthrie snorted. "Do you suppose I would have kept silent had I known?"

His father was at Alex's side, a calming hand on his shoulder. "The marriage was secret, my dear Alex, and with good reason."

Light dawned and a surge of hope entered Alex's breast. He fixed his sire with a compelling eye. "She's Apple's mother then?"

"Just so."

Lady Mere broke in, moving towards Alex, breathless and anxious. "Even I did not know until the deed was done, and I believe my brother would have kept it from me longer. Only

Cordelia thought it right to inform me, and thank heavens she did! I journeyed to Trubridge the moment I received your dear mother's letter."

"But the duke had told Vergette to warn me off." Suspicion, and cold rage, burgeoned in Alex, dispelling the rise of hope. "When was this marriage celebrated? Before Christmas?"

"Oh, in November, I believe, for —"

"November? The villain was married to Apple's mother in November and he still sought to suppress her origins?"

"Alexander, your conduct is perfectly appalling!"

He turned on his mother. "*My* conduct? And what of the wretch who has condemned poor Apple to oblivion?"

His father's hand was once more upon his shoulder. "That, my dear boy, is not the fault of Lady Mere."

True enough. Alex reined in his horns with difficulty. "Beg your pardon, ma'am, but this passes all bounds."

"Alexander, will you please allow Lady Mere the opportunity to speak?"

His mother's vibrant tone cut across the conflicting emotions churning in Alex's breast. He tightened his lips on retort and was as much astonished as touched when his sister took up the cudgels in his defence.

"Mama, cannot you see poor Alex is distraught with disappointment? Don't you understand how he feels about Apple?"

"I am neither so ignorant, nor so unfeeling as you suppose, Georgiana. But I will not have my dear friend Oriana subjected to his ill temper. Especially when she has done everything in her power to promote Appoline's cause."

She turned her gimlet gaze on Alex on this last, arresting his attention. He eyed her for a moment in frowning silence and then turned to Lady Mere.

"Accept my apologies, ma'am. I should not have spoken to you so."

The lady waved agitated hands. "Oh, it makes no matter, my dear Dymond. To tell you the truth, I was quite as dismayed when I learned from your mother that my brother had instructed Vergette to scotch any possibility of… But Cordelia insists he did so only to save her face. He had not told her of it, you must know."

"But you did, ma'am?"

Lady Mere shuddered. "You don't suppose I took such a tale to Godfrey? Good heavens! No, no, I went on the pretext of welcoming Cordelia to the family and seized my chance when we were private."

"So it was the duchess who wanted to meet Apple?"

Lady Mere put a hand to her bosom. "She burst into tears. It was so affecting. It was by no wish of hers, she told me, that the baby had been given away."

Veering rapidly back to hope, Alex took a step closer, eager now. "Do you tell me she knew Apple was her daughter?"

"No, how should she? But the very thought that she might be was enough to set her on a quest. She insisted on accompanying me to Dymond Garth, and then, as you see, we were all obliged to follow you to London once we learned of the intervention of Bow Street. Cordelia would not rest until she had ascertained the truth from Vergette."

Alex turned to his mother. "Why could you not confide in me, ma'am? Had I known of this —"

"My dear Alexander, were you not paying attention? The duchess insisted upon secrecy. She kept her room and used her former married name of Sutcliffe until the moment I presented her to Appoline."

Alex's mind flew to the interview now taking place across the hall. Consternation attacked him and his pulse speeded up. For two pins he'd interrupt, if Apple had not told him to leave them. What was the woman saying to her? From what Lady Mere had said, it seemed she was disposed in Apple's favour. But secrecy and staying here incognito? She must be terrified of raking up the scandal.

He felt a touch on his shoulder and turned to find his father at his elbow, armed with a glass of red liquor, which he held up. Operating on automatic, Alex took it and looked round. He had not realised he'd paced across to the window.

"Drink it, my boy," murmured Lord Luthrie. "It may serve to settle your mind."

Alex drew a steadying breath. "Don't think anything will do that, sir."

But he lifted the glass to his lips and tossed off the wine. Then he looked about the room. His mother and Lady Mere had their heads together. Georgy was regarding him anxiously from her chair by the fire, and his sire remained at his side. He tried to smile.

"You're always rescuing me, sir."

Lord Luthrie laughed. "A father's duty, my dear boy." He turned at the sound of the door opening. "Ah, but this, I fancy, signals the end of your purgatory."

It did not, much to Alex's chagrin. Instead, the footman Matthew entered bearing a letter on a silver salver. He looked round the room and then fixed his eyes on Alex, who strode forward.

"Is that for me?"

"It's addressed to Miss Greenaway, my lord."

"Good God!"

Alex picked up the sealed note and looked at the superscription. *Miss Appoline Greenaway*. There was no means of knowing who had sent it.

"Who brought it?"

"A lackey, my lord. I do not know the man."

Alex pocketed it, nodding at the footman. "I'll give it to her."

Matthew departed and the distraction of the little diversion faded. Alex crossed to his father again. "I've a good mind to go and find out what the devil is going on in there."

"You can do no good by interfering, Alex. Have confidence in Appoline, my boy. She is a capable girl."

Reminiscence lightened Alex's gloom for a moment. "Yes. Be surprised if she don't give the duchess snuff."

Lord Luthrie laughed and seemed about to speak, but Alex's attention became riveted as he heard a light footstep approaching the door.

The Duchess of Melkesham entered, leading Apple by the hand. Alex's gaze focused on Apple's face and he hardly heard the closing of the door behind them. She was looking dazed and a little frightened. He was all set to go to her when the duchess spoke.

"I would like to present to you all, in her rightful name, my daughter, Lady Appoline Damerham."

There was silence for a space, and then, as it seemed to Alex, several people began talking at once.

"It's true then!"

"Good heavens, Cordelia, have you run mad?"

"Oh, Apple, I'm so happy for you!"

"Go and speak to her, Alex," came quietly in his ear from his father.

He needed no further urging. Crossing at once to Apple, he caught up her free hand. "Are you all right? What happened?"

She clung to his fingers. "I scarcely know. I feel quite bewildered."

A fluttery laugh came from the duchess, catching Alex's glance. "I don't blame you, my dearest child. I hardly know myself whether I am on my head or my heels." She released Apple's hand and held hers out to Alex instead. "My dear Lord Dymond, I believe you have taken care of my dear girl here and I must thank you."

"Only lately, ma'am. Ran across her purely by accident."

"And thank heavens you did, or I might never have known her again."

"You're sure then? That she is your daughter?"

"Oh, I knew it the moment Oriana told me her name."

Apple's fingers tightened on his. "She gave me the name of Appoline, Alex. She really is my mother."

His world lightened all at once, and immediately dimmed again. What did the duchess intend by Apple? He went directly into the attack.

"What do you mean by this, ma'am? Presume you won't reveal it other than to us?"

"Then you presume wrong, Lord Dymond."

The ringing tone reminded him so strongly of Apple's occasional outbursts that Alex was startled. But whatever he might have said was forestalled by Lady Mere, bobbing up beside them.

"Have you lost your senses, Cordelia? The scandal!"

The duchess clicked her fingers. "That for the scandal, my dear Oriana."

"And pray will Godfrey agree with you?"

"He must be made to. Oh, it won't be easy, but I shall persuade him, never fear. He must legitimise our precious

Apple, and we shall introduce her to society as Lady Appoline Damerham."

Elation in his breast, Alex stepped in. "No, ma'am, you'll do nothing of the sort."

"Alexander!"

His mother's shocked tone did not deter him. He glanced at her, and at the other faces regarding him with varying degrees of surprise and disapproval. Then he turned to Apple and found her with question in her face. He smiled down at her. "Don't fret, Apple. I know what I'm doing." Her brows rose, but he turned back to the duchess. "She ain't going to make her debut as Lady Appoline Damerham."

"But it is the least I can do for her." The duchess's frowning annoyance made her look all too similar to Apple. "Why should you object?"

Alex felt a welter of emotion rush into his chest and his eyes went back to Apple. "Because by the time she goes into the world she'll be Lady Dymond."

Apple's mouth fell open. "Alex!"

From out of the plethora of gasps and exclamation came his father's amused tones. "It is customary, my dear boy, to enquire of the lady whether she is willing before making such an announcement."

Alex laughed out, his chest bursting with new happiness. "So I shall, sir, as soon as I can get Apple alone."

Then Georgy came skipping up, snatching Apple into an enveloping embrace. "Oh, famous, Apple! You'll be my sister."

"If she chooses to marry him," said Lady Luthrie on a dry note.

"Oh, she will, she will!"

"You seem to have as little doubt of that as Alexander himself, Georgiana. I should hope he will give the girl a choice."

"Naturally, ma'am. Ain't as autocratic as all that."

Apple's giggle pleasurably assailed his ears. "Yes, you are, Alex. You know you are."

He grinned. "Devil a bit. You'll soon tell me if you don't want to marry me."

"As if you would take no for an answer!"

He laughed. "Shouldn't, of course, but I'd find more gentle means to persuade you if you refused me."

"Refuse you?" Georgy was indignant. "Good heavens, Alex, she won't do that! She wears her heart in her eyes whenever she looks at you."

Lady Luthrie tutted. "Do be quiet, Georgiana!"

His father gently steered Georgy out of the way and took her place. "I suggest, my dear boy, that you retire with Appoline to discuss the matter."

"Mean to do so, sir, but must settle this first." He turned to the duchess. "I'm not going to have Apple subjected to all this legal argy-bargy, ma'am. Trust you to do the business while we're away. By the time we get back the tabbies will have oohed and aah-ed to their heart's content and gone on to something else."

Apple's suspicious tones cut in. "Get back from where?"

His father forestalled him before he could answer. "Ah, you mean to take Appoline away for the duration? That sounds an excellent plan, my dear boy."

"I agree with you, Charles. That is well thought of, Alexander."

"And so also am I in agreement," said Lady Mere, surprising Alex. "Amongst the four of us, I dare say we may contrive to brush through the business without too much fuss."

"Indeed, yes," agreed the duchess with enthusiasm, "loath as I am to lose her so soon, it will be much more comfortable for her." She reached out to Apple and stroked her face. "I will hope to have plenty of opportunity to get to know you, my dearest girl."

"I too, ma'am, to get to know you."

Alex was touched to see the unaccustomed shyness in Apple, but the duchess's evident pleasure was echoed in her eyes.

"Take her away with confidence, my dear Alex — if I may acknowledge our coming closer relationship? We will make all right here in the meanwhile, and give it out that my daughter has gone upon her wedding trip."

Georgy clapped her hands. "A honeymoon! How excessively romantic of you, Alex."

"Not a honeymoon, though I dare say it will be that too." He took Apple's hand in his and smiled down at her. "Going to take Apple adventuring — if she'll have me."

Chapter Twenty-eight

Dragged willy-nilly back towards the Little Parlour, in a whirling kaleidoscope of confused emotions and a trifle out of breath besides, Apple's first coherent thoughts concentrated upon Alex's conduct.

"This is typical of you, to be rushing me hither and yon."

He slowed a trifle, but grinned down at her. "Can't wait to get you to myself."

"To tell you the truth, I could do with a period of quiet reflection."

"That's the last thing you're going to get. Right now at least."

Apple was torn between indignation and a lively curiosity to know what he meant to do with her. She was not left long in ignorance. The moment he thrust Apple through the door and closed it behind them, he captured her into a stifling embrace, hugging her so tightly she uttered a faint protest.

"I can't breathe!"

His hold relaxed a fraction, but he clasped her head against his shoulder and seemed as if he would never let her go.

Her heart filled to bursting and her throat ached for several moments until the warmth and comfort of her position, enclosed in so strong and possessive a hold, began to permeate through her body. A sensation of utter bliss made the desire to weep recede, and she sighed in deep content.

Alex released his clutch upon her, enough to allow Apple to raise her head. She looked into his face and tenderness rushed through her as she saw a trace of moisture on his cheek.

She put up her hand and smoothed it away. "Oh, Alex…"

He caught her fingers and pressed them to his lips, sighing deeply. "My Apple."

"My Alex," she returned, and the beam of his smile lit up his whole face in a way she'd never seen before.

"I think I must have fallen in love with you the moment you produced that pistol in my coach."

Apple giggled. "No, you didn't. Don't be ridiculous."

He grinned, beginning to sound more like his usual self. "Had me at your mercy all too dashed fast, young Apple, with your hare-brained schemes and your propensity for doing exactly the opposite to anything you were told."

"Well, you shouldn't be so high-handed."

A hungry look entered his face, and he brought up a hand and captured her chin. "May I kiss you?"

Apple blinked at him. "You are actually asking permission?"

A quirk of a half-smile teased her. "Yes. Might be high-handed, but I ain't a beast. If you're unwilling…"

"But I'm not! I'm more than willing. I want you to kiss me."

His ran a finger across her lips and a flitter ran down her veins. Still he hesitated, his eyes on hers, their colour seeming to darken. "You won't pretend you don't love me too, for I know it. Felt it."

Apple was far from pretending anything of the kind, but she was growing impatient. "Must I say I love you before you will kiss me?"

His lips quivered. "Yes, that's it."

Her heart melted. "Then I love you."

He drew in an unsteady breath and she felt his fingers tremble against her skin where they held her face. Apple's breath became trapped in her chest and she could not say another word. Then his forehead was resting against her own and she had to close her eyes. She felt butterfly touches down her cheek, and at each one the flutter in her veins increased.

At last the lips reached hers and stilled for an endless moment. Apple's veins thrummed like a hive of bees waiting to swarm. Next instant she was crushed against Alex's chest, and the assault at her mouth left her breathless and shaken. Heat seared her and her limbs lost all strength.

When she came to herself, she was hanging about Alex's neck, her toes barely touching the floor. He let her down, and as his embrace loosened she nearly fell.

"Alex, I've got to sit down!"

Without a word, he lifted her quite off her feet and swung her up into his arms. The sensation of helplessness was oddly pleasurable, and even more so when he sat on the sofa, holding her imprisoned in his lap.

"Never want to let you go again."

He buried his face in her neck and blew hot breath there that made her shiver.

"Alex, what are you doing?" She pulled away and turned in his hold to stare at him.

He grinned. "I'm cuddling you, which is what I've been wanting to do for weeks."

Consciousness overtook her and she giggled with embarrassment, only to be kissed again.

Breathless, she chided nevertheless. "What if someone came in?"

"Doubt any of them would be so tactless."

"Yes, but the servants?"

He rubbed her back. "Want me to lock the door?"

"Yes! No!" He grinned and made to kiss her again, but she held him off. "Don't, Alex!"

"Do you dislike it?"

Warmth rushed into her cheeks. "You know very well I like it, but we've so much to discuss and I can't think when you … when you…"

He drew her against him and whispered into her hair. "When I do this?" Then he found her mouth and murmured against it, "And this?" kissing her so thoroughly that she went limp in his embrace. She sighed and gave in, throwing her arms about his neck and allowing herself the indulgence of enjoying the sensations his ministrations were arousing for some little time.

But at length, Alex sighed and put her from him. "Got to stop, or I'll disgrace us both."

"And I was just getting comfortable."

"Too dashed comfortable, that's the trouble." With a rueful grin, he ran his fingers through her hair. "You look a complete romp."

"It's your fault!"

She put her hands to her head and discovered her hair had come down. With a shriek of dismay, she scrambled off Alex's lap and went to a convenient mirror set above the fireplace. Hastily removing pins, she did what she might to repair the damage, all too aware of Alex's regard, grinning at her from the sofa.

"Can't believe the turn of events, my lady Appoline Damerham."

She glanced over her shoulder. "Nor I. I wish you won't call me that."

"Much rather call you my lady Dymond." He held out his hand to her, and she finished prinking her hair and came to sit demurely beside him. "You are suited with that, aren't you, Apple? Marrying me, I mean."

"If it's the only way I can be with you, then yes. Though I can't imagine how I shall cope."

"Don't fret. You'll learn all you need to. My mother will see to that."

Indignant, Apple glared at him. "If that is designed to comfort me, let me tell you it does nothing of the kind. Your mother terrifies me!"

He put an arm about her and gave her a hug. "What, when you were ready to brave the world quite alone? Nothing terrifies you, young Apple."

"If that's what you think, you don't know me."

He grinned. "I will by the time we're done adventuring. Though for my part, I know you already through and through." He took her hand, playing with her fingers as he spoke. "Never thought I'd get the chance to keep you. Believed it was hopeless from the first."

"So did I." A thought struck her and she gasped. "Marjorie and Walter will be wild when they find out."

Alex's hand stilled on hers. "Wonder if it's they who sent that note?"

"What note?"

He struck himself in the forehead. "If I'd not forgot it!" Diving his hand into an inner pocket, he brought out a somewhat crumpled paper and gave a rueful sigh. "Wrecked the thing, sorry. Broken the seal."

Apple took it from him and her heart jumped when she saw the superscription. "It is Marjorie's hand! Oh, will she never leave me alone?"

"No need to fret, Apple. Be out of her reach in no time."

Apple held the letter between her fingers, staring at it with a faint degree of anxiety creeping through the unaccustomed joy in her heart.

"Open it, love!"

The endearment on Alex's lips made her look round at him, startled. "Me?"

His brows shot up. "What do you mean, me?"

"You said love."

He gave her a quick kiss. "You are my love, aren't you?"

Apple's bosom felt as if it was exploding and her voice almost failed. "Yes... Yes, I am!"

His arm tightened about her. "No need to cry about it now, sweet."

Tears trickled down her cheeks. "Oh, don't!"

Alex removed his arm, digging into his pocket, and laughing the while. "What, I'm not to call you sweet either?"

"No! I mean, yes, please! Oh, Alex, I do love you so very much!"

He produced a pocket handkerchief and applied it to her cheeks himself, murmuring softly, "My love, my sweet, my darling. There! Now, blow!"

This proved too much for Apple and she burst into a fit of watery giggles, taking the handkerchief out of his hand, her face disappearing into its folds.

Alex's heart swelled, and he had all to do not to snatch her back onto his lap and start all over again. Instead, he retrieved the errant letter that she'd let fall to the floor.

She reappeared, sniffing and stifling her giggles, her enchanting little face quite blotched. He could not resist kissing her again, but contented himself with keeping an arm about her as he presented her with the letter.

"Are you going to open this or not?"

She sighed. "I suppose I must."

He watched her unfold the sheet and spread it out, reading over her shoulder. A rise of satisfaction took him. "Changed her tune all right!"

"Mr Vergette must have told her who I am really. Listen, Alex: '*I know when you are rich and grand you will not forget your loving cousins.*' I don't know how she dares suppose any such thing!"

Alex snorted. "Devil a bit. She don't suppose it at all. Hoping to turn you up sweet. Vultures! Won't have to worry about them anymore."

Apple turned dismayed eyes on him. "But we will, Alex. Marjorie is quite capable of turning up on your doorstep."

"*Our* doorstep. And we won't have one for some little time."

But agitation was getting the better of Apple. "What does that signify? Besides, I must go home for my things."

"Not until we're married you won't."

"But, Alex, I've got very little with me. You know I had to borrow from Georgy."

"Don't matter. In a couple of days you'll be swimming in lard and you can buy yourself a whole new wardrobe."

Apple brightened. "I'd forgotten that." All at once she recalled the conversation she'd had with her mother. "Oh, Alex, can you believe it? The duchess says I may have as much as twenty thousand pounds!"

"Good God!"

"Exactly so. Can you imagine? My grandfather put ten thousand in the trust and she says it will have grown. Alex, you may take it for my dowry."

He caught her close for a moment. "That's like you, Apple, but I don't need it. Want you to have your independence, sweet. It's what you've dreamed of and I won't take that from you."

Apple gazed at him, tenderness gathering in her bosom all over again. Of her own accord she leaned up and gave him her lips, a kiss he returned with fervour. When she was able to think again, Apple was struck by a fresh notion.

"I know! I shall buy a travelling chariot. I always thought I would if I could, for it makes sense to be as comfortable as one can, don't you think?"

Alex was laughing. "Incorrigible! Certainly buy one, if you wish for one. Dare say we'll need an extra coach to cope with the luggage, not to mention my valet and your maid."

"But I don't have one."

"Well, you don't think I'm going to let you blunder about the world without one, do you? Who's going to keep your clothes in order and make sure all's right in these foreign inns?"

"But —"

"Now don't start to argue, Apple, for my mind's made up."

Apple eyed him in frowning silence for a moment, taking in the inflexible look in his face that had so often driven her into fury. So typical. A bubble of happiness rose up and her lips quivered on a laugh.

"I can't think why I love you so much, for you are perfectly abominable, Alex, you know you are."

His countenance relaxed and he broke into a grin. "Being high-handed again, aren't I? Can't help it, that's the trouble. And if it comes to that, I can't think why I love such a feather-brained rebellious little monkey. Fact remains that I do, and if you keep on giggling in that fashion, Apple, you'll induce me to put you back on my lap and kiss you senseless."

In no way cowed by this threat, Lady Appoline Damerham dissolved into helpless laughter.

A NOTE TO THE READER

Dear Reader,

I started the Brides by Chance series during the later recovery months after major operations that had left me physically debilitated. Each story built on the previous one, in terms of getting my writing mojo back. With *A Winter's Madcap Escapade*, the writing flew. Before I knew it, I had 80,000 words — my normal output with Regencies — and at last the Inner Writer had returned to full strength.

The idea for this one had been around for several years. All I had was the hero finding a strange girl in his coach, who produces a pistol and insists on being taken to the next stage. I had no idea who she was or why she was doing this. As for the hero, he was a closed book to me, as it were.

Then along came Alex, ready made from *A Chance Gone By*, and there was my hero, ready and waiting to fall in love. As for Apple, don't ask! Where that name came from I simply cannot tell you. But the moment it popped into my head, there she was: my madcap little heroine, a whole character leaping straight onto the page and telling me just what to write.

I had a lot of fun with these two. It was one of the most effortless stories to come out of the Inner Writer, the dialogue seeming to flow naturally between Alex and Apple, and the development of their adventurous romance happening without my intervention.

Perhaps I should explain what I mean by the Inner Writer. Any writer will tell you that they don't really know where the words come from. Especially if the work is running well. In acting, Stanislavski called it the subconscious mind. All his exercises were geared to helping the actor get in touch with that elusive personality somewhere between the conscious and the unconscious. So it is with writing.

This is why the best advice to beginners is to get it down any way you can, and don't worry about the quality. Plotting and editing engage the analytical mind. But you don't want that part of your mind interfering when you are writing the first draft. Just write. Anything. Once you start, sooner or later the Inner Writer kicks in and takes over. When it happens, you don't really know it until you kick out of that mode again. That's why you can write for a couple of hours and not even notice.

When we talk about a treacle book, it's one where the Inner Writer is so elusive you find it hard to get in touch with her. It then feels exactly like wading through treacle, word after word after word. But this book had none of that slog. It was sheer enjoyment from start to finish!

If you would consider leaving a review, it would be much appreciated and very helpful. Do feel free to contact me on **elizabeth@elizabethbailey.co.uk** or find me on **Facebook, Twitter, Goodreads** or my website **www.elizabethbailey.co.uk**.

Elizabeth Bailey

Sapere Books is an exciting new publisher of brilliant fiction and popular history.

To find out more about our latest releases and our monthly bargain books visit our website:
saperebooks.com

Printed in Great Britain
by Amazon